Ravin Noow

MoreThanOneSees

Volume No. 1 (**English**)

Ravin Noow

MoreThanOneSees (English)

Young and Adult Fantasy, Urban Paranormal

Bibliografische Information der Deutschen Nationalbibliothek: Die Deutsche Nationalbibliothek verzeichnet diese Publikation in der Deutschen Nationalbibliografie; detaillierte bibliografische Daten sind im Internet über http://dnb.dnb.de abrufbar.

Die automatisierte Analyse des Werkes, um daraus Informationen insbesondere über Muster, Trends und Korrelationen gemäß §44b UrhG („Text und Data Mining") zu gewinnen, ist untersagt.

© 2025 Ravin Noow

Publisher: BoD · Books on Demand GmbH, In de Tarpen 42, 22848 Norderstedt, bod@bod.de

Print: Libri Plureos GmbH, Friedensallee 273, 22763 Hamburg

ISBN: 978-3-7693-5305-1

Table of contents

Chapter 1 - FAMILY

"Thank God," Kaito thought, the school bell dismissing him for the weekend. The timetable on Friday was hell, and then the whole day with this pedant, "all completely pointless, for today, for tomorrow and for the rest of eternity," he thought, tomorrow he would have forgotten it anyway.

"Now finish the lesson, you pain in the ass!"

"Don't make any trouble over the weekend, understood, students!" The teacher looked at the class one last time and left. The class shouted the obligatory "Goodbye, teacher". Almost everyone hurriedly packed their things and disappeared home or somewhere else.

Kaito packed more slowly, he still had time before his appointment with 'father', he thought. But he had to admit that he was curious what he wanted from him. It was the first time that 'Father' had asked him for help. While he was thinking about it, he looked at his classmates who were leaving the room one by one. "Classmates, should he really call them that?" he asked himself. He could count on one hand how many times he had talked to them until today, in the second year of high school. Half of them in this class even seemed quite nice, but he didn't know them. Their interests were too different. He was one of the outsiders here at this school, and he knew it would stay that way.

"The different types in the class are clearly recognizable," he thought.

The extroverts were always the first to stand out. They were always the first to shout during recess to show their arrogance coupled with stupidity. Talking a lot and loudly and saying little was their motto. "They'd make good politicians if they made it that far," he thought, laughing to himself. He'd heard that the guy over there, always well dressed, was a successful influencer. "It's not that hard with the good-looking men, they just have to talk shit, while the pretty women have to come up with different arguments, but they get more likes for it," Kaito laughed to himself. If they had any brains, they could have provided for their entire lives in ten years with their current income, but most of them were too stupid. "Well, that's how unfair life is.

On the other hand, there were the quieter characters, smart and intelligent at the same time, some still self-confident, "Yuma is close to that," he thought. Some even helped outsiders or victims of bullying, like the gangly boy with glasses over there, who now dared to go back to school. Another 1.5 years to graduate. The boy now had a real chance to make it again. "Well," Kaito thought, "you can divide them all into groups, but no two are alike, everyone has at least one characteristic that makes them unique."

He remembered his first day at middle school, when the pecking order was determined by the bullies. Strangely enough, a rumor soon spread that a classmate who had been bullying him for almost two years disappeared from one day to the next and was never seen again. At the time of his disappearance, Kaito was about 13 years old. Now, so much later, it was a strange thing to say, he recalled. Since he started school, he hadn't found out who spread the rumor that he had something to do with it. "What was that person thinking?" Obviously she wanted to hurt him, but it couldn't have worked out any better. No one had hit him since middle school. "Strength is everything, no matter how you get it," he told himself, smiling.

He knew that his future was set in stone anyway. That was the reason for everything in his life so far, that he never had any friends, that his parents no longer existed, that he almost died several times, that his 'father' was more of a guardian, and, and, and. If you looked at it logically, it was all very easy to understand. As long as he could remember, he had the ability to see spiritual life forms. Colloquially just 'ghosts'. The problem was, as always, the same in a modern world of the 21st century, or even the third millennium. What the majority cannot or does not want to see simply does not exist.

Lucky are the children who grow up in a family where these abilities are part of their community and where they are taught how to deal with them, especially in the company of normal people.

Growing up in a 'normal' family with this ability could only go wrong, he knew from experience. Especially if you entrusted it to an adult, hoping for help. And it could be fatal if that person hated you enough to try to kill you. Either you're smart enough not to, or you die. About eleven years ago, he was stupid enough to do just that, but luck was on his side. Seven years later, he was lucky again and got a new 'father', Hiroshi Tanaka. He owed him a lot, a great deal, he had made his current and above all self-determined life possible, for which he would always be grateful, if possible even beyond death.

Because of his alleged spiritual abilities, his "father" had dragged him to an order one day, who examined him and, to his surprise, wanted to keep him, which his "father" of course laughingly refused. His new father, who was used to oddities due to his profession, began to accept Kaito's view of his world, even if he didn't believe in it himself.

Unfortunately, he didn't get along well with the many people of the order he visited regularly for a while, which is why he left the order at some point and instead, thanks to his father, started his own small business with which he earned a meager income, though with initial difficulties that made him almost independent of his father, which in turn annoyed his father.

He had not lived with his father, Mr. Tanaka, for a long time. Mrs. Tanaka was a very loving woman, but she was afraid of Kaito and about her daughter, who was 10 years younger than him. That's why she was always against taking him in, but she did it anyway and was always there for him during that time. At the age of 15, even though it was against the law, everyone had agreed that Kaito should move out and live on his own from now on, even though Mr. Tanaka, unlike Mrs. Tanaka, came by from time to time to check on things, which he, Kaito, didn't like, because he liked the situation the way it was.

But he had bigger things in mind, as he knew when he arrived at the bottom of the gate and stepped out of the school.

Now he had to pick up Dawn and then go to his father, Mr. Tanaka, at the café. He hoped that Dawn was where he had told her to wait, in front of the school building, but she wasn't there and he realized now that he would have to look for her in the park.

"You have to train kittens properly," he thought, knowing it would be difficult with this one, and smiled.

She wasn't at the beginning of the park, behind the park was the cafe where he had an appointment with Mr. Tanaka. "Damn, you little beast, where the hell are you again, shall I ask Shy?" he thought and continued walking towards the exit of the park.

When the exit was already in sight, he wondered why that unpleasant visit from earlier this year kept coming back to him. That arrogant supposed government representative with his arrogance and his ridiculous statements that Kaito should help save the world from evil and that he had therefore agreed with the Order that he should explore the spiritual world with them. "Of course, you scum, as if the Order would get involved with something like you," he thought and was actually glad that it had turned out this way. Now he knew he had to be more careful.

"MIAU!" it snapped him out of his thoughts and he said to himself "Found it, you beast" and smiled. He looked to his right at the trees. It was so clear that Dawn was watching the people in the park. "Come here, now!" he called, holding out his arm.

As Dawn jumped in his direction, he noticed three girls sitting on a park bench under the tree. "Oh man, they must have misunderstood," he thought as Dawn landed on his arm. The girls' eyes met his and the bickering began. "What was that all about?"

"No time to argue with you idiots," he thought, trying to clear things up quickly and amicably. "I meant my cat, not you, so don't panic, I'm already gone."

"Sure, what do you think?" said the aggressive animal on the right. "Oh damn? The one in the middle is from my class, Sato..., Mato... Moto... or something like that, whatever. I'll just call her idiot number two." "Do you have a problem?" he asked forcefully in her direction, scowling at the beast on the right. The girl in the middle flinched slightly. Only now did he see that the three beauties from his school were sitting together on a park bench. Just as the girl on the right was about to start her next sentence, the nervous-looking girl in the middle whispered something to her. The girl on the right immediately froze, and there was silence. Probably the old story, "I told you so, perfect," he thought. He walked on and from a distance he heard the third girl say, "Did I get scared, I thought a person was going to jump down from the tree on us.

"Well, well, if you only knew," Kaito thought and continued walking towards the end of the park.

After 100 meters, Dawn jumped from Kaito's shoulder onto the road and walked to his right as usual. 200 meters later, he was at the exit.

"I don't know anyone who despises people who do stupid things as much as you do, Kaito. What's the first sentence of the Order? Look around you when you talk to spirits, or people will think you're crazy! And now it's happening to the nerd Kaito himself," Dawn said, looking at Kaito with the sneering expression of a cat.

"You little beast, I'm going to give you 'nerd' and tonight there's something on...", that was all Kaito could say. The loud "meow", which was audible for normal humans, was for Kaito an obviously derisive laugh and a mocking comment: "Today you're the nerd, look to your left, meow.

"No way," Kaito thought. A couple, a bit older than him, looked at him with a grin. "Probably from the third grade of our school. So no problem, the three girls from before would have been worse," Kaito thought and quickly went to a café on the other side of the street.

"Hello, Mr. Tanaka," Kaito greeted the stocky man who looked friendly and sympathetic and was about 40 years old. "The stocky build suits him, otherwise he's much too friendly for a policeman," Kaito thought, but he knew that this man was very successful with his appearance and had contacts to many influential people. "I am curious what he wants.

"When will you finally call me father, my son?" asked Mr. Tanaka.

A little overwhelmed, Kaito replied, "Forgive me, but it will be a while before the word 'father' no longer makes me nauseous.

"A family with a wife, a daughter and a son like you, that's what I've always wanted," Mr. Tanaka said and his expression showed that he meant it. "Damn, he knows how much I hate such sentimental ramblings," Kaito thought. Avoiding direct eye contact, he looked at Dawn, stroked her head and said, "I'm sorry.

"Take your time, my son, and let's get to the subject I want to ask you about.

"Thank you," Kaito thought.

"But first!" He paused and explained, "So many strange things happen in my job. Only the solved cases make the papers, nobody ever hears about the many unsolved and strange incidents. So why shouldn't spiritual beings like Yokai be responsible? I guess I'll just have to put up with it," he said, grinning.

"Please don't blame the incompetence of the police on the Yokai," Kaito thought.

"But what I don't believe is that Dawn is actually a cat Ayakashi whose human form can only be seen with spiritual abilities like yours. Are you gay or is that just an excuse because you don't have a girlfriend?

Kaito looked 'Father' in the face, "He's joking, I'm sure of it," and he thought he could read it on his face, otherwise he would have gotten up and left now.

"So one last time for the obtuse cop in front of me. Dawn looks like a manga catgirl to me," Kaito said quietly and very annoyed, "and you know I told you that in confidence."

Mr. Tanaka grinned and spoke a little louder than usual, "What will your children look like later?"

Kaito looked around embarrassed and hissed, "Did you come here today just to tease me? Dawn is not a Yokai and therefore not an Ayakashi, I've already told you several times.

"Then what is she?"

"She's not a god, even if she'd like to be and sometimes acts like she's by the grace of God, but she's in the class of divine beings, so have some respect."

Kaito looked at Dawn and then said, "She is comparable in rank between a Nekomata and a lesser deity.

Suddenly, Kaito had to fend off Dawn when she suddenly tried to attack him.

Mr. Tanaka leaned forward and grinned at the sight. First a little confused, then laughing, he said, "I don't believe it, as if she understood us and now she's angry that you took away her divine status.

Dawn hissed at Mr. Tanaka, who backed away.

"You interpret correctly, Mr. Policeman. Enough Dawn, people are already looking at us," Kaito said as he tried to avoid the claws. Accept what you are, after all you belong to the class of the gods and are more important to me than anything else".

"Idiot," Dawn said, turning away angrily and lying down. Mr. Tanaka's eyes widened and he thought, "I can't believe this, what was that all about?"

"Before I come to my point, please enlighten your disbelieving father and explain to me what spiritual life forms we are supposedly living with.

Kaito looked at him, "Is this a normal family conversation?" he thought and considered why he should do this, but came to the conclusion that there was no point in arguing with policemen.

"Well, roughly speaking, there are the following forms of ghosts in the spirit world.

First, there are simple ghosts, as I call them, which can arise from the spiritual echo of any living being that is left behind when it dies. They stay in the area of the echo and wander around until they have achieved what they wanted. When the echo fades, they move freely. If they are not eaten by Yokai or Demons, they will become Yokai themselves after a long time. Until then, interaction with humans is rare, and when it happens, it is usually harmless."

"Wait, wait," said Mr. Tanaka, "you can see where a human has died. Did I get that right?" he asked.

"Oh dear," Kaito thought, "I better not have mentioned that.

"Well, as long as the echo hasn't faded, you know that a living being has died in this place."

"Explain that to me in more detail, can you tell the difference between the echo of humans and animals and how long you can recognize it?"

"What a pity, is he trying to poach me for the police now?" he thought.

"The echo of a human being is different from that of an animal or a plant, including the duration of its existence until it dies, so yes."

"Then you can identify a crime scene!"

"You can do that too, or have you gone back to the Middle Ages?"

"We can see if a person died or was dumped at the scene, but we can't easily find a place where a person died unless we find clear evidence."

"Well, then everything is fine. You'll be fine. Writing bills to the state is always a bit stressful," Kaito said, barely able to contain his sarcasm.

Mr. Tanaka looked a little irritated, but then laughed and said, "I'll get back to you, but now on to the spirits.

Positive energy ghosts are an exception. They are still very similar to humans, and aside from the fact that they are spirits, it is difficult for someone who can recognize them to tell them apart from humans. They can look like you and me. Their goal is to protect those who were important to them when they were alive. When this goal is achieved, they ascend or, after a very long time, become what we call guardian spirits or angels themselves.

Sounds, things falling or disappearing are common signs of normal spirits with negative energy. Spirits are also eaten by demons, who can then take on the characteristics or even emotions and feelings of those spirits towards other people. Then it becomes dangerous for people, especially those who knew the spirit.

However, it is quite rare for a demon to infect a person. Given the number of people in the world, this is not reflected in any statistics, but it usually ends fatally for the person affected after a few weeks. Usually, however, the demons absorb the negative energy of the Ayakashi. They are weaker and less aggressive than Yokai. As a result, they have no chance even in a fight against a lower demon. The origin of the higher demons in particular has yet to be determined. Many say that they are the result of human hatred or a tragic death. But then there would be tons of them, as much hatred and tragedy as there is every day. Fortunately, this is not the case. Because unlike a ghost, demons can kill a person directly, but that is dangerous for the demon itself, so they prefer to sneakily and slowly suck the life energy out of a person and then turn it into negative energy. However, they only do this if the person looks 'excellent' to them. Unfortunately, it is still unknown when this is the case and what exactly causes a demon to attack a person in order to drain their vital energy. It is only believed that people with a special kind of aura are more at risk.

The great class of Yokai, including Ayakashi, are not created by echo, but by the accumulation of high concentrations of negative spiritual energy. This is usually caused by fluctuations or superimpositions of spiritual energy streams that constantly emanate from humans or animals.

The same applies to the class of gods, except that they are created from positive spiritual energy, and since positive spiritual energy is much rarer for whatever reason, there are many more yokai than divine beings. Dawn was created from positive energy. That's rare, and that's why she's special.

Kaito stroked Dawn.

"By the way, Dawn's sister is a pure Ayakashi and doesn't like humans at all. There are Ayakashi who live with humans. They absorb the energy they emit and grow bigger and stronger over time, which can lead to accidents, just like ghosts. The rest of the Yokai, especially the powerful ones, can also suck life energy directly from humans like demons, and this can actually be dangerous for humans if they drain too much energy from them."

"How powerful are all these powerful beings?" asked Mr. Tanaka, listening with interest.

"Divine beings have the power and the task to protect their territory, for example a shrine, from demons and to perform purification there with their positive energy; they also destroy invading demons, otherwise they would not be gods. Therefore, they are on the same level as high-level demons, and both are above the Yokai.

"Positive and negative energy, that sounds like physics," Mr. Tanaka grinned and scratched his head.

"Well, that's my term, but you're not wrong. Names change over time and culture. Call it what you will. Light and shadow, light and dark, good and evil, or divine and demonic.

By the way, the spiritual energy of living beings is considered neutral; it is transformed into positive or negative energy when it leaves the body. This is exactly what I do when I fight demons, I transform my spiritually neutral human energy into positive energy and thus destroy the demon, which is pure negative energy. I dissolve it, so to speak. Haven't you had a case where someone was dissolved in acid, so you can imagine," Kaito said and grinned at Mr. Tanaka.

"Hey, don't make jokes like that, it was really disgusting back then, I don't want to think about it anymore," but he grinned back.

"Is there anything more powerful than demons and gods that you can't handle?"

Kaito looked at Mr. Tanaka a little longer and said, "You are asking strange questions today. Is this an interrogation?"

"No, just curiosity," Mr. Tanaka said. Kaito looks directly at him and says after five breaths, "Yes, there is, but points of relevant contact between a human and these beings are extremely small."

"How small?" asked Mr. Tanaka.

Kaito looked at Dawn, who looked at Kaito. Petting Dawn, Kaito turned his head to Mr. Tanaka and said, "I'd say 1 in 100 billion, if you want a number.

Mr. Tanaka laughed, "With only 8 billion people in the world, that can't be the cause of the problem I want you to investigate, then I'm reassured.

"Now tell me. What do you want?" Kaito asked slightly annoyed.

"Okay, do you remember Mr. Kato, the man with the light gray hair, around 60, the doctor who treated Mika-chan at our house when she was so unwell? Yesterday he told me about his niece and her son who is very sick. By the way, he is convinced that beings like the ones you described really exist, so he came to me when he heard about you."

"If he is a doctor, he should take care of his grandson first, right?" Kaito said, still a bit annoyed.

"Kaito!" said Mr. Tanaka, "that was unnecessary, let me finish. What do you think the poor child was examined for?" continued Mr. Tanaka. "Result. He's perfectly healthy, nothing, except that he can barely stand on his feet. He hasn't even lost much weight!

Now Kaito looked straight into Mr. Tanaka's eyes. "How long has it been like this?" he asked.

"I see I've aroused your interest! It started two months ago. Can you check if it's a ghost?

"If it's a ghost, then it's a demon, a ghost doesn't have that kind of effect on humans. What do you want me to do?"

Mr. Tanaka looked directly at Kaito, "Help the child as best you can! Can you do that? Or no, just do it, that's what I expect from my son!"

"If the problem is of a spiritual nature, I can do something, but it should be quick. If you can't even stand up, it's already close, very close," Kaito replied.

"Thank you, I expected that from you, but now to the real problcm."

"The real problem?" Kaito said questioningly.

"Mrs. Kato, she's divorced again and a well-known scientist and, oh wonder, believes exactly 0.00% in ghosts or demons. I know exactly what you're going to say. But go and help the child, do it anyway, at any cost, that's my request to you. I have to go to work now, otherwise I would have come with you.

Mr. Tanaka looked at Kaito kindly but firmly, "Grow with such tasks, my son.

Mr. Tanaka signaled to the waiter that he wanted to pay, pulled a business card out of his coat and slid it across the table to Kaito, "Here's the address. See you soon," he got up and left.

Kaito looked at Dawn, then at the street where Mr. Tanaka was getting into a taxi.

"Only a policeman could say such stupid things," he thought, looking at the business card. It was the standard cheap business card from Mr. Tanaka's office with a hand-written address on the back. Kaito stood up, looked at Dawn and said, "So Dawn, let's go kill a demon."

Dawn meowed in agreement.

Chapter 2 - DEMONS

"This can't be, two hours for eight kilometers, are we in the Middle Ages?" Kaito thought, pressing the bell and waiting for something to happen. It took a while before anything moved. When the door opened, a woman in her mid-30s looked at him. "What do you want, boy?" she asked gruffly.

"Mr. Tanaka sent me, he said I..." "Come in and don't shout so loud," the woman said and let the door fall loudly into the lock behind him. Kaito was about to form an opinion, but he didn't get that far.

"So you're the ghost hunter. My uncle is another one of those weirdos who read too much fantasy trash and got stuck in it." To their surprise, Kaito didn't answer as he looked around the house. "Hey, what exactly..." Kaito interrupted this time. By the way, this is Dawn, my cat, and I'm not here by choice, but it's the express wish of her uncle and Mr. Tanaka that I get a picture and exactly this," he emphasized it very clearly, "will take a sec-ond, then I can tell you if I can help or not," said Kaito to her, who looked at him a little confused.

"It all takes a second?" she asked incredulously.

"No, I need a second to see if something spiritual is trying to harm your son."

"And if that's the case?" she asked somewhat maliciously. "Then, assuming you agree, I can perform some sort of cleansing.

"Then you want what, 1 million? 10 million?"

"Since it's Mr. Tanaka's wish, I didn't count on money," Kaito replied.

"What kind of person are you?" she asked him.

"Someone who was hired to help you by a friend of your family who cares about you and your son, otherwise I would have left already," Kaito said, slightly annoyed and trying to stay calm.

The woman looked at him, then to the stairs leading up, then back to Kaito. "One second?" she asked again.

"One second, then I can say more."

"Come with me," she replied, going to the stairs and climbing them.

"Even if you are freaks, if I can satisfy my uncle with one second, it's okay with me. My son is getting weaker and weaker, even if they didn't find anything at the hospital, I'll bring him back tomorrow," she said, slowly pushing down the handle of the door to the children's room upstairs.

"One second," the woman said, opening the door and closing it again a short time later.

Kaito looked at Dawn who was sitting on the floor. "Your cat is strangely affectionate! And what did the spirits tell you?" she asked mockingly. "Or will it take you a while to come up with something?"

"They said nothing could be found."

"Yes, are you listening to me?" she asked.

"Your son must have told you that he has pain or pressure in his heart area, right?" Kaito asked.

Silence fell. --- Mrs. Kato looked at him for a full ten seconds and said nothing. --- "Meow" Mrs. Kato startled, looked down at the cat that made the sound, then back up at Kaito, "How did you know?"

"Thank God I guessed right, otherwise it would have been over. Now I just have to find the right words. So, Kaito, hold back," he thought.

"A demon has seized her son and is draining his strength," Kaito said, while he thought he could have said, "A huge armored demon is hovering over her son and has drilled its long, barbed spike into his heart, slowly and gleefully sucking out his life energy, while he waits for him to die in agony so it can feast on him. That would be more scientifically correct," Kaito thought as he waited for Ms. Kato's reaction.

"And what..." she didn't get any further, Kaito interrupted her.

"I need ten minutes. Then your son will be better. I don't have to examine him or touch him. I just need to draw a kind of magic circle on the floor with chalk.

The hallway became quiet again and Kaito hoped that he had chosen the right words.

"Go!"

"Damn, scientists are such an annoying race," Kaito thought.

"If I leave now, your son will die!"

"Now the truth is out, there's no going back," Kaito thought.

Mrs. Kato's arm went up and her hand pointed to the door. She was about to repeat herself when Kaito said, "If you let me do this, the worst you'll have to do is watch an idiot make a fool of himself in front of you and your son for ten minutes. Isn't that worth it to you? Are parents like that?"

"Go on, what did your father Mr. Tanaka think?"

"He's not my father."

She looked at Kaito, "What is he then?" she asked slightly confused.

"My guardian."

And again she looked at Kaito, "where is your father?"

"Somewhere in hell," Kaito answered and thought, "That's it, tomorrow the boy will be dead.

Kaito took a step towards the stairs.

"Wait, boy," she looked at him, "ten minutes, not a minute more, what should I do," she said.

"Okay, no time to think about why she changed her mind. Not that she's going to change her mind," Kaito thought as he entered the room.

"Sit on the bed to your son, I'll draw the circle quickly."

"Mom, what's that man doing here?" a weak voice asked from the bed.

"He wants to drive out evil spirits, Yuto-chan. He'll be done in a moment and then leave."

"That is good, then please drive away these voices as well," Yuto said.

Kaito smiled slightly, "Well, parents", he thought and said to Dawn, "get in position, the bastard is getting nervous."

Kaito stood up, walked to the door, turned around and stood at the edge of the circle he had drawn, which was about two meters wide.

"It's four meters to the bed, that should be enough. The demon won't suspect anything from that distance. Now let's see how much she loves her son," Kaito thought.

"Mrs. Kato, put your arms around your son, hold him tight. No matter what happens in the next minute, don't let him go," he said.

"That wasn't the agreement," she said.

"Let's silence the voices you hear and prove to your mother that you were right," Kaito said to Yuto.

Yuto looked at his mother. She looked at him.

"If you love him, then don't let him go in any way, Mrs. Kato," Kaito said, clutching the amulet he wore around his neck.

Just as Mrs. Kato was about to answer and look at him, she saw Kaito's hand wrap around the jagged amulet and her eyes widened as she saw blood oozing from between his fingers.

"SHY NOW!"

"This power of words, did it really come from the boy? No. Yes, from whom else? What a commanding tone, it's hard to believe it came from the boy. She hasn't had anything like that for a long time ... what's going on?" Mrs. Kato panicked.

The bed she was sitting on with her son suddenly accelerated, causing her to tip backwards slightly as the bed moved faster and faster across the floor towards the door where Kaito was standing. In shock, she immediately wrapped her arms around her son and screamed "What the hell is happening here", no it was just thoughts, she couldn't get words out, just screams. She looked into Kaito's eyes as the bed slid further and further in his direction and she came closer and closer to him.

Only about one meter separated Kaito from Mrs. Kato. She tried to scream again as the bed suddenly stopped about a meter from the door. Still paralyzed with shock, she looked at Kaito and noticed that his expression had changed. "Is he grinning," she thought, "no, he's smiling slightly, what was that about?

"DISINTEGRATION!" Kaito shouted calmly but commandingly as he looked Mrs. Kato in the eyes beside him while pressing his bloody hand to the chalk circle on the floor where the bed now stood.

It was getting bright in the room, "the lights are dimmed and the windows darkened, where is the light coming from," Mrs. Kato thought as she tightened her arms around her son and looked at Kaito. "Where is the boy looking, not at me, no at the source of the light," she slowly turned her head in that direction.

Shock! It went through her like an electric shock. She jerked back, "No, you're not getting my son, you monster," she screamed inwardly. A glowing something, huge, enormous, with muscle plates all over its body, abstruse and surreal like a Dali, sat, no, hovered above the bed, half a meter away from her and her son.

"Go back where you came from and die," Kaito said calmly but commandingly with a smile on his face to the demon.

Only now did she notice that her son was screaming, struggling, and that something was trying to tear him away from her. Automatically, without thinking, she screamed, "It's trying to take my son away from me!

"I told you to hold on to your son or he'll die," Kaito replied without taking his eyes off the demon. Mrs. Kato grabbed her son even tighter. The pulling became more violent, the child seemed to want to tear himself from his mother's arms as he screamed louder and louder in pain.

Mrs. Kato closed her eyes, clutched her son even tighter, and screamed, "Die you beast, get out of here, leave my son alone. She didn't know how long she did this. Eventually, she realized that something had changed.

"Yes, Yuto's screaming and struggling has stopped," she realized. Startled, she looked down at him, the child looked at his mother and smiled a little, "No, there's nothing wrong with Yuto," she looked at the demon that was still hovering directly above them.

"Is the demon shrinking, is it getting weaker or am I just imagining it?" thought Mrs. Kato.

"Ten more seconds," Kaito shouted, knowing that ten seconds was an eternity for Mrs. Kato in this situation.

"It's getting weaker, it's disintegrating and the falling particles are starting to glow, now you can see it clearly," she thought and understood Kaito's words, the demon was dying right now, the boy, Kaito, was about to extinguish it here and now.

"Die, you scum, you'll be with your father in ten seconds," she shouted at the creature, which became visible in the light of golden particles that detached from it and floated back and forth in the room, while the demon tried to escape with her son at the same time.

"Dawn, no, not yet," Kaito shouted, thinking, "Damn, that creature was bigger than I thought, this is really getting close.

Only now did Mrs. Kato see the cat, hissing as she aimed at the glowing something above the bed, "What was her name again, Dawn? What's she doing there? What is she waiting for?"

The cat turned her head and looked at Kaito. Automatically, Mrs. Kato looked at him as well, her arms still wrapped tightly around her son.

"Damn, don't let up, boy, the demon looks ready," she thought.

"Now, Dawn," but the cat had already jumped and was now diving above the demon into the glittering, radiant particles that lit up the room.

Mrs. Kato's eyes grew wide, bigger than when she was first shocked by this monster. The cat distorted. The faint light from the lamps in the room, which had made the cat visible before, was now dwarfed by the bright golden particles, and where the cat dipped into the area of the particles, it transformed out of nowhere into a beautiful young woman, moving through the air like a cat leaping. She resembled a predator approaching the demon from behind at high speed.

Shocked and fascinated at the same time, as if paralyzed with horror at the whole situation, she saw the young woman reach out and with a mighty blow smash her hands, no, paws with claws or still hands, through the visibly weakened body of the monster, which disappeared in a sea of myriads of glowing particles that illuminated the room as bright as day.

The young woman came up like a cat after jumping right in front of Mrs. Kato, their faces only about half a meter apart, when she saw cat ears and a bushy tail appear behind the creature. She didn't know why, but she had to touch the creature that had saved her son, and slowly her hand separated from her son and reached out to the strange creature. The creature smiled at her, shook its head slightly and pointed at her son. She understood immediately and pulled her arm back, holding her son tightly with both arms.

"Mom, what happened?" Yuto asked his mother with tears in his eyes.

With one bound, the creature jumped over her and landed on the floor like a normal house cat.

"You were dreaming, a nightmare, and your mother woke you up," Kaito said in a panting voice.

"Where's the kitchen?" asked Kaito.

Mother and son looked at each other. "How are you?" she asked.

The son cried, "Everything hurts." "Where does it hurt?" she asked desperately.

"Everywhere," he shouted loudly, crying and flailing. But Mrs. Kato noticed that her son had much more strength than before, and that the crying was more from fear than pain. She smiled at him and he smiled back.

Mrs. Kato looked at Kaito who was just walking out the door. "That is normal after such a dream. Everything will be back to normal in a week. Dawn, take care of yourself a little longer and you'll catch up," Kaito said and went downstairs.

Mrs. Kato slowly stroked her son's head and then asked, "Something to eat?

"Yes, I'm very hungry, Mom."

"Then I'll make you something." She looked at the door, the cat sitting motionless, its gaze fixed on Yuto.

Mrs. Kato walked out of the room, looked down at the cat, looked back up and said, "Thanks, kitty," and walked down the stairs.

When he arrived in the kitchen, Kaito was sitting on the floor with a beer in his hand.

"Do you always raid your client's fridge after a job like this?" asked Ms. Kato.

"As a high school student, you are never 20," she said.

"Maybe," Kaito replied curtly.

Ms. Kato rolled her eyes, "I didn't see anything and I don't want to know, what do your, hmm, ... Mr. Tanaka say?"

"I got a little carried away, the armored demon lived up to his name. Alcohol simply helps with regeneration better than a soft drink, a scientist should understand that. But your beer is not very good, Ms. Kato."

"And you threw up in the sink too, great. Shall I call an ambulance for you?

"Quite the old lady, how fast it goes," Kaito thought.

"So it's called an armored demon and why could I see it, I thought only people as sublime as you could see these creatures," she scoffed, emphasizing the word 'sublime'.

"Stardust, the golden particles created when a spiritual being like that demon disintegrates, reflects light into both dimensions, believe it or not. I don't care. My work is done."

"Two dimensions? Is that some kind of parallel universe or something?

"No, I interpret it as another spatial dimension to our three, so a scientist should understand that too, Ms. Kato," Kaito said with a slightly mocking laugh on his lips.

"And you believe what you're saying?"

"How many spatial dimensions has string theory just reached, Ms. Kato?" and took a big sip from the can. "One more dimension doesn't make much difference, does it?"

"What do you get from me?

"I told you, I don't take money for it."

"What would you have taken if it was a normal job?"

"I charge 100,000 yen per hour."

"A high hourly wage, you must not have many customers," she said somewhat disdainfully as she went to a closet and took something out.

"I reduce the number of annoying customers and thus my workload. So I have more time for the really important things."

"Here, so you don't have to raid other customers' fridges," Mrs. Kato said, placing an envelope on Kaito's lap.

"You will keep what happened today confidential, and I will reach you through Mr. Tanaka if I have any questions!"

"Of course, and thank you very much. By the way, your son only has a weak spiritual aura, which is good because demons usually ignore such people. The fact that an armored demon attacked your son is quite unusual. There are only a few situations I can think of that would lead to something like this, and they all have something to do with an innocent soul that has built up a tremendous hatred due to the betrayal of a close person."

"Boy, you've talked enough now, you seem to be feeling better, your cat is waiting for you at the door!"

Kaito stood up, said "Goodbye" and went to the front door, where Dawn was indeed waiting for him.

"Goodbye, and if we do meet again, I hope it won't be because of something like this!" she said coolly.

"What really happened today, what consequences does it have for my son, for our family, for people's lives in general? Can I tell anyone? No, who can I tell without making a fool of myself and my team at work?" she thought and watched as Kaito closed the door.

"The demon is history, the particles seemed to come out of nowhere when the demon disintegrated and dissolved back into nothing. It all took no more than a few seconds, even though it seemed like an eternity. In the end, there is no evidence that the demon was killed, scary what that means," she thought as she walked up the stairs to her son and said, "What kind of monster is this that hunts monsters!"

"Phew, what a bitch and now all the way back," Kaito thought and walked to the bus stop. It was already dark when he entered his one-room apartment on the tenth floor of an old high-rise building with a broken elevator.

"Small but nice, and thanks to the bitch I can pay the rent again, she was very generous in the end and I don't have to ask Mr. Tanaka again," he thought.

"You seem to be feeling better," Dawn said, leaning against the table in front of him.

"Well, the two beers..." He didn't get any further, Dawn took a step towards him and gave him a resounding slap in the face.

"You ass, are you going to leave me alone, or what was that today? An armored demon, unprepared, when you've barely slept for two days and made a huge amount of protective seals with your spiritual energy for the Order on the side. That was really close today, you know? Do you understand that? Or should I tell you again what would have happened if we hadn't vanquished him completely," Dawn shouted at him.

Kaito sat down, looked down and then back at Dawn.

"I'm sorry, I made a mistake. I really didn't expect anything like this, it was a mistake that won't happen again. But the child really could have died at any time, so I put life before logic. It won't happen again in the future, I promise."

"Meow, woe betide you, you're more important to me than any other person."

Chapter 3 - EXPANSION

"My son, I'm so proud of you," said Mr. Tanaka. "Old Mr. Kato called me and thanked me a thousand times, the boy is doing great again, he's even going back to school on Monday. Come on, let's order something good to eat. By the way, Mr. Kato is coming by again and ..."

"Oh, please don't," Kaito interrupts, "besides, I've already been talked into something, I really don't need this."

"Oh damn, didn't you want to take the money in the first place? In all the excitement, I forgot to tell you that the family is very wealthy, so you can just write a big bill."

"What did she give you, only if you want to tell me?"

"300,000 yen, that's very good."

"Wow, if you're satisfied. Do you have enough other customers?

"They will come, I have an agreement with Mr. Nakamura from the Order, and I'll also get some money for making the protective seals."

"You've become a real young entrepreneur," he laughed cheerfully at him, "keep up the good work."

"So I can't answer your question Kaito, why Mrs. Kato agreed at least, it's funny how that happened. But maybe she knows that my children are all just great," Mr. Tanaka said to Kaito with a laugh.

"You can't choose relatives like your father, mother and children. But you can choose someone like me. Maybe you're closer than you'd like to admit," Kaito thought and said, "Maybe the despair was greater than it seemed.

"By the way, what you said to Mrs. Kato about `close person', please forget it quickly. Her husband couldn't handle the situation of the wealthy Kato family, had overreached himself out of male pride and ambition, causing great upheaval, and then kidnapped the child in anger over the divorce. A chase with the police led to an accident, the son survived, the father died. Legally it's all settled, morally it's no longer our business. In any case, the father was not innocent."

Kaito looked at Dawn who was sitting next to him. "I guess that's what they told you," Kaito thought and said, "Of course, water under the bridge, we have a test tomorrow, that's more important."

The already high sun that illuminated his room woke him up, "Monday, I hate Monday. No! I love Mondays, but only this semester," Kaito thought with a grin and sat up. "Man, I slept well. 9 o'clock perfect, then I'll be on time for third period and won't have to listen to that witch of an English teacher, so these Mondays are really great. If I can stay in the middle of the pack on the test, that's good enough, anything more would just attract attention."

"Dawn, do you want to get up?" he asked, blowing gen-tly into her cat ears, which twitched slightly in response.

"MIAU!" Dawn pulled the covers over her cat ears.

"I only understood 'meow', but that was probably a clear no," Kaito thought.

"Dawn, I have to go, see you later."

Kaito went out the door, turned around and looked at Dawn who was lying peacefully in bed.

"My personal catgirl. Just for me. How you would envy me. I'll take care of you, forever. I'd kill for you, Dawn," Kaito thought as he closed the door and made his way to school.

The school bell had rung at the end of math class. "Not that I need it, but math is interesting and the teacher is above average and nice. Luckily, I didn't run into the scarecrow. A perfect day. I'm going out for lunch."

"Where is the best place to sit today? Oh, that's where the outsiders sit today." Kaito sat down nearby when one of the students at the table got up and left.

"Huh, was that a coincidence?" There was a low murmur from behind, something like, "Did you hear that guy is supposed to be in the Yakuza?"

"Aha, so the wind is blowing, a new rumor about me and a lot of stupid people who believe it, and in a year you'll be allowed to vote. If the right to vote were taken away from these idiots, our country would be a very different place.

"I guess I'm the outsider's outsider now," Kaito laughed to himself.

"That bitchy girl from Friday is sitting over there too, but she won't move even though she saw me."

"Hey Mio-chan, come on, I'll show you my ghost collection too," came a slightly louder voice from a neighboring table.

Kaito looked over and saw the third girl from Friday in the park sitting at the table with two guys who obviously wanted more of her. "What a stupid pick-up line, but if it works, he's hit the jackpot," Kaito thought.

"Listen, kid, I'm not coming to the party, and certainly not with you, and you shouldn't make fun of ghosts."

"Now, now, so rude and bitchy all at once, if you want to see ghosts, we can have the party at the cemetery and leave a little early so Mom doesn't worry.

"Idiot, that's enough!" the girl said, getting up and walking away. The boys laughed after her.

"Just try the next one, the beast from Friday is still there. That would be fun. It'll work with someone," Kaito thought, looked at his tray and continued to eat.

Kaito was about to put his tray back into the cart when he saw a moving shadow between the trays. His hand moved between them almost automatically, reached out, pulled something out and saw a small Ayakashi that looked like a cross between a fur ball, a rat and a hedgehog.

"I told you to stay away from the school," he hissed softly, barely audible to anyone else, as he walked out of the cafeteria.

"Do you want me to cremate you? Playing dead won't help, otherwise you'll be dead in a minute."

"Please, please, great creator of all things, let me go, I won't do it again," the Ayakashi said.

"The forest begins at the southern end of the city, 2000 paces into the eastern forest, you can stay there. Tell your kind that Kaito has given you permission."

"I will never steal food from humans again," the Ayakashi said.

"That was just garbage anyway and not the problem, I just don't want to see you here at school, okay?"

"Yes, Master of all things.

"If you know me, why are you here?"

"I was hungry."

"For human spiritual energy?"

"No, no, I would never allow myself to do that, the human food is so good, I usually only get seeds and roots."

"Stick to that, it's healthier, otherwise you'll become even fatter than you are now.

"Master, what ..."

Kaito lunged and made a throwing motion, but only he saw the ayakashi flying through the air to the south.

"Hey, what did you throw?" a girl's voice asked behind him.

"Nothing, I'm doing gymnastics, English was stressful," he turned around and looked Mio in the eye.

"Really," Mio asked, "I thought something flew, but at least I didn't see anything. You know you can't run or throw anything on the schoolyard, school rules paragraph 5a."

"Are you from the student council?" Kaito asked with a laugh.

"Yes, I am," Mio said.

"Oh bitch, you're annoying," Kaito thought and said, "Well, like I said, I was just loosening my arm."

"Because of English?" asked Mio.

"Yes, exactly."

"So because of English, so, so, even though you missed the first two lessons, like almost every English lesson for almost a year and a half," Mio said.

"How do you know that?" Kaito asked in astonishment.

"Everyone is talking about you, Mr. Tanaka. The boy who has been seen in English at most ten times this year and last year and yet always does well. Is it because of your contacts with the Yakuza?"

"Do you believe those stories?"

"Of course not, how stupid is that, but how you manage to stay in the top third in English, that would interest me."

"The longer you talk to me, the more you run the risk of my negative aura sticking to you," Kaito said, wanting to end the conversation quickly.

"Nice try, I'm from the student council and I have to talk to outsiders like you. I'll keep an eye on you from now on, Mr. Tanaka," Mio said, took a step back, looked at him, nodded once, turned around and left.

Kaito looked after her and thought, "I underestimated that bitch, she'll go far, but what was her name again?"

Then he looked to the ground and said, "If you say a word, you will become stardust and now go after your friend without a word."

The Ayakashi on the ground was startled and fled in the direction Kaito had thrown his friend.

"This could be fun," Kaito turned around and went back to his class.

"What book are you reading today, Kaito?" asked Dawn in the late afternoon.

"A Japanese translation of a treatise on the killing of demons in the French Middle Ages," Kaito said as he sat in an office on an old swivel chair at a completely outdated wooden table on which he had put his feet.

Dawn was lounging on a sofa three meters away from Kaito's desk. There were a few chairs and a shelf full of books and folders in the 25 square meter room.

Kaito put the book aside, looked around and thought, "I really need to replace these chairs, they're almost embarrassing for an office. On the other hand, if customer don't like it, go somewhere else. The rent is very cheap for this location, especially considering the age of the building and the broken elevator, hopefully they'll never fix it."

Dawn got up from the sofa and sat down on Kaito's lap, who was still sitting in the chair at the desk.

"So, Dawn, are you bored?" Kaito asked.

"Meow, yes, meow! Let's go to the forest to the Ayakashi and play with them."

"You know that you and I are not welcome there, that Ayakashi can give something back is foreign to them."

"Then let's tease them and pretend to hunt them," Dawn said to Kaito, putting her arms around him and pulling him close.

"The office door burst open and a panting ten-year-old boy stood in the doorway.

"Can't ghost hunters afford an office where the elevator works?" he asked into the room, still panting as he looked down at the floor.

"What do you want, boy, speak," Kaito said slightly annoyed.

The boy looked up and pointed his finger at Kaito.

"What kind are you and what is this seemingly horny girl with the cat ears doing on top of you?"

Silence, Kaito was stunned, what kind of boy is this that could see Dawn. Did he even know how outrageous this was? The boy wanted to say something again, but Kaito was quicker, "Dawn," he said.

Dawn jumped at the boy, who ducked in fright. When he saw Dawn slam the door and grin at him, he jumped away from her. But Dawn was faster and wrapped her arms around him.

"What exactly am I, say that again, you little prick," Dawn said, glaring at him.

"I'm sorry, I'm sorry, I didn't mean it. Please let me go," the boy said, starting to cry.

"Tell me, what do you want from me?" said Kaito.

The boy looked up and said, "Look at this on my body, only I can see it, no one else can, but I want it to go away, my parents don't believe me and my sister doesn't see it either. I keep trying to make it go away and it keeps coming back," he babbles without a period or comma.

Kaito looked at the boy. Yes, there was a little Cling-Ayakashi attached to him, harmless but annoying, feeding on the radiated spiritual energy of a human being and not like demons that suck it directly and then transform it for themselves.

The little Ayakashi was the kind that couldn't communicate with humans.

"Still, I can understand the boy, I wouldn't have had the courage to seek out a 'ghost hunter' at his age," Kaito thought.

"What do I get if we get rid of this?", Kaito asked.

"Whatever you want."

"Dawn, send him up."

When the boy saw Dawn approaching him again, he was startled, closed his eyes and yelped slightly.

"Meow, you scaredy-cat," it ended. Small glowing particles floated to the spot where the Ayakashi had clung and quickly disappeared into the sunlight.

"That's how you make a billion yen, kid."

"What kind of person are you?" the boy asked provocatively.

"You said I could have anything I wanted."

The boy got nervous, looked around, and was startled again when he saw Dawn's sardonic grin.

"But I don't have that much money," he said and started to cry again.

"Then we'll sell you to a man-eating Yokai," Dawn said.

The boy looked up startled, "What, what, what are you going to do to me?"

"Oh, you got scared, pantser?" asked Dawn, shoving the boy.

"Dawn, enough is enough!" said Kaito. "Hey you! Catch," said Kaito, throwing a crumpled note to the crying boy.

"What's this?" he asked fearfully.

"You don't want this to happen again. Follow the instructions on the note and it won't happen again, okay?" said Kaito commandingly.

"Dawn, throw him out."

"If you're that cheeky again, I'll eat you," Dawn said, opening the door and pulling the boy out by the collar.

The boy bowed to Kaito, then looked at Dawn, stuck out his tongue, said "horny cat" and ran off.

"Dawn!" said Kaito.

Dawn turned around, laughed, walked over to Kaito, said "Meow, what a fun day" and gave him a kiss.

Almost a week and two sparse missions later, Dawn and Kaito were back in the office and Dawn was moaning again, "Now we haven't had an exciting mission for over a week, I'm so bored.

"I'm more worried about my bank balance and the next rent due, maybe I should offer more cleaning rituals, every little helps", Kaito thought and closed the banking application on his tablet.

"Meow," Dawn said, Kaito looked at the door, there was a knock. "Come in."

"Hello, my name is Mio Yamamoto and I..." Mio, the girl from his school, didn't come any further. Kaito and Mio's eyes met in the room.

"Mr. Tanaka, what are you doing here?

"I should ask you that, you're in my office, Ms. Yamamoto.

Mio looked at Kaito for a long time and then said, "Come in, he's not lying to us.

Another girl of the same age, but wearing a different school uniform, entered the office, startled and slightly frightened.

"It was so clear that something was wrong with you, you can see them."

"What exactly?" asked Kaito.

"Spirits, demons, Yokai, whatever you call them."

"Well, what's the point? After all, you came to me," Kaito asked.

"This is Yuki Watanabe, a very good friend of mine. Her father is sick and getting weaker and weaker, although no doctor can find anything. I keep telling them that it could be a demon, but they won't listen, so I dragged her here today. It can't go on like this. Her father will lose his job.

"Then we have a problem," Kaito said.

"Why, what do you mean?"

"I only accept assignments where the client is also the person being spiritually attacked, the spouse or legal guardian, which is probably not the case with you.

"Now she's getting angry," Kaito thought.

"Okay, I see, what do you want for an exception?" asked Mio.

Kaito looked at Mio, "Okay, that's not the answer he was expecting, rather something arrogant like 'come with me', 'go there', 'move'. Had she gone through something similar like him in her childhood?"

"I stay out of trouble and that's the way it is..."

"There won't be any trouble, I'm coming with you and no one will question anything, I promise," Mio interrupted him.

"How bad is he?

"Sometimes better and sometimes worse, depending on the day. But since he's been home, it's gotten worse," Mio said when the other girl started to cry.

"Maybe a demon or Yokai has taken up residence in the house, you don't have to fight it right away," Kaito thought and said, "Tomorrow after school, is that possible?"

"Yes!"

"Then sign the contract here!"

"I'll do that, I'll read it and bring it to school tomorrow, is that okay?" asked Mio.

"That's fine."

Mr. Tanaka here "I read the contract yesterday and signed it too, your prices are adventurous but not as high as the one billion for my brother and don't you dare lie to me. Let's go right now. This is the way," Mio said and walked ahead.

"So the boy was her brother. The similarity in personality and manner was clearly a result of their being related", he thought to himself, smiling and saying "That boy was your brother. Do you know that he can see ghosts too?"

"Yes, but he's already afraid of a little Ayakashi, so I can't let him look for a demon."

"An existing ability like that fades with most children when they reach puberty," Kaito said, "and then they forget it, or want to forget it quickly, from then on, other things are simply more important. Your brother will be no exception."

"That's what I thought, it's just stupid that I didn't know that when I was five," Mio said to Kaito.

"Okay, that's why she reacted like that, she could see some Spirits even as a child," he thought.

"How did you get through that time, you could help your brother with that, couldn't you?"

"You can't compare that. It was much worse for me. I didn't go to my grandfather's funeral or my grandmother's funeral, I didn't go to their graves until I was eleven, even though they meant so much to me."

"Was it that bad what you saw?"

"Hell, I was five years old, nobody believed me. I was scared to death. I pretended to be sick every time, just so I wouldn't have to go to the cemetery and pray that my parents would come back in one piece. And then, at the age of eleven, it was all over, like a bad dream I woke up from. Today I see things differently. The spirits never attacked my parents, why? What about my grandparents, are they ghosts too, can I apologize to them? Now that I want to know and I'm ready, I can't see ghosts anymore, what a bummer, right?"

"How did your parents react to your behavior back then?" Kaito asked carefully.

Mio looked at him, "Well, the way parents react when you say you're sick, they always came home as soon as possible to nurse me all day."

Kaito swallowed.

"Meow."

"Thanks Dawn, just the right time," Kaito thought and said to Dawn, "come here."

"You can get into a similar situation again so quickly," Mio said as Dawn jumped up to Kaito.

"My classmate was really pissed off, she really thought you were hitting on her, she's still a little upset, but I took care of it. There's nothing more to it."

"It almost sounds like I was the culprit."

"Well, men almost always are, aren't they?"

Kaito rolled his eyes, but before he could say anything, Mio interrupted him, "So you're the catgirl Dawn my brother wanted to see, by the way, I slapped him for his insolence towards you."

"Meow," came from Dawn.

"Yes, that's exactly what I mean," Mio replied.

"As if you knew what Dawn said," Kaito thought.

Mio rang the doorbell at the Watanabe's house and her friend from yesterday opened the door. "Come in," she said, "we're all sitting in the living room."

"A small but cozy house," Kaito thought. The Watanabe's were sitting in the living room, Mr. Watanabe on the sofa, you could tell he wasn't feeling well.

His wife was sitting at a table with a child who was playing with building blocks. Everyone was looking at the guests who had just arrived.

The child jumped up and ran over to Mio. "Hello Mio, hello Mio," he said.

The father tried to stand up, and the mother jumped up anxiously to support her husband. "Welcome to our house, Mr. Tanaka, would you like to sit down?"

"Please bring us something to drink, Yuki."

It became increasingly clear how depressed the mood was and that Mrs. Watanabe was at the end of her tether.

"Mr. Watanabe, please sit down again. May I ask what Mrs. Yamamoto told you?" Kaito asked.

"Well, that you are a ghost hunter, no, she expressed herself differently, but forgive me, I forgot. Mio said that if there is a ghost here, you might be able to help us, me."

"You don't mind if I take a look around, do you?"

The look on Mrs. Watanabe's face spoke volumes, but she didn't say a word and just nodded friendly when Kaito looked at her.

"No, no, no one could find anything or even help me, now we just have to go another way," Mr. Watanabe said.

In the meantime, Dawn had gone to the child and he began to stroke Dawn and talk to her. His mother watched and smiled slightly.

"Damn, why always such orders. Cleaning jobs are much less complicated."

"Shy, look around, now," Kaito ordered.

Everyone in the room looked at him, Kaito didn't move and looked at Dawn who was playing with the child.

"Is everything to your satisfaction?" asked Mr. Watanabe.

"A guardian ghost is looking around, it only takes a minute."

"Oh, that's good, I hope he doesn't find anything bad."

"If he doesn't find anything bad, you've got a much bigger problem, sick man," Kaito thought, but kept it to himself as he continued to watch Dawn.

"Well, Mr. Watanabe, my guardian spirit told me that a larger and more troublesome Yokai has taken up residence in the place in your house where he finds you most often, which is why you are at your worst when you are here in the house."

"Should we leave my parents' house?" asked Mrs. Watanabe slightly hysterically.

Kaito tried to smile at her, but he couldn't.

"No, we kill the Yokai," Kaito said without looking back.

"Then he's probably in the bedroom?" said Mr. Watanabe.

"Why there?" his daughter asked.

"Well, because I spend at least eight hours a day there," he said.

"Right, Mr. Watanabe, and since I am too lazy to go up the stairs, we will kill the Yokai down here," Kaito said, thinking that Mrs. Watanabe would never let him kill the Yokai up there in the bedroom.

Kaito took some protective seals from his pocket and spread them around the room.

"And how are you going to destroy him here if he's up in the bedroom?" Mio asked slightly annoyed.

"We'll lure him down, Ms. Know-it-all", Kaito said, also annoyed.

Mio was annoyed but said nothing more.

"Please all go to Mr. Watanabe's sofa and stay there, no matter what you think you see, don't move, you'll be safe there," Kaito said to the group.

"Mrs. Watanabe, please take the child by the hand."

Mrs. Watanabe takes the child in her arms and gives Kaito a slightly angry look as she walks over to her husband.

"And how do we lure the Yokai down now?" asked Mio.

"We summon a spirit," Kaito said and drew a magic circle on the ground.

"Huh," a loud murmur went through the room.

"I wish I hadn't said anything," he thought.

"This kind of yokai is very possessive, if it senses a spirit near its victim, it will try to extinguish it, just like this yokai. Such a yokai will never allow a spirit to approach its victim.

"Isn't that dangerous?" Mio asked.

"No, ghosts are not dangerous, we'll get rid of him later."

"There, stand right there, don't worry, it's all half as bad, I'll call the spirit and off we go," Kaito said, looking around, took a small needle from the lining of his jacket and pricked his finger.

"What are you doing?" shouted Mio.

Too late, at the same time Kaito said "*RISE UP, NEAREST!*" and pressed his finger on the circle of magic.

There was silence in the room, no one dared to speak, even Mio was silent. A light breeze came from the front. "It's coming," Kaito said.

The wind from the front became stronger. Everyone except Kaito looked around in amazement, trying to locate the source of the ever stronger wind. The wind and its noises became a soft pounding and rushing. The child in his mother's arms began to cry and Kaito thought, "Remember, next time remove the child and mother from the room first.

Now the wind became very clear and above all colder, the door to the living room swung open in the wind, hit the wall of the room and everyone but Kaito flinched.

Mio said loudly, "Kaito, damn it, what's going on, it's getting cold!

"Stay where you are!" Kaito shouted in Mio's direction.

"*HOLY LANCE!*" Kaito said clearly in the direction of the open door where the wind came from.

"What's he doing, what's he flicking away, a stone, a paper ball, what's that?" Mio thought and tried to follow the object with her eyes as it moved away from Kaito's hand.

A flash, a flash in the middle of the room, had the object hit something that wasn't there before?

Mio shielded her eyes by slightly squeezing them shut and holding her hands in front of her eyes with her fins slightly apart so that the bright light where the object had hit wouldn't blind her too much.

She couldn't make out exactly what it was, everything was blurred or...

Mio's breath stopped for a moment as an abysmally ugly grimace with a much too small body on four legs appeared a few meters in front of her. Wrapped in a cloak of glowing particles, the Yokai could be seen as a golden lance inside it slowly dissolved the beast the faster it squirmed.

"Die you beast," she thought without realizing what she was experiencing.

Mio looked at Kaito, who stood not a millimeter away from the first starting point, calm and relaxed, with a meaningless expression on his face, watching the spectacle indifferently.

The Yokai wriggled one last time and then dissolved completely. New particles appeared, illuminating the room and disappearing just as quickly. The cold also gave way to the cozy warmth of the house. It took no more than ten seconds.

Kaito looked around, everyone had retreated except Mio, who was still staring wide-eyed at the spot where the Yokai had disappeared.

"It's over, they'll be better tomorrow. Dawn, let's go!"

"What about the spirit you summoned?" asked Mio.

"Oops, oh that one, he's sticking to you Mio, I think he likes you, do you like older men?" It was the ghost of an older man who seemed very confused and didn't know exactly where he was or what was happening to him.

"You little wanker," Mio said, "get rid of him now."

"Dawn, send him up," Kaito said, "Sorry old man, but it really is time for you."

It happened so fast that Mio only saw the cat move over her head out of the corner of her eye. Golden particles again, and in those particles she recognized a cat girl with her eyes wide open.

That brief moment lasted less than a second, but it was burned into her memory like a favorite childhood photo. "My brother wasn't lying about how sweet and beautiful Dawn was, much too beautiful for that bourgeois," Mio thought.

Mrs. Watanabe left the room with her child in her arms.

"This was probably too much for her, I hope she recovers," Kaito thought.

Mr. Watanabe and Mio's girlfriend, on the other hand, had realized what had happened, but didn't really know how to deal with the situation and kept thanking him.

"What do we owe you?" asked Mr. Watanabe after several thanks.

"Well, the contract was signed by Ms. Yamamoto," so you don't owe me anything.

"I'll take care of it, we'll go then and I still have to talk to Mr. Tanaka about something," Mio said with a slight grin.

After Kaito and Mio had said goodbye to the Watanabe family, Kaito asked, "What else do you want, Dawn and I want to go home."

"Actually, I should smack you for what you did to me, but I forgive you for your rudeness, I don't want the day to end like this. I found what I was looking for, I'll bring you the money tomorrow."

"Oh dear, that doesn't sound good," Kaito thought and made his way to the train station.

In the afternoon of the next day, Dawn lounged on the sofa again while Kaito drew protection seals and thought: "Why do I do these time-consuming drawings, they get my blood almost for free, then the Order could have them drawn as well. Sometimes, I really am a fool."

"Hello everyone, Mio is here with yesterday's wages," Mio said as she opened the door and came in.

"I haven't finished the bill yet," Kaito said.

"Never mind, you won't get any money anyway."

"Huh?"

"You will be paid in kind," Mio said, grinning maliciously.

"Do you want a child from me?" Kaito asked sarcastically.

"No, you little pervert, I'll work off my debt here in the office and then you'll be so positively overwhelmed by my performance that you'll officially hire me as a part-time employee.

"Give me one reason why I should do this."

"Because someone has to clean up around here, because you need someone who can talk to customers without them going down your throat, because you need someone who knows the subject matter and isn't afraid, because you need someone who can get orders, because I can shut up, because I can shield you, because I can be a super cute figurehead, because..." Mio didn't get any further.

"Got it, okay," Kaito said, remembering yesterday when Mio's eyes had shown no fear and she hadn't backed down an inch. He smiled to himself and thought, "Yeah, you're a super cute figurehead too," he turned away from her embarrassed and explained,

"I won't be able to pay much later."

Dawn meowed loudly and Kaito realized that he had probably looked at Mio a little too long.

"That was easy, when do we start?" she said.

"As far as I'm concerned, I'd like some tea, Ms. Yamamoto."

"Oh yes, and from now on you call me Mio and I'll call you Kaito, except at school of course. I already blew it in the fight yesterday anyway," Mio laughed a little embarrassed.

It was a very nice laugh, Kaito thought, not artificial, but honest.

"Then I'll call you Mio-Chan," he replied.

"No, no, I'm five days older than you, Kaito-chan."

"What the hell, how do you know ..."

"I just looked it up, student representatives have divine rights, you know," Mio grinned at the overwhelmed Kaito.

"Tea coming up pervert Kaito-chan."

"Meow, pervert Kaito-chan," came from Dawn. Kaito looked over, she was sitting on the sofa with a big grin and looked at him with amusement.

"You were just what I was missing, my overgrown hunting ferret", Kaito said, turning to the window of his office, looking at the sunset and muttering softly

"Shy, leave Mio alone, she's with us from now on."

Chapter 4 - OFFICE WORK

"She's been here less than a week, and she's doing the work like she's been here a year. She's quick to learn, one explanation is enough. The perfect employee. In complete contrast to the divine being on the sofa to my right," Kaito thought as he saw Dawn lying lazily on the sofa again, playing with her tail.

"Didn't you want to search the house for Ayakashi like we agreed, Dawn?"

"Meow, I'm not in the mood right now, why don't you send Shy?"

"Well, at least she looks cute when she plays like that, cuter than Shy anyway.

Mio, who was studying books, looked up and said, "I think I've understood everything. I'll summarize it again.

Firstly, very importantly, the corner to the right of the window is the place for your house ghost 'Shy', I can't disturb him there under any circumstances.

Second, the number of folders on the bottom shelf are empty and can be used for new cases, then they need to be moved to the top shelf. Where there are so few," Mio said smugly.

"Third, the books on the left shelf are copies of books from old works on spiritual powers, as long as I put them back where you put them, I can read them. In time, I will scan them and archive them.

Do you even have permission to do that? Don't look so annoyed, it's not cool, copyright is important," Mio said with a grin and moved on to the next point.

"Fourth. Monday to Friday from 3 to 6 p.m. and Saturday from 10 to 6 p.m. I'm supposed to take customer calls and sort out the ones that are 'too stupid for this world', those were your words Kaito. In between, I answer emails and greet everyone who dares to come here.

I'm surprised you have any customers at all, Kaito-chan.

Kaito kept a straight face.

"Now I would like you to tell me if I have understood the ways of fighting demons. Sensei!"

"Come on then," Kaito said.

"Dark spirits, can be fought from a distance, for example with banishing orbs, in which the 'deriver' has stored positive energy through his blood. You can only use the energy stored in the orb, so the effect on a demon is rather small, but you can keep your distance.

Pressing a banishing seal on the demon can release all of the Deriver's energy, so it's much more effective, but more dangerous because you have to get close and touch the demon.

In a pentagram, the ley lines created transmit a spiritual secondary field over a large area, which is very ineffective, especially against strong demons and yokai, but covers a large area.

Depending on how they are used, magic, protection, or sealing circles are symbols drawn on the ground. They are limited in space and fixed in place like pentagrams, but they have the advantage of being able to amplify incoming energies and even store them for a certain period of time, so that they can release energy for a period of time even without further energy supply and thus maintain their function independently. Therefore, they are a good tool against strong demons, both for attack and protection. And what do you say, Kaito?"

"Copy and paste from the older church manual 'Modi pugnae contra ignobiles daemonas eorumque socios, anno Domini MDLV', since you forgot to cite the source, zero points. Ms. Yamamoto!" Kaito said laughing as Mio tried to hit him on the head with a book and he held his hands protectively in front of his head.

"Should I feed Dawn?" Mio asked a little later after she had calmed down again.

"Dawn is a 'Spirit', a supernatural spiritual being from the class of gods, they don't need food. Her body is maintained by her divine energy." Mio looked at Dawn, who was sitting on the sofa, basking in the sun.

"Wow, if only our dog Kaito was this easy to look after," Mio said with a slight grin.

"You have a dog named Kaito?" Kaito asked a little annoyed.

"Oh, Freudian slip, I meant Kuro," Mio grinned, "but unfortunately he hasn't been around for a long time."

"Does that mean Dawn doesn't eat anything?"

"She doesn't need anything, but she eats like a combine, especially if it tastes good and is expensive."

"Okay, I take it all back."

"Meow."

"What did she say? It sounded like she didn't agree with you."

The phone rang and Mio answered it.

"Spirit-KT Science Institute, Spiritual Deriver Department, how may I help you?" said Mio, listening to the other side.

"So, Mr. Ono, you're saying that the faucet in the kitchen has been running irregularly for a week now and you're afraid that there might be a ghost behind it?"

Kaito rolled his eyes and Mio had to suppress a laugh.

"We'd like to come over," Mio said. Kaito jumped up and waved his arms wildly, but Mio waved him away.

"But it's much more likely that there's a problem with the pump, and a plumber is a lot cheaper than having an institute examine it and find nothing. Especially since you would have to pay us in advance, don't you think, Mr. Ono?" said Mio and listened.

"Of course, Mr. Ono, if the plumber doesn't find anything, you're welcome to call again."

Mio looked at Kaito, "Happy?" she asked.

Kaito walked over to Dawn, sat down next to her and said "Sufficient!" and smiled contentedly at Dawn.

Two days later, Mio, Dawn and Kaito were on their way to a place in the north.

"Is it really okay for me to come with you, there's no one in the office?" asked Mio.

"You need practical experience, so no problem," Kaito said and thought, "Negotiating with the old bag is your job too."

"Hello Mr. Inoue, we spoke on the phone about the spiritual cleansing, we are on site," Mio spoke into her smartphone and hung up shortly after.

"He's coming to pick us up."

A well-dressed, very confident gentleman approached them.

"So you are the 'Gostbusters'. We've agreed on an all-inclusive price for the whole property, and I'll get a confirmation! Then let's go!"

"I'll give it to you, you little rat in a suit, and stop ogling Mio like that, it's really disgusting," Kaito thought.

"How long will this take?"

"About two hours," Kaito said.

"Good, then I'll come back for the final inspection, don't break anything or you'll have to pay for it."

The man left and Kaito asked, "He signed the contract, didn't he?"

"Yes, of course, everything came in writing, checked and filed," Mio said.

Kaito opened the tray.

"Here is the satellite map of the house from above, I have drawn a pentagram for the ley lines, the protective seals must be aligned at the ends of the points.

The more precise the pentagram, the greater the effect and the less effort for us. I aligned the pentagram so that the inner pentagon encompasses the entire house, that's where the effect is greatest. If you put the two points there and there, we should be on public ground. Make sure you're not on private property. I'll set the others, here are the coordinates and the GPS tracker. Align the sigils with the center of the pentagram as accurately as possible.

Dawn, see if Ayakashi is ready to leave the compound."

"Wait, isn't cleaning like this dangerous for Dawn?" Mio asked, startled.

"I always wait until she's behind me, and no, positive spiritual energy only affects negative energy and vice versa. It's more like the positive energy would also have a positive effect on Dawn and she would even like to stay inside the pentagram, but since things can always go wrong, she stays outside. She gets enough energy," Kaito said with a laugh and looked at Dawn, who meowed.

"I understand, thank you," Mio said, taking the GPS tracker and Kaito's coordinates and setting off.

Dawn sprinted towards the house while Kaito ran the other way.

"Phew, the terrain is so large that I had no visual contact with the individual peaks of the pentagram in places, the GPS tracker is only accurate to 10 meters, I had to run and stake out several rounds to get an average, is that enough?" Mio asked when she returned to Kaito and Dawn an hour later.

"We'll see once we try it. Increasing mental performance is much less effort than realigning in this large area. Dawn, how did it go with your task?"

Mio only understood a "meow" from the cat and Kaito said "ten, thank you Dawn". Dawn meowed again and Mio saw her put her paw on Kaito's leg.

"I wonder what it would look like if I could see what Kaito sees," Mio thought and grinned, "definitely naughty."

"Mio!" said Kaito, "what's up, ready? I want to start."

"Yeah, right, sorry, I was distracted."

"Then let's start," Kaito took a needle out of his jacket.

"I know what you do in theory, but how does it work in practice?" asked Mio.

"This is the source seal and the drain seal all together on one seal paper at the same time, so it is much more intricately drawn than the others, which are reflection seals. I bring in the positive spiritual force from the source seal. This is refracted by the reflection seals until it falls back onto the drain seal and is absorbed there, which is why the exact positioning of the pentagram is so important. The angle of refraction is defined in the seals. The resulting ley lines of the closed pentagram then create the positive spiritual force field. This force is doubly concentrated in the inner pentagon. The blood serves both as a means of transportation and as an energy store. Therefore, the amount of blood is important. It determines the maximum power that can be transferred from the body. Multiplied by time, the result is energy. Just like high school physics. Energy = Power x Time.

If the amount of blood is too small, it limits the power like the eye of a needle; you can also think of it as an electrolyte. Powerful derivers can even convert their blood directly into the desired positive or negative form of energy and then fight directly with it, otherwise it has to be converted by the seals, which has the advantage of amplifying the energy. So they also act as a kind of catalyst.

"The further transfer of spiritual energy from one's own body through the blood into a seal is triggered exclusively by the power of imagination. If you can't do that, nothing happens. That is why many people who have spiritual energy, although they cannot see the spirits, are not able to use them. They simply lack the power of imagination. Do you understand?" asked Kaito.

"Um, yeah, sure," Mio said, laughing embarrassed.

"Does that mean I could also use spiritual energy if I can imagine it?"

"Well, if you have enough energy and can make it flow by imagining it, it would be possible. You wouldn't see it, but the effect would be there. If you want, we can try it sometime."

Mio was hooked and wanted to try it right away, but Kaito blocked.

"We'll try it later. The job comes first," he said in an authoritative tone, and Mio accepted.

"Let's do it then," Kaito said, lightly pricking his thumb once and pressing it on the source seal.

Mio looked intently at the seal, which was slowly absorbing Kaito's blood and turning red. She waited and looked, waited and looked and saw... nothing. "You can't see the ley lines and the spiritual field it creates, you know that, look at the terrain," Kaito said slightly sarcastically.

Mio looked up, nothing. Then suddenly "POP!", what was that out of the corner of her eye, there again directly in front of her, yes, there was a particle cloud about ten meters away, hardly visible during the day under the bright sun, "POP" here and there. Very briefly, less than two seconds. Mio pulled out her smartphone and switched to video recording. POP'

"You got it, why did it take so long?" she asked.

"It was a wandering Yokai."

"Are there any good Ayakashi among them?" Mio asked, slightly depressed.

"Some of them are Ayakashi too, but only those who can't communicate with us. Those who could communicate with Dawn have left the place, almost everyone got a chance, the rest fall through the cracks. That's the way it is.

"No, it's okay, I didn't mean it like that, I know you're careful not to catch the wrong people. The situation at school was also an Ayakashi that you chased away even though you could have taken him out, right?"

Kaito smiled and nodded at Mio, took his thumb off the seal and said, "Perfect, that's it, well done Mio. There are more than expected here, no negative spirits will enter the grounds for the next few years."

Mio watched the video on her smartphone intently and then said disappointedly, "Why can't I see any gold particles on the video?

"Because only the eyes of living beings can see them."

"Why is that?"

"No one knows for sure, but it is believed that only the eyes of living beings who are endowed with spiritual energy can see them, and all electronic technology is not designed for that. If the wavelength doesn't match the detector, nothing happens. High school physics," Kaito said and grinned at Mio again.

"Yes, I understand," she pouted.

"Maybe life is more than just a machine with an engine and fuel. Otherwise, something like this would have been researched long ago, don't you think?"

"Oh crap, I thought I was the first to record something like this. Say, can you see these ley lines?"

"Yes I can, I can see almost everything spiritual!"

"All what?"

"All kinds of spirits, ley lines, positive or negative spiritual energies that have been ejected and are floating around before they dissipate, and the echoes of the dead. What I can't see is the aura of people or spirits. This is really annoying because it says a lot about the object, such as its nature, its spiritual strength, and a little about its attitude toward life.

"I've read that an echo is a kind of light or flame that is created when a living being dies and then goes out after a while," Mio said questioningly.

"You can think of it that way."

"A few years ago, long before we were in high school, a girl is supposed to have thrown herself off the school building, you know ..."

Kaito interrupted her, "Do you really want to know?"

No, Mio didn't want to, he had already given the answer.

Mio became pensive. "What?" Kaito asked.

"You probably see the world very differently from me, or like everyone else, ... almost everyone else?" she asked.

"Now, where normal people enjoy a beautiful field of flowers, I might see dark, billowing streams of energy drifting across the field, enveloping it, blocking out the light, and echoes of dead creatures in various colors illuminating the surroundings. But it also has its charm, a kind of mystical attraction, I've gotten used to it.

"As a child I could only see ghosts and some Yokai, but that was scary at the time. How did your parents react?" Mio asked thoughtfully.

Suddenly, the good mood changed. Dawn hissed loudly at Mio, who was startled and realized that she had broken a taboo.

"I shouldn't have asked," it flashed through her mind, "damn, it was so obvious."

Kaito paused for a few seconds and Mio tried to find a way to quickly change the subject when Kaito said, "Dawn, it's okay.

"Some in the order actually envy me for this ability, while others probably wonder why they have it. Any skill or trait where you could have an advantage by birth, such as logical thinking, high attractiveness, beautiful charisma, quick comprehension, easy learning ability or good communication skills are probably more interesting than this for the world of humans", Kaito said, turning to Mio and trying to smile.

"But I'm not complaining, I was lucky."

Mio still tried desperately to change the subject and finally asked,

"What about the beings with positive energy? Are they also kept away by the purification now?" although she was sure that she already knew the answer.

Kaito laughed lightly, "That would probably be counterproductive, because everyone would like to have gods in their house, or don't you want a god in your neighborhood?"

"Kaito, you're awesome," Mio thought and was glad that she got her act together.

Chapter 5 - GODS

"Can you sign the cleaning certificate?" Mio asked two days later.

"Did the bum pay?"

"Kaito!" she lectured, "The bum didn't pay, but Mr. Inoue, our valued customer, paid his bill without hesitation and is now waiting for the certificate."

Kaito took the pen offered by Mio and put his seal under it.

"An effect of the student council, or did she get it somewhere else? Maybe from her family?" Kaito wondered, put the seal away and asked, "Have the protective seals reached the Order yet?"

"Yes, Mr. Nakamura confirmed it by e-mail and thanked me. He's always so nice, I'd like to meet him personally, why did you leave the Order?"

"There was a difference of opinion, you said something earlier about an important mission?"

"A shopping mall is to be built in the middle of nowhere, everyone is happy except for the workers who believe it is haunted and have stopped working due to unexplained accidents. The job is already confirmed. A shutdown like this is very expensive, we have an appointment there on Sunday morning," Mio said.

"Oh, that was the Sunday appointment, do you want to come?"

"Sure, or are you going to leave me here and scare the customer away?"

"Kaito put a key on the table in front of Mio. "I'm going shopping, will you pack and lock up?" asked Kaito.

Mio looked up, "You're giving me an office key?" asked Mio.

Kaito was a little embarrassed but didn't show it, "I think you deserve it."

Mio beamed, but quickly calmed down and said, "Sure, I'll do it."

"Come on Dawn, we're going shopping, see you tomorrow Mio, thanks," Kaito said and left the office.

Mio stood up, turned to the window and looked out. Still a little confused, she felt a tear trickle from her eye.

"Oh Kaito, if only you were a little more my type," Mio thought.

"It's very generous of them to buy us the tickets for the Shinkansen," Mio said as they left the train compartment together.

"The final bill has to be paid from the departure station. It's faster and the customer saves money, too," Kaito said.

"Oh, if you look at it that way," Mio said, "but I'm glad the trip only took an hour."

"Mr. Tanaka, Ms. Yamamoto?" a voice asked behind them.

They both turned around. "Yes."

"My name is Yuki Mori, from Kato-CityCenter Corporation, assistant to Hiroshi Kato," a perfectly dressed and styled woman in her thirties introduced herself. There was another man in the background, "probably the driver or security guard," Kaito thought as Mio introduced herself and bowed.

"Can we go now?" Kaito asked a little fast, too fast for Mio's taste. The woman looked a little confused, turned around and walked towards the exit. Kaito and Mio followed her.

"Yes, security," Kaito thought as the man got into the passenger seat.

Mio, who was visibly uncomfortable with the situation, sat together with Kaito, who was quietly looking out of the window, with Ms. Mori in the area of a very long limousine screened off from the driver's cabin.

"Then tell me, Ms. Mori, what happened," Kaito said simply.

Mio flinched slightly and thought, "Geez, Kaito, a little more respect, please."

The woman looked at Kaito and explained: "Four accidents in seven days, that's a negative record for our company. Fortunately, there have only been injuries so far, one serious, but no fatalities. All the accidents have one thing in common: they are mysterious. Mr. Kato is here in person to greet you. I ask for your patience."

Kaito continued to look out of the window, "what a beautiful deserted area, what reason does someone have to build a shopping mall here?"

When Kaito saw that Mio was getting more and more nervous, he asked, "Should we stop?"

"No, of course not," Mio looked at him, blushed a little and then got angry.

"Ouch," Kaito looked down, Dawn had dug her claws into his arm.

"What was that all about?" Kaito wondered.

About an hour later, the limousine pulled up in front of the huge construction site. Kaito and Mio were given a hard hat while they were led into the office, Dawn walked beside Kaito who looked at the huge construction site and was happy to see that Mio had calmed down again.

They all entered a rather plain office with a folding table at which an old man, who must have been over 90 years old, was sitting. "Well, as announced, Mr. Kato himself, this will be interesting," Kaito thought.

Ms. Mori was about to begin the introductions when Kaito took a step forward and said in a calm, concise voice, "My name is Kaito Tanaka, I am the director of the Spirit-KT Science Institute. It is an unspeakable honor for me to be received by Mr. Kato himself, the founder of one of the most powerful buying organizations in our country. I suppose I also have Mr. Nakamura to thank for this interview," Kaito said and bowed to Mr. Kato.

Mio was now at her wits' end, she hadn't expected that, "so he can be friendly and formal at the same time if he wants to," she thought.

She looked from Kaito to Mr. Kato and back. Kaito made a head movement towards Mio with the suggestion to introduce herself.

"Mio Yamamoto," Mio said startled, "it's an honor," and blushed.

Mr. Kato stood up, laughed and said, "Today's youth," pointing to the chairs in front of him. They sat down and Mr. Kato said, "I want to tell you a story."

"Now this is getting interesting," Kaito thought.

"Do you know where I was born?

"You were born in September 1933 in Yamashiro Prefecture, 5 km north of here, so to speak, in a small village called Sai," Kaito said.

Mr. Kato looked at Kaito and said, "What do students learn in school today?"

Kaito replied, "I don't know, you have to ask my colleague Ms. Yamamoto," and laughed.

Mio blushed again and looked away, but Mr. Kato asked, "And Ms. Yamamoto, what do you learn there, your colleague doesn't seem to be there often?" and laughed.

Mio was visibly uncomfortable in this situation and seemed to be the one who was overwhelmed this time, she didn't know what to say, but then she said as everyone looked at her, "Well, language, science and...", she didn't get any further. Mr. Kato laughed and Mio's expression changed from uncomfortable to extremely annoyed. Mr. Kato stood up and said, "Let's go outside, I'll explain it to you on the spot."

Right behind the office, the current excavation started, after the excavation, there was still an uncleared forest about 200 meters away, in whose direction Mr. Kato led everyone around the excavation.

"Mr. Tanaka, you are right, I was born in this area 92 years ago. When I was about 9 years old, I had only one friend, Ken, my faithful dog and really my only friend in those difficult times. The rest of my family was dead, frozen or starving, and when the rats I hunted with Ken for our group ran out in the winter, there was nothing left to eat," Mr. Kato said.

Mio swallowed as she heard this and a cold shiver ran through her body as those words manifested in her mind and she thought of the sumptuous meal her mother had prepared for her family on the weekend. She swallowed again and looked at Dawn who was walking dutifully beside Kaito.

"When I came back from digging roots one winter, Ken was gone. He had an injured paw and was supposed to stay in the village. When I looked for him and asked where he was, one of the hunters laughingly offered me a leg bone that had been gnawed off three quarters and made it clear that this was my share of Ken.

That was too much for Mio, she stopped, that was all she wanted to hear. Mr. Kato, Mrs. Mori and Kaito walked on unimpressed. She lowered her eyes and Dawn meowed at her. Mio smiled, knelt down and at the same time Dawn jumped at her while Mio caught her.

"Oh Dawn, why is there so much suffering in the world?"

Dawn meowed.

"Thanks Dawn, let's catch up again," Mio said and quickened her pace.

"I was so angry that I wanted to kill the hunter, but I just got a bloody nose and ran out of the village into the forest, screaming wildly and ready to die." Mr. Kato points to the forest in front of him. "As I sat there bleeding and freezing, not knowing what to do, I saw him. Ken, he was shrouded in golden light, sitting in a tree, barking at me as if to say, 'Survive, don't give up, keep living for me!' "

"I don't know if it was my imagination, a hallucination from the shock or the cold, but that's exactly what I did. And how I did it. I went back and worked hard for the village. The hunter who killed Ken fell into the river one day and drowned, what bad luck," he laughed. "Ten years later I met my wife and through her I was able to study in Tokyo. At some point I told Ken's story to a priest who explained to me that I must have seen a benevolent God who guided me on my path and took the form of my best friend.

Sadly, my wife passed away much too soon, but I'm doing better than ever, especially since I started this project. Shall I explain what drives me?" said Mr. Kato, looking at Kaito.

"Of course," Kaito said nonchalantly, even though he noticed that the mood had changed.

"It all started ten years ago when I woke up one day and could not remember the most important thing in my life. My wife's face. Someone had stolen my memory," Mr. Kato said, continuing to look directly at Kaito.

"Damn, old man, now it's getting difficult!" Kaito thought, making sure that Dawn and Mio were close to him.

"My wife died 40 years ago, I have many memories and pictures, but my wife's face has only been a blur to me for ten years."

"It was bound to happen, getting involved in another stupid case like this," Kaito thought.

"Luckily Mio hadn't realized the situation yet," he thought as he saw Mio with Dawn on her arm, who to Kaito's surprise seemed to get along quite well.

"The old man isn't blaming this god for his memory loss, is he?" he thought.

"What is the purpose of the construction here?" asked Kaito cautiously, looking at Mr. Kato.

"Exactly what you think, Mr. Tanaka."

"That's not an answer to my question, old geezer, and now talk, but if you think, old wreck, that I'm afraid of you, you're wrong," he mused.

"I want to find out who stole my wife's memories and thank him," Mr. Kato said, smiling unrealistically at Kaito.

"Okay, now we have the salad, a crazy old man," Kaito thought.

"Mr. Kato, no god, no demon can erase memories, they're just legends."

"You think you know that? How old are you? What if it was a tribute from the being or god of that time that he now claims or not?"

"Fanaticism can only be fought with something higher," Kaito shouted in his head.

"The gods have given me the power to destroy demons. I will not go against them. Do you really want to anger the gods that protect your wife?" Kaito said directly to Mr. Kato's face, trying to get a reaction, even a small one.

But Mr. Kato remained unmoved.

"I want this god to bring my wife back to me, just like he did with Ken. Gods should be able to do that, otherwise it's not a god, and then I ask myself, 'Do we need these beings?' "

He pointed to the excavators at the edge of the forest.

"The reason for your Supercenter, is it to prove God?" asked Kaito with mixed feelings.

Mr. Kato grinned broadly.

"How much money and time do you think it takes to level a nature reserve in our country? Since the accidents, I'm sure I've gotten close enough to this thing. It must be around here somewhere, and now you come into play, Mr. Tanaka."

"Like I said, I'm not going to help you with something like that," Kaito said unimpressed.

Mio stood with her back to Kaito and Mr. Kato, pretending to look into the distance, but you could tell at first glance that she understood every word and would rather not be here.

Meanwhile, Kaito thought, "There's something wrong with this whole story. The man may have been old and had nothing to lose, but he wasn't stupid. Religious fanatics usually don't survive 90 years.

"One more time, so you understand. This god has nothing to do with the loss of your memory, it's a heavenly law and if you don't believe me, you'll end up empty-handed," Kaito said directly to Mr. Kato's face while he thought, "I hope that's enough now, I haven't rambled this much in a long time?"

Mr. Kato's expression became unexpectedly friendly as he said, "Please help me regain my memories of my wife," Mr. Kato said, placing a hand on Kaito's right shoulder.

"Now I understand," Kaito thought.

Kaito relaxed a little, "Then let me make a suggestion..."

"I'm all ears!"

"The trees of the gods are sacred, destroying them has serious consequences for everyone involved, you understand that, don't you?"

"Every word, boy, and now for your proposal!" replied Mr. Kato, slightly annoyed. Mio jumped when Ms. Mori put her hand on her shoulder.

"Relax, Ms. Yamamoto, games between men are always like that."

"Is that still a game?" Mio thought.

"Up ahead, where the row of trees starts, is that the center of the mall?" asked Kaito.

"Yes, well seen, but damn, are you trying to annoy me, Mr. Tanaka? I want to hear your suggestion right now."

Mio looked at Mrs. Mori who shrugged and rolled her eyes. Mio realized that she was hugging Dawn way too tightly, looked down and loosened her grip.

"Sorry Dawn," Mio said.

"Very simple Mr. Kato, you integrate a piece of forest into the shopping mall, build a shrine around it and let the people worship the god there, in return you get the memory of your wife's face back."

It became quiet. Mio froze, Mr. Kato looked into Kaito's eyes and came even closer.

"Are you kidding me?" asked Mr. Kato.

"No, this is my proposal, I will negotiate with the god," Kaito said.

"You know where he is?"

"Yes.

"Where?"

"What do you think of my proposal?"

"Who can guarantee that I will get my memories of my wife back if I accept your proposal?"

"We can settle this tonight, here and now."

Mr. Kato's eyes grew wide, he now put both hands on Kaito's shoulders, looked deep into his eyes and said: "Boy, are you serious?"

"Absolutely!"

It became quiet again, even the light wind was louder in the ears of the bystanders.

"Agreed!" he took his hands off Kaito's shoulders, turned around and said, "When?"

"Give me 30 minutes to negotiate."

"I'll wait in the office," Mr. Kato said and walked toward the office they had come from.

Mrs. Mori ran after Mr. Kato and talked to him, "This will cost us billions, it's impossible, no one has ever built anything like this before".

Kaito watched as Mr. Kato ignored Ms. Mori for a while and finally silenced her with an angry gesture. Mio approached him with Dawn in her arms.

"What now? Are you sure you can do this?" she asked, looking around a bit worried. "I don't feel comfortable here.

"Come on, let's negotiate with a god," Mio's eyes widened and you could see that her fear had faded and curiosity had won out.

200 meters deeper into the forest, Kaito stopped and said, "Hello Master of the Forest, you were the one with the accidents, right?"

"Who wants to know?" said a short, fat dwarf who was sitting on a branch but didn't see or hear Mio.

"It's obvious," Kaito said.

But nothing was obvious to Mio, she thought.

"This is a dark forest and Kaito is talking to a tree", thought Mio.

"Whoever destroys my tree will be destroyed himself, that is the law," the god said rather curtly.

"At least he's still in a good mood," Kaito thought. Mio looked around and still saw nothing, but then she saw Dawn looking in the same direction as Kaito and tried again.

"Damn, it's still not working," Mio thought and looked at Kaito again.

"You heard everything, didn't you?"

"Sure, or do you think I am hard of hearing at 565 years old?"

"And what do you think, is that okay for you?"

"And if not, will you monster kill me?"

"I take it all back," Kaito thought, "you fat little rat."

"You could get a shrine, have gifts and people worship you every day, it's up to you if you want to live on leaves for another 500 years or get something better."

"And if I don't want that. The forest is my home," he said arrogantly.

"Should I explain that to a little god like you?" said Kaito angrily.

"You little runt of a human who was shitting his pants just a few summers ago!"

"I can eat you too, you fat thing," Dawn hissed at the god.

"Tell that mangy, half-naked cat woman to stay away from me, she will defile me."

"And if I don't," Kaito said, pointing his finger at the god.

"Then you won't get what you want, human."

"For a little god like you, this one tree is important, not the forest around it, but we are welcome to take a few more trees, and Mr. Kato will also be happy to reforest elsewhere, if possible."

The small figure looked up and turned away from Kaito.

"Humans are pathetic creatures."

"Okay, okay, you're a great wise deity, I bow to you," Kaito said exaggeratedly loud, thinking elsewise to himself.

"I am a god of luck, I bring prosperity and fulfill dreams, so respect me."

"Mr. Kato and the many people who come here will worship and respect you, also think of all the extra energy they will give you."

"I will not bring his wife back to him."

"Those arrogant, no-good little gods," Kaito thought, now understanding everything.

"That is clear to me. You can't do it, I don't ask for it and Mr. Kato doesn't ask for it either. Nobody can bring a person back," Kaito said lecturingly.

"You didn't voluntarily turn into his dog back then. You can't do that either. You probably didn't care about the child back then. A lucky god always appears to a person in the form of their deepest desires, but only if they are strong enough to show themselves. That's not you, so it was just a coincidence, a ghost probably passed by at that time, and just as Mr. Kato was looking in your direction, which you probably didn't even notice, you vanquished the ghost and Mr. Kato was able to see you in the form he wanted most."

"Hmm, the tyke is clever for a human? Is the woman next to you what you want most?"

Kaito had no desire to negotiate further, but he understood that the little fat god had made his decision.

"Then you will show Mr. Kato that there are gods, then you can stay or go!"

"You little human monster, you snot spoon," the god looked at him and finally said, "I guess I have no choice, woe betide you if I don't get any offerings worthy of me."

"Yoo," Kaito thought, "you square little god should lose weight anyway," and said, "humans are selfish, they always take more than they give, always remember that and act accordingly."

"Mio, please go get Mr. Kato," we are ready, Mio looked up.

"You want me to get him," she asked softly.

"Is my fearless fellow ghost hunter afraid of an old man?"

"No, of course not, hmm, maybe a little."

"Everything will be fine, trust me!"

"Dawn will stay with you. I'll get everything ready!"

"Okay, sure," Mio nodded and walked slowly towards the office building as the sun set, while Kaito started to draw a circle in the ground, thinking "Hopefully she won't take too much from today and she'll be back on Monday" and finished the magic circle.

"Here they come, why did it take so long, the sun's already gone and you can hardly see anything, it's gotten so dark," he said.

"What the hell... Mr. Kato and Mio are laughing together, is the old man flirting with Mio, hey, hey, hey," Kaito thought with a smile as Mio, Mr. Kato and Mrs. Mori ran towards Kaito with flashlights in their hands.

With a hearty and adorable laugh, Mio said, "How long has this been going on, when did you notice it, Hiroshi-senpai?" Mio asked Mr. Kato.

"Hello, what, Hiroshi-senpai?" I've gone crazy, 30 minutes ago she almost fainted in front of that man and now this and I'm still worried about her. What happened there? Never mind, I want to go home," Kaito thought.

"Mr. Kato!"

"Mr. Tanaka, I think we can start, Mio-chan has already explained everything to me."

"Hey, you old bastard, pull yourself together, this could be your great-granddaughter!" thought Kaito and said, "Yes, I'm ready. Since it's already dark, you have ten seconds, is that enough?"

"One second is enough."

"What you see is up to you!"

"I know what I want to see, Mr. Tanaka, go ahead.

"Everything as we discussed?"

"Yes, you are a troublesome little boy."

"Look at the circle from over there," Kaito pointed to a spot Mr. Kato occupied.

"Dawn ready?" Dawn meowed.

"*RISE UP NEAREST!*"

Dawn jumped, golden particles illuminating the circle and its surroundings, the eyes of the viewer widening and a smile appearing on Mr. Kato's face. Kaito looked into the circle for a moment and immediately looked away. "Damn, I forgot that," Kaito thought and quickly looked at Mio, who was also looking at the circle with wide eyes.

For Mio, it seemed unexpectedly long this time, it was beautiful, a memory she had always carried in her heart and hopefully would never forget. Tears ran down her cheeks.

"I will be there soon, my love," Kaito understood Mr. Kato's words.

As Kaito had estimated, it took about ten seconds, then it went dark again, no one said a word. Mr. Kato looked motionlessly in the direction of the circle for another two minutes. Then he suddenly bowed 90° to the circle, turned to Kaito, bowed back and said, "Tell him he gets what he asks for," turned around and walked wordlessly towards the office.

Mio looked after him a little sadly and thought, "I hope you saw what you were hoping for."

"Let's clean up," Kaito said, wiping away the circle and collecting the seals he had placed. Then he bowed to the tree and said, "As agreed! Not another word from you!"

Mio also bowed to the tree and followed Kaito to the office.

When Mio and Kaito arrived at the office, they could clearly hear Mrs. Mori's excited voice.

"I told you, there in the circle was a half-naked catgirl with beautiful cat ears and a gorgeous tail, licking her paws."

"Ms. Mori, you should sleep more and read less manga, it's sick," Mr. Kato could be heard laughing amusedly.

Mio grinned, looked down at Dawn and said, "You've done some damage, Dawn."

Dawn meowed maliciously.

Mr. Kato and Mrs. Mori came out of the office. Mrs. Mori approached Kaito somewhat shyly and explained that they would be taken to the station now.

"Mio-chan, I'll be in touch," Mr. Kato called, waved and went back into the office.

Mio waved goodbye.

"What are those sinister figures standing around?" asked Mio as the car left the premises.

"Security personnel," Kaito said. Mio's eyes went wide and an "Oh" came out of her mouth.

At home, Kaito was lying on the bed looking up at the ceiling, Dawn was lying next to him with her arm around him.

Carefully and sympathetically she asked Kaito, "Meow, do you want to talk about what you saw in the circle?

"No," Kaito said coolly, but no matter how hard he tried, he couldn't hold back the tears.

Chapter 6 - SCHOOL DAYS

"Yay, Monday morning, I'll go to the office first and skip English," he said to himself and was about to unlock the office door when he realized that it was unlocked. Had he forgotten to lock it?

He slowly pushed the handle down and opened the door. He wondered if someone had broken in, but quickly dismissed the thought, "Nobody could be that stupid," he thought, then the door opened to reveal the view.

"What are you doing here Mio?"

Mio grinned, "I'm picking you up for your first English lesson! Let's go now, we can still make it."

Kaito rolled his eyes, he had never thought that they would see each other again so soon, eight hours after they had parted at the station. Especially not after what had happened yesterday.

Shouldn't she be angry that he, Kaito, had put her in such a situation?

Even if there was never any real danger for Mio, she didn't know that at the time. After all, he had brought her to a man who had practically confessed to having committed a murder 80 years ago.

But what the hell, at least Mr. Kato had addressed her as 'Mio-chan' in the end, and she had even addressed him as 'Hiroshi-senpai', Mr. Kato himself.

"Mio looked in her school uniform again today like ...", he thought, no, "we're just colleagues, that's all," he told himself. But still, who wouldn't want to go to school with Mio like that?

"Though, English with the old scarecrow, is Mio really worth it?" he thought again.

"Come on, let's go, see you later, Dawn," Mio said and pulled Kaito out of the office.

"Let's clear up a few things on the way to school," Mio said.

"Ouch, now she's mad about yesterday," Kaito said to himself.

Mio stopped, raised her hand in Kaito's direction and pointed her finger at him, "Kaito, I've been thinking all night, but I couldn't come up with anything. How on earth did you know that his lost memory would be restored by the god?

"Phew, really, that's her only problem from yesterday and I was up all night trying to figure out the best way to explain to her that we were never in any danger."

Kaito laughed in relief and said, "It was too easy. Much too easy. Someone as rich and powerful as Mr. Kato, who has set his mind to something and really believes in what he says, isn't impressed by a few words from a high school student like me. Ms. Mori was too calm for me, too. The way he reacted, he wasn't demented, and when memories are lost because of something like that, it's not just one memory, and especially not such an important one. That leaves dissociative amnesia. But that doesn't fit because he probably idolized his wife and wasn't traumatized by her, not to mention the stupid story with his wife's blurred face, something like that could happen in a bad movie."

Mio had to cough and kept her thoughts to herself.

"I think he played us a story from the beginning so that I would react faster to his wishes. He didn't want to make a request, he wanted me to tell him what I could do for him."

"His wish was obviously to see his wife again in the same beautiful yellow and white light that he had seen his dog in as a child. That experience as a child must have made a big impression on him. It made an impression on you too, didn't it?"

Mio understood now, "Yes, of course, what she had seen and how she had seen it was beautiful. Would she remember it as intensely as Mr. Kato?" she thought.

"Couldn't he have had it easier?" she asked.

"Maybe! Or maybe Mr. Nakamura had explained to him that normally you can't agree to something like this, or that it would be difficult, and then he came up with this plan."

"He spent billions of yen on a shopping mall in the middle of nowhere just for his plan? Why did he do that?"

"Because he's old, rich, very powerful and even richer," Kaito laughed.

Mio looked at Kaito, "How rich is Mr. Kato?"

Kaito looked at Mio. "What do you learn in school?" he laughed at Mio. Mio slapped him on the head. "Ouch! ... Mr. Kato is one of the 50 richest people in Japan."

Mio's mouth formed into an 'O', but it stayed that way. A little later she said, "Damn, I should have accepted his offer."

"MIO!!! What the hell happened at the office?"

"Shh, that is and will remain a secret!" Mio smiled sweetly and maliciously at the same time.

Two hours later, Kaito was still introverted, he hadn't listened to a single word the teacher had said in the two English lessons and was admonished several times for having to repeat questions to him. "What did Mio mean earlier? Damn it! And now all those warnings from Mrs..., damn, what was that old bitch's name?"

End of school, home and then to the office to see Dawn, he thought to himself.

"Attention, Kaito Tanaka, please report to the disciplinary committee immediately," came the loudspeaker.

"What's going on now, is there really stress because of all the warnings from the old lady?" Then he could at least ask her her name, he thought. Some of the students grinned at him, but quickly turned away when they felt he had caught them out.

"My dear classmates, why don't you all throw yourselves off a cliff," Kaito thought to himself and started walking.

He had no idea where to go, where was the disciplinary committee anyway?

And suddenly again.

"Attention Kaito Tanaka immediately and I repeat immediately to the disciplinary committee."

Damn, he thought, maybe he shouldn't ask the old lady for her name after all.

A boy from a higher class was kind enough to tell him where to go. A minute later, he knocked on a door. "Come in," he heard and entered the room.

"Kaito Tanaka, with what..." he didn't get any further when he saw Mio sitting at the table, laughing and slapping her hand on the table.

"You little bitch, that was you," Kaito thought to himself and looked around the room.

Next to Mio sat a well-dressed boy who looked a bit older, probably from the class above him. Otherwise, it was a normal office, nothing special.

"What are you doing Ms. Yamamoto," Kaito said.

"Calm down Kaito and keep calling me Mio. This is Taro Suzuki, the student representative and the client for our next case."

"If Mio is telling all this to someone from the school, he should be trustworthy, otherwise she's risking a lot," he knew as he looked at Taro and said, "Mr. Suzuki, I take it this is all Mio's doing?"

"Forgive her, she was already so sneaky in kindergarten."

"So the famous sandbox friend, how nice for him, for her," he thought.

"I suppose it's not about Mrs. ... Damn, how ..."

"Ms. Kobayashi is the name of your English teacher," she blurted out and Mio couldn't stop laughing.

"No Mr. Tanaka, I'm moving to the university soon and I'm already starting to pack," Taro began, trying to calm the situation. He too was visibly uncomfortable with the situation.

Did he need a pack mule or what did he want from him, Kaito thought.

"Actually, I don't believe in ghosts, unlike Mio, who has been trying to convince me of that for years. Actually! But strange things have been happening for a while now, I told Mio and that set her on fire and now we're here."

"Then tell me, I'm all ears," Kaito said and looked angrily at Mio, who could only just suppress her next fit of laughter.

"As I said, I'm moving soon and I'm packing all my important things. I keep finding things turning up in places where I took them and then packed them. At first I thought there was something wrong with me, but now I'm sure it must be something else, and I don't want to leave the house without knowing that my family is safe. Mio had said there was no one better than you, Mr. Tanaka.

Family. Childhood friend. Kaito was annoyed again, but he didn't know why himself, but he knew, he just didn't want to admit it.

"When?" Kaito asked. Mio, who had just managed to hold back her laughter, suddenly became serious again and interrupted: "Right now, let's go, it's not far."

Big house, Kaito thought as they stood in front of the door of the Suzuki family. Taro opened the door and invited Mio and Kaito inside. The house was furnished in European style, very elegant, very expensive, Kaito thought, while Taro called, "I'm home, mother."

A friendly middle-aged woman greeted Taro. "Hello mother," he replied and hugged her.

"Hello Mio, nice to see you again," she said and hugged her. "This must be your school friend you were talking about," she took a friendly step towards him.

Kaito took a step back.

Mio was shocked, "what just happened," she thought.

For Kaito, it was some kind of reflex, like a protection program that had switched to automatic. How could that happen? Damn, Kaito thought. He bowed and said, "Sorry, I have a bit of a cold and don't want to infect anyone, I won't be staying long either," he said, annoyed at himself.

"My God, if that's the case, I'll quickly make some tea for all of you," Mrs. Suzuki said and went to the kitchen.

It was Taro who broke the silence and said, "Let's tackle the problem," as he climbed the stairs to the second floor.

Kaito entered the room. "What does Mio think of me now, that was really embarrassing."

"Sorry Kaito, my mother is very outspoken, she exaggerates a bit," Taro explained.

Kaito wanted to forget the topic. As soon as he entered the room, he saw the reason why Taro had invited him, a stranger. He looked in the direction of a small round carpet at the foot of the bed and thought, "The faster this goes, the faster I'll be gone.

"There on the carpet is a little ghost dog with a stumpy tail, it has black fur. But it's white around the eyes, does that tell you anything?"

A soft cry from the right, startled him, he turned to Mio, who held her hand over her mouth.

"Mimi," she said and collapsed. Kaito tried to help her, but she pushed him away.

"It's okay," she said.

"What was that about," Kaito wondered, "is she mad about short before?"

Kaito looked at Mio who was still sitting on the floor with one hand over her mouth and the other leaning on the floor. Then he remembered that Taro was still in the room and turned to him. But he hadn't moved since then. Kaito, somewhat amused by the slow-motion situation, was about to say something stupid, but caught himself when he remembered the situation with Mrs. Suzuki. He refrained from doing so again and preferred to watch the still picture and remain silent.

After a while, Taro looked at Mio and put his hand on her head.

"What is wrong with you, you should see yourselves in the mirror like this," Kaito thought.

Taro broke the silence. "Why do you think he did that?" he asked in Kaito's direction.

"A simple spirit reflects the most intense wishes of his life. He probably realized that you wanted to leave the house and wanted to stop you. You were probably his most important caretaker?"

"Let's make him visible," Mio said. "No," Kaito replied immediately, "what's the point? Mio looked at him and started to cry.

"Hey, hey, hey, what the hell is this?" thought Kaito.

"No, Kaito is right and took Mio in his arms, nobody should interfere in God's work.

Kaito looked at Mio and Taro who were hugging each other, "I wonder what Dawn is doing right now?" he thought.

Taro continued to hug Mio while telling Kaito the story of a dog that had been run over as an abandoned puppy in front of Mio and Taro. His parents had allowed him to take it in and raise it. It had lived with him for five years, then died too soon, probably from poisoned bait.

"What would you do, Kaito?" Taro asked him.

"Send him up," Kaito said and got a really nasty look from Mio.

"Can you take him with you or is he somehow dangerous, Kaito?

Kaito was annoyed by the small, black, rat-sized ghost dog.

"Did he die here?"

"Yes, in this room. He wasn't feeling well, he didn't want to eat, so I put him in his basket and the next morning, he sadly passed."

He looked around, no more echoes. That was unlikely with such a small barker.

"He's harmless. As it is, Taro is his master, so if he doesn't take him with him, he might become bitter and cause trouble. If you take him, you'll have to live with his jokes or you should end it."

"How long would that last?"

"A few years or decades for the spirit. Eventually, it might leave on its own or become an Ayakashi. Then it would follow you for all eternity if it wasn't eaten or sent up. If you were no longer there for it, it might turn into a yokai out of grief and hatred over time. But we're talking about a few hundred years. No one knows for sure. It's just a theory," he said to Taro, who nodded gratefully.

Mio's hands touched her mouth again and her eyes widened.

"That means that all pact ghosts or pact ayakashi become bitter when their master dies and become yokai," Mio said.

"No, if the pact is ended before then, the Ayakashi can continue to live normally, but you can't make a pact with normal spirits, this one seems to be directly bound to Taro, that's a problem. But we should all have enough time, right?"

"Thank you for everything and I apologize for putting you in this position. If I take him with me, how should I proceed?", Taro asked.

"Give him a small offering once or twice a week at the same time and then talk to him for five minutes about what you're up to, maybe that will help. Do this even if you can't see him. That's all I can tell you."

Taro's mother knocked and opened the door, she had a tray with three cups and wished everyone a good evening as she passed the cups around.

"Damn, now I have to finish my drink before I can leave," Kaito thought and thanked her.

She asked if anyone wanted something to eat. Taro said no and Mrs. Suzuki left the room to go shopping.

Mio and Taro looked at Kaito, who didn't know what was going to happen next or whether he could leave.

Mio said, "Shall we go, Kaito?"

Kaito would have liked to be home with Dawn by now, but he didn't know how to do that before and took the opportunity, "Yeah, I think it's time, Dawn's waiting."

"I'll come with you," Mio said.

"Better not, I'm going straight home, why don't you explain to Mr. Suzuki what else he should consider?"

Mio realized that she had better not argue and said, "Sure, we'll make sure you get down safely."

What a shitty day, Kaito thought when he got home. How could this have happened with Mrs. Suzuki, luckily she was out shopping when he left the house, what had gotten into him? "I don't know what I'm imagining, I know for sure!", he mumbled.

Meow, meow, meow, Dawn said, while she poked Kaito in different places, but got no reaction and repeated it more and more. Kaito took advantage of the surprise and pulled Dawn towards him, pressing her head against him and grabbing her cat ears.

"So cute, I love your ears Dawn!"

"MIAU, you know you can only do that with permission," Dawn meowed a little annoyed, "they're very sensitive."

Kaito looked at Dawn and said, "Okay then your tail," and held out his hand.

Dawn jumped up from sitting, then out of bed and ran to the bathroom, turned around once more, hissed and closed the bathroom door.

"How long are you going to stay in there, Dawn, or am I going to the office?" Kaito asked amusedly.

Dawn came out again and said, "I'll see if Mio's here yet, at least she respects me.

Kaito got ready and went to the office. Actually, Mio was already there and Dawn was complaining to Mio about Kaito, but Mio misunderstood the meowing and thought she should check on Kaito and was startled when he suddenly came in. Kaito had to laugh and Mio thought "when he laughs, he doesn't look so scary". After Mio had made tea, checked the mails and Kaito had made a note of yesterday's case, Mio said, "Taro sends his thanks again. He and I would also like to apologize for yesterday."

"Why is she apologizing," Kaito thought, "I screwed up."

"Well, I guess I made mistakes too, let's just forget about it," Kaito said and was glad that Mio nodded in agreement and turned back to Dawn.

He knew that Mio's relationship with Taro was none of his business, but he was interested and he knew he shouldn't ask, but he asked anyway, "Are you with Taro?"

Mio paused for a moment. "Damn," Kaito thought, "that wasn't good, we're just colleagues."

But Mio just laughed and then said, "No, but it could have happened almost two years ago."

"Okay Taro probably didn't want to, I hope I didn't open any old wounds with my curiosity."

"But he's like a big brother to me," Mio said.

"Wrong again," he thought, realizing that Mio had left him.

"What about you and Dawn?" Mio asked back with a smirk on her face.

Dawn jumped up and hissed first at Mio, then at Kaito and then at both of them together and disappeared into the kitchen.

"Ah ha," Mio said loudly, "So you're together!" and laughed again, while Kaito thought, "Yeah, Dawn and I have more than just a pact!"

The doorbell rang and Mio looked up. A young man came in. Mio stood up and went to greet the new customer.

"You still look so grim, Sensei."

"Don't call me Sensei and aren't you a week early?"

"Yes, but it's more convenient now and I wanted to see Dawn again," he said, catching Dawn as she ran out of the kitchen and jumped up to him.

"I have something tasty for you too, my goddess. You must have been neglected, doesn't he give you anything to eat?" he said as Dawn cuddled up to him and licked him.

Kaito got angry, "Payback for just now, you mangy cat," he thought and said.

"Hey Dawn, is that enough or are you a mutt now?"

"May I introduce Yuma Shibata, he is a student at the local university and a specialist in IT security, he checks our IT for vulnerabilities from time to time. And this is Mio Yamamoto, a classmate from the parallel class, she mainly does administrative work in the office.

"What a hot guy," Mio thought and greeted him.

Yuma greeted her friendly and thought, "You stinking boot hires someone and then such a hot girl, I didn't expect that, how did you manage that?"

"Is our network so insecure that we need to protect it?" asked Mio.

"On the contrary, that's exactly why the data is secure and I want to keep it that way, I can well imagine that there are some who would like to know what Sensei knows," Yuma said.

Mio thought about it, she had never asked herself this before, but maybe this was the reason why her smartphone wasn't on the local network, why she had to turn it off when talking to customers, and why she was only allowed to use the tablet or notebook on her desk for office work? Was there really someone out there who wanted that information? Wouldn't that be dangerous for her as well? Kaito had never mentioned that, even though he was such a cautious, rather paranoid person. "Strange," she thought.

Yuma was still holding Dawn and Mio just noticed again that Dawn had a human form for Kaito. How the hell did that look to Kaito, what Dawn and Yuma were doing? But Kaito remained calm.

"Hey Yuma, I'm Mio, tell me, can you see ghosts and what about Dawn?"

Kaito went over to Yuma and took Dawn from his arms, who struggled a little but then gave in.

"Pretty bold girl, I like that," Yuma thought and walked over to the desk where Mio was sitting, she stood up and let him sit at the desk. He pulled the tray over, opened the notebook and said, "Mio-chan, I can't see ghosts, but why shouldn't I be able to see Dawn?"

Mio smiled mischievously and said, "Yuma-chan probably wants to stay formal and can see the cat, I'll make a note of it for further research and file it away."

"Okay, okay, I get it, let's stay with Mio," he said, glancing briefly from the screen to Dawn and back again, thinking to himself, "what else was I supposed to see?"

A slight shiver ran down his spine when he noticed Kaito next to him, staring at him angrily.

After two hours, Yuma declared his work done.

"You'll get the minutes tomorrow, nothing special, just the usual," he said. Kaito put a book aside and Mio put down her smartphone, on which she had taken about 100 photos of Dawn in various poses.

Yuma packed his things and was about to leave when Mio said, "I'm leaving early today, there's not much going on and everything's done, is that okay with you, Kaito?"

"Go on, there's nothing going on today, will you be there tomorrow?" asked Kaito.

"As usual," Mio said, picking up her things and following Yuma.

"If he doesn't have a steady girlfriend at the moment, then he probably has number 945 right now," Kaito thought when he heard Dawn's voice from the sofa, "they would make a good couple, wouldn't they, Meow?"

"Are you talking to me again?" He'd better not say more as he watched Dawn lolling on the sofa in her usual pose.

Chapter 7 - SEE OR NOT SEE

"The books in the office read like the thoughts of crazy people, how can this babble be true?" Mio thought and closed the next book. Mio remembered Yuma again, he really was a student and apparently one of the best in his semester. And he was so handsome, too damn handsome for a single. She didn't believe him.

Mio had questioned Kaito, so she knew that he knew Yuma through his father. His father had many contacts, everywhere, supposedly even up to the mayor. Yuma had visited Kaito once and wanted to organize a spiritual cleansing of his estate for his father, which had been so impressive and successful that Yuma and Kaito had stayed in contact and now helped each other or commissioned each other to do so.

Mio wondered if Yuma would get back to her as promised and looked at Kaito and Dawn who were playing a board game together on the sofa.

"I hope you'll both be happy," she said to herself and thought of Yuma again.

She looked back at the sofa and said in surprise, "Hey, since when can Dawn play board games?"

There was a knock and an older man in a black suit entered.

Kaito got up from the sofa and thought, "Great, a lawyer, he brings money."

Mio brought coffee and sat down at the table, Kaito stood next to Mio at the table and was still thinking "somehow the roles are reversed here" when Mio introduced himself and Kaito. The man asked for discretion and Kaito pushed him a contract, which he signed after reading it several times and trembling slightly.

"Okay, this isn't a lawyer", Kaito thought after watching the nervous man reading.

He introduced himself as Kenji Harada, a confidant of the honorable lady of the house Shimizu.

"It's like this", he began.

"Every year, Lady Shimizu holds a reception for friends and relatives of the Shimizu family, and this year is no exception. This year, she is also introducing her grand-daughter, who is now 21 years old, to the guests," Mr. Harada said and started shaking, took the cup from the table, wanted to take a sip, but spilled it because of all the shaking, got scared and dropped the cup.

Mio jumped up, Mr. Kimura apologized and was on the verge of tears.

Mio supported him and helped him back to the chair. She knelt down on the floor in front of him, took his hands in hers and asked in a sincere, sympathetic voice, "Mr. Kimura, just tell us what happened and we'll help you."

Mr. Kimura looked at her and said in a broken voice, "Your granddaughter, Hana Shimizu, died in an accident with her whole family a long time ago."

Kaito said soberly, "Then that's probably something for the fraud squad."

Mio looked at him as if she wanted to kill him.

"She looks just like the Miss, her behavior, her knowledge from her childhood, everything about her seems genuine," Mr. Harada continued.

"Are you sure that she was among the dead?" Kaito continued to ask.

"I was at the funeral, I stood at her grave!" he sobbed and looked at Kaito.

Mio spoke reassuringly to Mr. Harada and Kaito thought: "This will be interesting."

"Did Mrs. Shimizu ask you to look at it?" asked Mio.

Mr. Harada looked down, embarrassed and with a trembling voice, and then said, "No, I want you to look at Hana Shimizu."

Mio looked at Kaito, her expression saying, "We're both thinking the same thing, a big conflict of interest. Mr. Harada had acted without the consent, probably even against the will, of the lady of the house, Mrs. Shimizu.

"That's a problem," Mio said.

Mr. Harada continued to look at the ground and said, "I could never forgive myself if Mme. Shimizu was in danger."

"Interesting, how do we get to Hana Shimizu?" asked Kaito.

Mio looked at Kaito disdainfully, "What was the prime dircctive of this company again," she let him know.

Kaito waved her off. Mr. Harada looked from Kaito to Mio and back to Kaito.

"I would invite you to the reception. Hana Shimizu will be there and you can't miss her," he said as the man visibly regained hope.

Kaito explained to Mr. Harada that Dawn, his cat, would have to be present to first check if an 'evil spirit' was up to mischief and only if that was the case would he take action, but not without consultation.

To Mio, it looked like the man didn't even understand what Kaito was saying, nodding eagerly and probably just happy to have found help.

A few days later, the time had come, Mr. Harada had passed on invitations and instructions, ordered a chauffeur and informed them who would take them where and when.

The whole thing had the feel of a grand conspiracy involving the entire household staff to protect Ms. Shimizu from danger.

Mio had been dressed by Mr. Harada in a very tight and very noble looking evening dress and Kaito had immediately recognized Mr. Harada as an old lecher.

He, on the other hand, had probably been given a suit from the 'second-hand, class B' category, at least that's how he felt.

Mio had Dawn on her arm because it was less conspicuous. They both got out of the limousine and went to the main entrance as agreed. There they were intercepted by Mr. Harada and handed over to an elderly housekeeper who led them to a room right next to the banquet hall. When Hana Shimizu appeared, the housekeeper would lead her unnoticed into the banquet hall. Since everyone would be watching Ms. Shimizu at that time, they would have plenty of time to observe her. If that wasn't enough, there was still plan B.

So they waited. Mio looked around and was overwhelmed, this room alone was as big as Kaito's entire office with all the rooms put together and probably 10 times as expensive to furnish..., no, she laughed inwardly, more like 1000 times as expensive to furnish.

Kaito had taken Dawn in his arms in the meantime and then suddenly everything happened in quick succession. Voices, then clapping and a toast was shouted several times. The housekeeper opened a side door and gave the agreed signal. Kaito and Mio entered the large banquet hall from the back.

Mio's eyes shone with excitement when she saw the splendor, but Kaito only had eyes for the young woman who just came down the grand staircase arm in arm with an older, very elegant lady. "There is no mistaking the kinship," Kaito thought, and also that this woman was far too beautiful, far too perfect, for a human to be coming down the stairs in front of him. But he couldn't recognize anything. Kaito knew very well that he couldn't see the auras of living beings. He could only see spiritual energies that were not bound to a living being, and no matter how powerful his spiritual powers were, auras were his greatest weakness.

He knew that unlike nonhuman beings, very few people could truly see and evaluate auras. But he had Dawn for that, she was a master at recognizing and perceiving auras. A divine gift.

"Dawn, what do you think?" Kaito said and waited, looking down at Dawn.

"Dawn is hesitating?" Kaito thought, "That's not possible. This isn't a human standing in front of us, is it? "Dawn, is that a human?" Kaito asked again, but Dawn still hesitated and said, "I have to get closer.

"Plan B," Kaito thought. At first, he thought that someone from the Order was trying to lure him into a trap, but now he was sure that something was wrong on a spiritual level and they went back into the next room.

This new 'Plan B' was to wait until the end of the banquet and then walk past Hana Shimizu as she left the banquet hall.

In the meantime, Mio was enjoying herself at the banquet, keeping an eye on everything and would join them shortly before the end or inform Kaito if anything unusual happened. "As pretty as she looks in her evening dress, she'll hardly attract attention," Kaito thought sarcastically, recited parts of the fairy tale Cinderella and retired to a small adjoining room three rooms away for the waiting time.

"What happened, Dawn?" he asked.

Dawn was silent. "Hey Dawn, aren't you talking to me anymore?"

"A very faint aura, like from a human, but then again not. I don't know, let's just wait until I get closer."

"I've never heard an answer like that from Dawn, what's going on?" he thought.

Suddenly there were voices, screams, a cry of pain outside the door. Dawn turned to the door, which burst open at the same moment. Mr. Harada was pushed rather roughly into the room, more like thrown, and fell on all fours in front of them.

"You old bastard, you brought that monster into the house of your mistress, didn't you?" came from the door in the voice of an angry young woman who turned to Kaito and closed the door behind her.

Reflexively, Kaito and Dawn jumped back. Hana Shimizu stood in front of them and looked at Dawn and Kaito with a deadly stare.

"So a demon emperor in human form makes a pact with a demigod. You treacherous little cat, I should send you to your god for this.

She gave Dawn a threatening look and took a step towards her.

Kaito was still reeling from the shock of being discovered, but he recovered just as quickly. He had played out a situation like this too many times. As if he had internalized it, almost as a natural reflex, he grabbed the amulet around his neck with his left hand and pulled a magic seal on paper out of his pocket with his right hand, clapped both hands together in front of him and at the same time took a big step to the side, blocking the dawn from Ms. Shimizu and breathing out "DESTRUCTION" loudly while holding the blood-soaked seal in his hand towards Hana Shimizu. Hana Shimizu abruptly stopped her attack on Dawn and backed away in a flash. Only now did he hear Dawn scream, "Stop, stop, Kaito, stop!"

"She attacked us, Dawn," Kaito said and looked at Dawn for a tenth of a second. That was enough time for Hana Shimizu to make something appear in her hand and point it at them. Now, Kaito didn't care, no one in this world was more important than Dawn. The banishing orb from his pocket that he threw at Ms. Shimizu was completely covered with his blood and fully charged with positive energy, no dark being would survive such a thing unscathed, he knew that, he looked at Ms. Shimizu and said loudly: "HOLY LANCE". The small, inconspicuous ball glided across the room at high speed towards Shimizu Hana and again he heard Dawn scream, "Stop, stop, she's a goddess.

Shimizu Hana grinned, made a hand gesture and slammed the incoming sphere to the floor, where it burst unspectacularly. Hana Shimizu straightened up, scowling at Kaito and Dawn, while at the same time, the room around Ms. Shimizu bent strangely, distorting her body. In an instant, a female fox stood in front of Kaito, considerably taller than Dawn, with longer ears and, most importantly, with nine tails. Any Otaktu would probably be overwhelmed, Kaito thought as he realized why this Hana Shimizu looked too perfect, too perfect for a human. "Perfection, the perverted arrogance of the gods," he knew.

Mr. Harada had just managed to get to his feet when Hana Shimizu transformed into a fox god in front of him. With a scream, he toppled backwards faster than his legs could react and fell backwards onto the ground.

He tried to continue screaming, but all that came out of his throat was a croak.

Hana Shimizu looked at him disdainfully, turned to Kaito and said, "Are you human, you disgusting individual?"

Kaito pulled another seal out of his pocket, but now he heard Dawn screaming even louder, "Stop it, stop it now, she doesn't want to hurt us."

At that moment, the door opened again and Mrs. Shimizu, the lady of the house, entered the room, shouting, "What's going on!"

Kaito, Hana and Dawn stood still, only Mr. Harada pointed his finger at the goddess and stammered something incomprehensible.

"Who are you and what are you doing here?" Mrs. Shimizu asked in Kaito's direction.

Kaito immediately realized that Mrs. Shimizu, who was now standing right next to the goddess, saw her and concluded that she had somehow managed to make a pact with such a powerful fox goddess. Most enviable, he thought as he bowed and said, "Your household servants who worship you were very concerned about your welfare and wanted to protect you. I now see this as unfounded and apologize for intruding on their sphere. I wish you well. I commend myself." What a hackneyed and ridiculous phrase, Kaito thought, but he couldn't think of anything better in a hurry and now get out of here, he said to himself and pulled Dawn towards the door.

Ms. Shimizu was speechless and busy trying to make sense of the situation, but then she said, "Mr. Harada probably hired you, didn't he?" and looked at the terrified employee cowering on the floor.

Kaito rolled his eyes, he probably wouldn't get out of here that fast, he thought, turning around and walking towards Mr. Harada.

"If someone suddenly enters a house who doesn't actually exist," he avoided the word 'death' so as not to provoke any more, "then the reaction of the staff is pre-programmed, at least if they are loyal. Mr. Harada would have rather died for you than put you in danger and you didn't even tell your most loyal vassal!" he said as he helped the still frightened looking Mr. Harada to his feet and then went back to the door.

Mrs. Shimizu looked at Kaito and said, "What kind of monster are you, young man?"

"Apparently the only one here with brains!" and started to open the door.

"Not so fast," the goddess said, grinning, taking a step towards Kaito, looking him in the eye and pointing her finger at him. Distracted by her mocking fox look, Kaito saw too late that she reached her other hand in Dawn's direction and touched her arm. Kaito jumped at Dawn, the goddess backed away with a grin and said with a laugh, "Equal rights for all," while Dawn let out a scream. Kaito was back in battle mode. He glanced at Dawn for a moment, then turned back to the goddess, who continued to grin and back away. But what was that, what had he just seen? Was it real or imagined and he looked back at Dawn. Dawn yelled at him, "Don't look at me. Dawn stood naked in front of him in her human form, seemingly visible to everyone in the room, her cat form lifted, only without clothes.

The goddess laughed, walked over to Mrs. Shimizu and changed back into Hana in a song beat, reached out her hand to her grandmother, looked at her and said, "Let's go back to the festival, grandmother."

Mrs. Shimizu looked at Hana, "Hana-chan, you're being naughty today," she said, smiling and taking her hand. Dawn was kneeling naked on the floor and everyone could read 'kill' on her face. Kaito took off his jacket and put it around Dawn. He refrained from commenting even though he found the situation very cute and thought "how cute Dawn is right now".

Just before Ms. Shimizu closed the door, she looked at Mr. Harada, who was looking at the floor, not knowing what to do.

"Mr. Harada, give the woman something to wear and then throw them both out."

"Very well, Ms. Shimizu," he replied.

Kaito knelt down beside Dawn, both waiting for Mr. Harada, and Kaito tried to turn Dawn's face to him, but she looked away and hissed, "Don't do that. He tried to take her in his arms, but the same thing happened again.

When will that butler finally come, he thought as the door opened and Mr. Harada entered, followed by Mio, who immediately rushed towards Dawn and yelled at Kaito, "Let go of Dawn!

As always, it sounded like he was the guilty one, Kaito thought.

"Mr. Harada, Kaito out of the room," Mio ordered. Kaito stood up and angrily left the room with Mr. Harada, closing the door behind him.

Mr. Harada, still depressed, opened his mouth to say something to Kaito, but he was not in the mood, interrupted him and said, "The creature is a fox goddess of the highest order, her mistress knowingly made a pact with her. The goddess will not harm your mistress and will disappear when the time comes. Just allow your mistress to spend the rest of her earthly time with her granddaughter and keep the secret for her protection". Meanwhile, Kaito looked at the door, saw a bow out of the corner of his eye and thought: "Oh, just get out of here.

The door opened and Mio came in with Dawn and said, "Tada! Kneel before Goddess Dawn." Mr. Harada was about to kneel when Kaito said, "Hey, old man, get us out of here, now."

Mr. Harada looked back and forth between Mio and Dawn, but then decides to grant Kaito's wish and leads all three to a side exit.

The car stopped and all three got in. Kaito looked at Mr. Harada, who flinched slightly, but Kaito just nodded and thought, "What an embarrassment today."

When she arrived at the office, Mio of course didn't want to go home until she had heard the whole story, three times and slowly, so that she could absorb it. Again and again, Mio pulled Dawn to her and danced with her or went to the bathroom with her in front of the mirror. Kaito just thought, "Dawn's clothes are probably two sizes too small and your clothes, Mio, would fit better somewhere else. Unfortunately, Mio suddenly realized that selfies now worked with Dawn's human form, and it took another hour for her smartphone's memory to fill up and for Mio to calm down again.

"Why didn't you realize it was a divine being right away?" Mio asked.

"It seems difficult to unmask a nine-tailed fox. Maybe it balanced its aura with negative energy so Dawn couldn't tell the difference from a human, I don't know everything either. Foxes are sneaky and cunning, but most of all, they are powerful.

"If a god can do that, there could be thousands of them out there."

"Hmm," Kaito thought, "Mio is right, that could be real, he never thought of that before," but clarified that it was just a theory of his.

But what did the fox mean by "demon emperor", another new word creation for him. Or was the Fox just teasing him? On the other hand, what if there was a deeper meaning behind it? He knew from Dawn that his aura was huge, no, gigantic. No wonder with the amount of spiritual energy he could use, which was one of the reasons for the pact with Dawn. But should his amulet not hide that, or did it only work on demons? Again, something he didn't know. If it did, then it was clear why the gods acted the way they did, they were intimidated by what they saw. But his energy was human and not like that of the gods and the Yokai, neither positive nor negative. They had to be able to see that or not. "Leave it, it's no use, foxes are sneaky," Kaito thought.

"I would have liked to see the fox, why didn't you call me?"

Kaito was a little annoyed, "Um, where were you all the time, you could have warned us that we were found out, you must have been busy talking?"

"Hey, I was supposed to contact you when the party was over and..." Mio blurted out angrily.

Kaito interrupted her. "And here you must have thought you were hitting on everyone!"

Mio continued angrily, "No, I didn't need to, they all came on their own."

"They're just not suitable for observation because..." Kaito broke off.

"Say it out loud because ..., because ..., I'm too pretty, you wanted to say, admit it."

"Maybe, now go home Mio," Kaito said slightly embarrassed.

Mio grinned, "Sure, but I'm taking Dawn with me."

"Out," Kaito counted three, two ...

"Dawn, see you tomorrow and keep that pervert at bay," Mio called to Dawn and slammed the door.

Dawn came out of the bathroom and looked embarrassed at Kaito.

"How long will the condition persist?" she asked Kaito worriedly.

"Forever as far as I'm concerned", he thought and explained that he was expecting two to four weeks.

Dawn got up and went back to the bathroom. Kaito watched her and thought, "Isn't my kitty cute today?" He had to laugh as he imagined Dawn and Mio running around outside together in their current outfits and some of the older men falling over at the sight.

"He should thank the female fox and Dawn should thank her too," was his last thought before he fell asleep.

The next morning, Kaito woke up next to Dawn. "Everything is back to normal. Dawn's calmed down," he noted with satisfaction, "but the effect hasn't worn off yet. Luckily!"

Dawn meowed half asleep and Kaito was making himself a cup of coffee when the doorbell rang.

Kaito looked at the coffee cup in his hand, grimaced and thought, "This can only be ... Then I'll fire her," and opened the apartment door. Of course, it was Mio. "What?" Kaito asked angrily, actually wanting to insult her, but he refrained, he didn't know why.

"Where's Dawn?" Mio asked as she entered the apartment. "You do realize you're in the apartment of a boy who's only wearing pajamas," he said to Mio, who didn't seem to care.

"I want to pick up Dawn, she needs something to wear, we'll go shopping and give some money for Dawn."

"Dawn's not going anywhere without me," Kaito said again, but he quickly realized that Mio was right. Dawn had nothing to wear, everything was missing. He didn't even know if she needed to eat in this form. Not to mention care products or even special women's utensils. He looked directly at Mio and thought, "Pretty casual today," then said, "I'll go with you."

"To the lingerie store?" Mio asked mischievously.

"Don't overdo it Mio," he warned in a cold tone. Mio knew she had won and left it at that. "Great, then get dressed, we're going to have breakfast in town first."

Even the walk to the café was a gauntlet for Mio, but especially for Dawn. They were watched or even stared at from all sides. Not only the men, but especially the women could hardly contain their jealousy of Dawn. She looked like a top model, a mixture of Asian and European beauty, with dark golden shining hair. Something like that stuck out like a sore thumb here.

"She desperately needed an ID or at least a residence permit, even if no one would check her out," he thought.

If necessary, he could show his kitten's vaccination certificate, Kaito laughed to himself. At the same time, he sent a message to Mr. Tanaka, "why do I have the police in the fam..., the word made him sick, but he finished it, 'family'".

Arriving at the café, attention was drawn to the two beauties, and Kaito only hoped that no one from the school had breakfast here in the morning.

Fortunately, they had been assigned a somewhat secluded table in a corner, but for some reason, they were now being served by a waiter and not a waitress as they had been a minute ago. "I can understand that," Kaito thought amusedly.

"What would have happened if your seal had touched the fox?" Mio asked.

Dawn lowered her head, the topic seemed to make her uncomfortable for some reason.

"A normal demon would have been wiped out by both the seal and the banishing orb, or it would have fled if it still had a chance. I had also put negative energy into the seal. The fox must have noticed this and left us alone. However, the negative energy was not strong enough to seriously injure her, it was much too strong for that. But she probably didn't know that. The banishing orb was only positive energy, so she just swatted it away as if nothing had happened. Unfortunately, I don't know if this magic ball triggered her retransformation or if she just wanted to show us her power. Either way, the information would have been worth the trouble. My fear on this mission was that we would have to deal with a ghost in combination with a demon. I hadn't even considered a god. Gods don't usually attack humans, but they also don't make pacts with humans, at least not normal humans.

The Fox Goddess had probably realized that we didn't mean her any harm, but we had invaded her territory, and out of anger and arrogance she had shown us her power, I suppose.

Dawn meows. Kaito and Mio laughed.

Kaito watched for a while as Dawn and Mio talked to each other, and the two of them seemed to get along very well, when it got a little louder behind them. He turned around and thought, "If only the police were that quick when you need them."

A very friendly, but tall and strong looking man entered the cafe and walked past the waiters directly to Kaito, unimpressed.

"Meow," Dawn said and waved. Mr. Tanaka was taken aback, but waved back in a friendly manner and said to Kaito, "Move over and make way!"

"Yes, General," Kaito said, moving a little to the side and saying, "May I introduce Mr. Tanaka." Mr. Tanaka gave Kaito a light pat on the head and said to the group, "I'm his father, he never learns, nice to meet you."

Mr. Tanaka also noticed the excitement caused by the two graces in front of him here in the cafe and waited patiently until people's curiosity had died down before he listened to Kaito's incredible story.

"You are a bad liar, Kaito. I can always tell when you're lying," he explained, laughing softly, then he suddenly became very serious and said, "But I guess you're not lying here, or you believe what you're saying," and looked at Dawn, who was slightly startled. Then he smiled and said in a friendly voice, "So that's Kaito's girlfriend, I'm very pleased and I thought he was gay," and laughed at the group.

Mio could barely contain herself, quickly looking away and trying to think of something else, "Don't start laughing," she thought, but couldn't stop herself.

Kaito was annoyed and was about to get up and leave when Mr. Tanaka said to Dawn, "By the way, you have the same beautiful, deep, emerald green eyes as a cat, I know, a good friend's grandson always tells me that she saved him from a monster."

Dawn smiled shyly and thanked him for the compliment. Mio looked at Kaito and said with a mocking grin, "Maybe Kaito-chan should talk to his father more often, it might have a positive influence on him."

Now that he looked at Dawn, he also saw those perfect emerald green eyes, he had seen them on Dawn so often that he hadn't even noticed them. But now that he looked at them again, he realized that they were somehow even more impressive than before.

"Yes, they're beautiful," he said in her direction without realizing it. Dawn turned away embarrassed and Mio started to laugh out loud.

Mr. Tanaka also laughed and then said to Mio, "So you're the new colleague, Ms. Yamamoto, who actually gets along with my grumpy son. Please take care of him and explain the human world to him so he doesn't get lost. If he annoys Dawn again or doesn't understand anything, just let me know, this is my phone number. I'm always available for such things." Kaito watched him angrily as he pushed the same cheap business card across the table to Mio.

Mr. Tanaka then suggested that Mio and Dawn go shopping now and call him immediately if anything happened. In the meantime, he would talk to Kaito about documents for Dawn."

Mio and Dawn thanked her and left the cafe.

"Did you know that I know the mayor well?" asked Mr. Tanaka.

"I can't count how many times you've told me that," Kaito thought and nodded.

"The mayor wants to smoke out the yakuza and gathers like-minded people around him. Granting a residence permit to a Finnish exchange student shouldn't be a problem, but he expects something in return," Mr. Tanaka said.

Kaito rolled his eyes and thought how stupid it would be to give a residence permit to an illegal when he was supposed to be fighting the Yakuza. He would make himself vulnerable and jeopardize everything he wanted to achieve.

"Dawn doesn't speak a word of Finnish, how did you even think of Finland?"

"Our mayor, Mr. Takahashi, actually has connections there, and 99% of our fellow citizens don't speak the language, so it's risk-free."

"Dawn doesn't even speak English, let alone a word of Finnish," Kaito said, thinking, "That's not so bad, a lot of people probably don't even know where Finland is."

"Work calls and I'll take care of it. In two days, a Dawn from Finland is coming, who doesn't speak a word of English due to special circumstances, but speaks excellent Japanese, and you think of something to thank Mr. Takahashi," said Mr. Tanaka, getting up and going to the cash register to pay.

Kaito called Mio and went to meet them. When he saw them standing there with all kinds of bags, he stopped and thought about running away, rolling his eyes and thinking, now I'm a ducat-shitting pack mule too.

Kaito looked at the ten or more bags in front of him and thought it couldn't get any worse. It was getting worse, the number of stares Mio and Dawn were getting was proportional to the number of students on the train and they were probably at their maximum at this time of night. Kaito remembered the situation when he had called out to Ms. Kato that she had to hold out for another ten seconds, which was an eternity in her situation. But she had held out, protecting what was most important to her.

"So hang in there Kaito," he thought, "you're no worse than a bitch like that," and laughed.

When they got home, there was no room for Dawn's clothes and utensils, of course, but Mio tidied up mercilessly and threatened to call Mr. Tanaka, so he left them alone and went to the office. Towards evening, Mio let him back into his apartment and surprised him with dinner. Mio and Dawn were laughing together, Kaito was thinking about what else he could eat, when Mio noticed out of the corner of her eye that it was getting brighter in Dawn's direction. She looked at Dawn and saw clothes on the floor and a cat meowing.

Startled, Mio jumped to Dawn, took her in her arms and yelled at Kaito, "do something."

Kaito got up, walked over to Mio and took Dawn from her arms. Mio reluctantly let him.

"I would have thought the effect would have lasted longer," he said, remembering how Dawn had been terrified less than two days ago that she would have to go around in human form all the time from now on.

"There's nothing I can do, only the gods have that power."

"Then go to that bitch Vixen and kick her ass and make her realize that she should give Dawn that power," Mio said.

Dawn meowed disapprovingly.

"Let's wait and see, it may well be that the effect will be active again in the morning, as it certainly depends on the spiritual energy of the user," Kaito explained, stroking Dawn's head and giving her a kiss.

Mio scratched her head and said, "Hey, Kaito, lusting again?"

Like Kaito said, it was like that. The next morning, Dawn was human again, but the time it took for Dawn to become a cat again for everyone except Kaito was getting shorter by the day. So it was clear that the effect would wear off faster and faster and the original state would be reached again soon.

Mio blackmailed Kaito with his father until he agreed to let her and Dawn use the time as long as possible. A week later, Mio came into the office with Dawn on one arm and her clothes on the other and said, "So, now it's your turn, do something.

Chapter 8 - THE CAR IN THE RIVER

A few days later, Mio showed Kaito a letter from Mr. Kato.

"Look, Mr. Kato, um," she clears her throat, "Hiroshi-senpai sent us photos of the construction of the shopping center and invited us to the opening."

Kaito took the photos, which clearly showed the rapid progress of the construction. In particular, the circular section of forest that had been preserved was clearly visible as it was being integrated into the huge building.

"Well done, this is going faster than expected, hopefully it won't be a flop, there in the ass end of the world," Kaito said and thought, "The old man and the fat arrogant god go well together.

Suddenly, the office doorbell rang and Mio looked towards the entrance. A slim, unassuming man entered and looked over at Kaito who was still lying on the sofa with Dawn.

Before Mio could greet him, he said "Beauty and the Beast" with a laugh.

"Are you here again, Mr. Nakamura?"

"Friendly as always, I hope you remember that you asked me for a favor? And you must be Mio," he said, walking over and greeting Mio. Mio replied, "It's a pleasure to meet you in person, Mr. Nakamura.

"You should at least learn to be polite from your colleague if you're going to employ such a gallant and enchanting beauty."

Kaito rolled his eyes, looked at Mio, who blushed slightly, and then said to Mr. Nakamura, "Did you get what I wanted?"

"As rude as ever, no wonder you and he don't get along."

Mio listened, she was very interested, the Order was a subject Kaito kept as silent as the grave. He only kept in contact with Mr. Nakamura.

Mr. Nakamura walked over to Mio and said, "This is the reason I came," and held up a piece of paper, which he placed on the table in front of Mio and slowly slid it over to her.

What did it say, she thought, that Mr. Nakamura himself had come by and especially that Kaito had deigned to negotiate with the Order.

"This is going to be expensive for you little uh big monster."

"How expensive?"

"You accompany his son on a mission."

"You mean the little asshole?"

"Exactly."

"All right."

"Ms. Yamamoto, is he sick or have you drugged him, it's never been that easy?" he grinned in Mio's direction and let go of the note.

Mio didn't know what to do at first and laughed sheepishly. She would like to know what was written on the note.

Kaito straightens up, wants to get up but sits down again.

"Mio, what does it say?"

Mio looked at Kaito, not wanting to be told a second time, grabbed the note and read it. "Myojin Inari Shrine, Sakura-Dori, Kazehara."

Mio's eyes widened, she immediately realized that this was a fox shrine and why it needed a powerful fox god. She wanted to scream, but she managed to control herself.

Mr. Nakamura asked directly and without beating around the bush, "What do you want from the fox, you don't want to do anything stupid, do you?"

"No, I just want to ask him something, the door is behind you," Kaito said.

"Ms. Yamamoto, I've heard a lot about you, I imagine you want to take a look at the Order?"

Mio looked at Kaito.

"It's up to you what you do, just one thing, business matters are strictly confidential, but I would think twice about going with people like that," Kaito said.

"That's what he says when he takes his classmate to a shady old man."

Kaito looked at Mr. Nakamura, "Who gave me the order? Get out of here."

Mr. Nakamura went to the door, turned to Mio and said, "Come by whenever you want, unlike that monster over there, we don't bite, and if you're ever looking for a new job, just give me a call, it's not often you find someone who can wrap Mr. Kato around their finger. Oh yeah, and judging by the furniture and the skimpy clothes of his poor cat girl, the earnings can't be that great either, I'd pay you a lot more," he laughed and winked at Mio.

Kaito stood up and went to the door, said "Thank you" and closed it.

"You want to help Dawn materialize! That's right! Right?" Mio asked Kaito excitedly.

"I want to know what the conditions are, do you want to be there?" he asked in an undertone.

Mio didn't like this undertone, but immediately said, "Of course, you're not going without me.

"Then why don't you call Yuma and make an appointment for 3-5 days, during which he will serve as our taxi, we need a local car."

Now she understood the undertone and asked, "Why three to five days, isn't it enough to ask the fox and go home?"

"Mio, do you really think you can just ask a fox god without providing a great deal in return?"

"Why should I call Yuma?"

"Don't pretend or do you think I'm blind," Kaito said and grinned at Mio.

Mio was a little annoyed, but quickly recovered and looked for Yuma's number on her cell phone.

"I'm going shopping, Dawn, do you want to come with me?" Dawn meowed loudly and stayed where she was.

"She's probably mad that I'm deciding this over her head, but it's better for her future," he thought.

"If Yuma agrees, then book the hotel rooms, but watch the price, Chief Secretary," Kaito said and left the room. No matter how angry she was, he knew that Mio would do anything for Dawn, she was just too nice.

Three days later, Yuma was at the wheel, Mio was the passenger, Kaito and Dawn dozed in the back seat. "Thanks for stepping up, Yuma," Mio said.

"No problem, it's good that it's the semester break. But tell me Mio, I know Kaito is a cheapskate, wouldn't two hotel rooms have been enough?

Mio looked at Yuma, a little irritated and then annoyed.

"I mean you and Dawn and Kaito and me, of course," he grinned into the rising sun.

"Men!" Mio thought and started to explain to Yuma exactly what it was all about, whereby Mio threw in a few demons out of revenge, which then also had an effect on Yuma and made him think a little more about whether it was right to get involved in this trip. After the first stop, Mio corrected this at Kaito's command, whereupon Yuma set the tone again and Mio immediately regretted telling him the truth.

Kaito stroked Dawn and thought, "I hope this doesn't go on all the way.

When they arrived at the shrine, there was a cordon and various people, probably from the area, were demonstrating.

Mio looked questioningly at Kaito, who replied, "The shrine is to be torn down. That was part of the order to Mr. Nakamura, to find such a situation that we could use to meet the god there in the first place and have a possible option for negotiations. But now we have to get in there first."

The plan was set, Yuma stayed in the car with a line of sight to the shrine, Mio pretended to be a budding journalist from a school newspaper and interviewed people in front of the shrine. This served to gather information and distract them. Dawn and Kaito walked around the shrine to see if there was another entrance besides the main one.

There wasn't one, but that wasn't a bad thing because Mio attracted so much attention that the two of them could have walked through the main entrance slowly and waved without any problems.

Inside, Kaito immediately saw the fox and the fox saw that Kaito saw him and came towards him.

"Monster, what are you doing here and why are you bringing a cat into a fox shrine?" he asked in a deep voice and came even closer.

Kaito was not impressed by the slightly aggressive nature of the fox. He was well prepared for a possible fight, as he had learned from his last encounter with the female fox.

Kaito bowed deeply to the fox and said, "Dear Myojin, I have a wish, may I express it?" and placed an offering bowl with rice balls in front of him.

The fox looked at the offering and turned to Kaito, "Monsters like you shouldn't exist in this world. Say your wish," he said, swallowing the offering and then glowing with golden light.

"He gets this amount of spiritual energy from the believers in a year at the most, and the way things are going with his shrine right now, it's more like two years," Kaito thought, waiting a little longer until the fox was off the dope again.

Then he pulled Dawn, who was visibly uncomfortable in the fox's shrine, over to him and said, "I want Dawn to get the ability to materialize as a human at her request, how does she do that?"

The fox looked at him, came closer and then moved away.

"Is he drunk now," Kaito thought as he saw the fox running around inside the shrine, "did I give him too much energy?" he laughed to himself.

He looked at Kaito and said, "Is that all you want to know, why are you coming to me with this?"

"Damn," Kaito thought, "that sounded like beginner's knowledge, basics, if that's the case, why isn't it in any books, should he have asked the order first?

"No, he can't do that," he thought and realized that he had to go through with it now.

He improvised, "for you maybe, so what do you want for it?"

"Kill the man who wants to tear down the shrine."

That was easy, he thought, and said, "Killing people is unworthy of a god and a crime in the human world. I cannot serve you like this."

The fox circled him and Dawn several times.

"Anyone who tears down sanctuaries is not worthy to exist, evil must always be eradicated."

"What a lot of talk," Kaito thought. "That may be true in your world, but not in the human world," Kaito said, thinking about sending a demon or Shy after the man. But a certain policeman probably wouldn't like that if it got out.

"How about I get the man to leave the shrine standing," he said, remembering Mr. Kato, who in a similar situation had finally agreed to keep a shrine or some trees.

"That and one of your gifts once a year would be appropriate."

Kaito was annoyed, "That divine arrogance again.

"One more time, no more."

"Agreed, and now get out and take your pet cat with you," the fox said and lay down on the altar without giving Kaito another look.

Kaito was glad that it was so easy and left the shrine with Dawn. Mio was already eagerly awaiting her release. By now, she had gathered a lot of information about the man who had bought the shrine in order to tear it down, but when she ran out of topics, the demonstrators started telling her their life stories, many not suitable for young people, and Mio was finally just annoyed by the group of men who had gathered around her.

Mio said a friendly goodbye to everyone anyway and ran to the car where Yuma was sleeping, who was then rudely awakened by Mio with the words, "Did you ever really care about me!"

As they drove to the hotel, Kaito explained the deal he had negotiated with the fox and Mio proudly reported the results of her research.

The man who bought the shrine was named Katsuya Maeda, a small but well-known contractor in the area, and he wanted to build a "stupid parking garage" on the site of the shrine. A residents' association was formed to oppose this, as no one here needed a parking garage so far out of town.

"The association believes that Mr. Maeda wants to demolish the shrine because his daughter drove off the road and drowned in the river ten years ago. Mr. Maeda blamed it on the foxes that jump around in the valley, and people think he wants to take revenge on the foxes in the valley," Mio said.

Pretty stupid of the guy, but it couldn't have gone any better, Kaito thought. The fact that Mr. Maeda accepted the world of the gods and the Yokai should also be good for him. In fact, he should thank the fool and his daughter, Kaito thought.

"Anything else?"

"Ha! Ha!", Mio said triumphantly.

"Speak up, what is it?

"The coffin they buried was empty, the body of the woman was never found, only the car was found in the river and it was empty. What a shame for a yakuza, they all said."

"Do you know where the accident supposedly happened?"

"Yes, there is a memorial plaque at the site, Mrs. Maeda was very well known here."

"Yuma, drive me directly to the memorial plaque and drop me off there."

"You want to question the spirits and Ayakashi, please let me come with you."

"No, you go back to the hotel with Yuma."

"Why, is it dangerous?"

"No, I need to think in peace and I can't do that with you jumping around me."

Now Mio was really angry and looked out of the window.

"If Mr. Maeda is really still with the Yakuza, you shouldn't show your face there anyway and stay in the background."

"Yuma, make sure Mio doesn't screw up," Kaito said as he and Dawn got out after an hour's drive.

"Pah! After all I've done for you," Mio said, looking sourly in another direction.

Yuma led the way and Dawn said, "Sometimes you really are an ass.

Kaito ignored Dawn and walked to the tablet, muttering, "Truths are hard to bear."

Once there, he looked around. They were in a hollow. The road rose steeply in both directions and there was a bend right in the hollow, not five meters from the river, where Mrs. Maeda had left the road and her car had plunged into the river. It was all plausible. It was quite possible that she swerved into the river, or that she was distracted and did not see the road way. The fact that she knew the route argued against it. However, it is not uncommon for something like this to happen on a wet winter evening, even to residents who are distracted. Especially when something was running across the road. But something made him wonder.

Dawn snapped him out of his thoughts with a "meow" and Dawn said, "Nobody's died around here yet.

Exactly, that was the problem, he also had this suspicion and an indication of it was clearly visible, or rather something was not where it should be. There was no echo at this point, such echoes from the death of a young person took longer to dissipate, in the case of such a young woman it could be more than ten years, he estimated. Sometimes, a ghost would appear and stay in the area of the echo until it burned out.

There was plenty of dark energy, but no echo. Even stranger was the fact that there were no yokai or ghosts buzzing around.

Nothing, absolutely nothing, no yokai, no ghosts were here. If the woman had been thrown from the car and died in the floods later, an echo would have been expected by now, and if not here, it would have been seen somewhere on the way upriver from the mouth of the river. He hadn't expected to find her spirit, but maybe a ghost, or at least a Yokai, or better yet, an Ayakashi to negotiate with. This place was filled with dark energy. But there were no ghosts, no Ayakashi, no Yokai to be seen for miles around."

"Dawn, can you sense any presence. Any?"

"No," Dawn said and looked around, smelling and hearing in the light breeze. But nothing, nothing at all.

"Unusual for a place like this, isn't it, Dawn?" Kaito asked.

"No one has died in this river for a long time," he confirmed to himself. Everyone who travels here knows this dangerous place, strangers rarely come here and the road was well secured, maybe not as good as it is today, but certainly good enough.

"Let's go downstream towards the town, that must be the direction she came from."

Dawn, running up the slope in the darkness, called out to the sky, "What a beautiful, clear, divine night.

Dawn could hardly be stopped, she just kept going, but Kaito was annoyed by the ups and downs of the road, his legs aching after a long walk.

Two cars in that time and not a single Yokai, nothing, that couldn't be true, Kaito thought.

Further ahead, a lone lantern illuminated a small parking lot that they had passed on their way here. "Why is there a parking lot here of all places," Kaito wondered.

He looked down from the parking lot at the river that meandered picturesquely through the grounds and understand, "Parking lot with a view," he thought. But that didn't change the fact that he still hadn't seen a Yokai he wanted to question.

"Meow, over there!" said Dawn.

Kaito quickly looked in the direction Dawn was pointing. Now, he could see it. Two slightly glowing figures were jumping between the trees on the other side of the road. Why do Yokai glow, Kaito wondered. Kaito reached into his pockets, "Everything is there," he assured himself.

"Go Dawn." They ran towards the shining figures. They were moving at high speed between the trees further up the mountainside when they noticed Kaito and Dawn.

"Go Dawn cut them off," Kaito gasped and looked back, "only 20 meters and already done, not good," he thought.

He continued to climb up the hill on all fours, having long since lost sight of Dawn, when he heard Dawn's voice calling two foxes to stop. Then a laugh and Dawn's scream again, this time much more exhausted. He caught his breath for a moment and then climbed further up the mountainside. "Two foxes, then, probably divine beings, which would explain their glow. "This is going to be fun. Those sneaky foxes," he muttered, now looking with the last of his strength at a small plateau in the mountain.

He lay down on his back and took a deep breath. The stars were clearly visible. If the moon disappeared, it would be pitch black, and he was glad he could still feel his smartphone in his pocket. "Where would mankind be today without smartphones?" he laughed at the sky.

Dawn came back, panting herself, and lay down next to him, looking up at the stars as well.

"The beasts were too fast. Young foxes, no more than 120," she said.

Kaito laughed, "How young are you again, Dawn?" and had to cough.

"Meow, you know, I'm only 190!

"Still so young," he laughed and added amusedly, "in a thousand years our relative age difference will be only marginal," it came out of him, panting and breathing fast and regretting his lousy condition.

"Did you see where the foxes went?"

"With foxes, it doesn't matter," Dawn said.

"A human, a human who can see us," came two voices from behind their heads.

Dawn jumped up from her lying position and turned towards the voices while still in the air. Kaito could only look on enviously. He was still panting as he positioned his body.

"Human, human, he seems to see us," the two foxes who were sitting on a tree trunk five meters away from them repeated.

Dawn hissed at them and Kaito thought they would run away again, but they laughed at Dawn.

"That little cat thinks she's better than us. Female cat, female cat can only meow," they sang as a duet and Dawn was about to lose it.

"Dawn, leave her alone, you know how foxes are," he said and Dawn sat down angrily.

"Of course they toyed with us. What's the best way to start?" Kaito thought.

Kaito took a box out of his pocket, the two immediately looked interested and sniffed the air and Kaito had understood how to wrap them around his finger.

He took out two rice balls and put them in a bowl in front of them.

The two foxes immediately came closer and examined the two balls in front of them.

"Are you a human god, human god?" they asked in a duet.

"A normal human. Here for you, something better you'll never get again," Kaito replied.

They each swallowed the small rice ball, then looked back at Kaito and said, "Human god, human god, your aura is not of this world, are you sure you belong here?"

Kaito realized that it was going to be a long night and watched as Dawn lay down, but not without taking her eyes off of them.

"Do you want more?"

"Yes more, yes more," came out of them.

"Fox doping or fox drugging," he laughed to himself, "I just hope no fanatical animal cult finds out about this."

Kaito talked about the car accident in the hollow ten years ago, where a woman had died, but the two beasts had only looked at the box.

"What now? You know anything?" Kaito asked.

"Car, car, what's that?" they both said at the same time and jumped around him.

"The rolling vehicle, where people sit in to get around," he almost shouted at them.

"We know, we know, the noisy thing that people use because they are too slow and have too short a life."

"Just such a car. One drove into the river here ten winters ago, do you know anything about it?" asked Kaito, already desperate.

The car in the river, the car in the river, ten winters ago, ten winters ago. Of course we saw it. Do you want to know something?

Kaito listened electrified, he hadn't expected that or was this just the usual trick of a fox? He remained calm and continued to ask.

"Were you there when it happened?"

"We were, we were."

"Tell me what happened."

"Rice balls, rice balls, that's what we want."

Kaito realized that he might be in short supply and placed two more bullets in the sacrificial bowl in front of the two foxes.

"So, what happened?

"The car went into the river."

Kaito grabbed his head, Dawn meowed maliciously.

"Did the car have to swerve because a fox jumped in front of it and then the car drove into the river?"

"Fox, fox, lots of foxes here in the forest, but none there that day."

"Why did the car drive into the river?

"Ask the car, ask the car," they both laugh.

"We're not getting anywhere," he thought, and asked, "What happened to the person in the car when it went into the river?"

"person?, person?", they said, looking at each other.

"There was no person in the car."

Dawn straightened up, Kaito flinched, now, just now, he slowly began to understand.

He had asked the wrong question. It should have been the right one,

"The car rolled down the hill without people and then went straight into the river, is that right?" he asked simply.

"Man is clever, man is clever! Reward, reward."

That was the trigger he needed, the veil was lifted. Mr. Nakamura's tip had paid off.

Trembling slightly with excitement, he placed two rice balls back on the bowl in front of him.

"What did the woman who brought the car down the hill do?" he asked, thinking, "the good girl wanted a life without yakuza and faked her death and then went abroad."

"Woman, woman," they both looked at each other, "there was no woman."

Kaito looked at Dawn, Dawn looked back, it's harder than I thought, but it's going to be something big.

"Was it a man?"

"A man, a man, the human is smart!"

"But before the car went into the river, there was a woman in the car, where did she get out?"

"In the mountains, in the mountains, reward, reward."

Kaito looked at Dawn again and then asked the two foxes with a slightly trembling voice.

"Is the woman still alive in the human world?"

"Not for ten winters, not for ten winters," they said in a duet and he realized his mistake.

Okay, now he understood, his next questions were clear and would probably all be answered in the affirmative.

"Can you take me to the woman?"

"Can we, can we, reward, reward."

"The woman and the man met down here in the bay by the road?" He pointed to the parking lot from which they had climbed up the hill.

"The human is clever, the human is clever!"

The woman was murdered! By the Yakuza? Maybe even by her father himself, which would explain why no one was surprised to find no body.

Now it's time to stay calm, if it were like that, everything would fall apart.

Even the construction of the parking deck could just be a distraction to feign grief and hate. Should he call Mr. Tanaka and request the favor for Ms. Kato?

He placed two more bullets on the offering bowl and said, "Describe to me the man who made the cart roll down the hill and the man who meet the woman down there.

It was the same person. The description showed a man in his 50s with striking blond hair, a scar on his left cheek, and a missing left pinkie. That should be enough, anyone who knew him should be able to recognize him.

In any case, it wasn't Mr. Maeda, but that didn't mean he couldn't have hired someone to do it.

He pulled his smartphone out of his pocket and called Yuma.

"Please come to the parking lot, about 4,000 meters from the memorial plaque."

"Is something wrong, you sound strange."

"The case is solved, I have the woman."

Silence on the other side, then a scream and a clatter, then Mio on the line, "We'll be right there, we need about an hour, is that okay?"

"Take your time, she won't run away! Drive carefully, bring lamps and something to eat," Kaito said, realizing how he was thinking about the value of a life.

"How little a person can be worth," he said quietly and hung up.

"I have two more rice balls. I'll give them to you and then five each if you take me to the woman, what do you say?" and stroked their heads.

"Woman in the mountains, woman in the mountains, we want more."

Kaito didn't feel like smiling or negotiating.

"Fine, but not until tomorrow."

"Human god, human hod , we trust in you."

"Then let's go down the mountain and you two will show us the way to the woman."

"Yes, Human god, yes, human god."

Mio and Yuma arrived much too quickly, but Kaito was too tense to give a sermon now.

He greeted Yuma and Mio, who seemed to have forgotten their anger, and asked the two foxes, "Would you like a ride?"

"Ride along, ride along, it's fun."

"Well, at least it'll be faster," he thought.

Mio and Yuma looked around, but said nothing and understood.

Yuma, drove off, Mio next to him and Dawn sat on Kaito's lap in the back and seemed to enjoy the way he stroked her.

"Where are we going?" Yuma asked.

"Ten kilometers upriver into the mountains and then left, I'll let you know."

"Yuma, your car is officially a god truck as of today," he broke the silence.

"What does that mean?"

"Well, there are two divine beings to your left and right, so from now on you are a messenger of the gods."

Yuma flinched slightly and looked back.

"Hey, look at the road, damn, everything's fine."

"Such a coward", Mio said, grinning.

"Oho, all is not forgiven yet", Kaito thought.

Yuma remained silent and drove on.

"From here on, we have to walk, smartphones out and lights on", Kaito said.

The two foxes jumped around Kaito the whole time, trying to steal the box from his pocket. Dawn kept hissing at them, keeping them at a distance.

"That's really cute, but unfortunately I can't enjoy it right now," Kaito thought about all the consequences that would happen to him now.

"In here, in here," the foxes called.

Kaito called everyone together and said, "Yuma, please remove the boards from the entrance.

"I'll go check, you wait here and if..." he didn't get any further.

"I'll go with you, no arguments. I know it's a lot to ask, but then you'll have something good with me. Yuma and Dawn will keep watch and if anything happens, Yuma will get help," Mio said firmly to the group.

Kaito did not object and went ahead, Mio followed. The danger of collapse was clearly visible in several places; the mine had been secured for a reason.

The foxes were also romping through the tunnels.

"Hey, you two, if we get killed here, there won't be any more rice balls, that's for sure, so make sure you don't touch anything," Kaito called to the two, knowing full well that it wouldn't do much good.

Mio was a little nervous as well.

"Collapse, collapse, the human-god is afraid."

"Damned if this is a fox trap," Kaito thought and stopped.

"How much further?" he asked.

"Not far, not far," it came back.

He was about to say something when the two foxes stopped and pointed at the wall.

"Woman here, woman here," they said and backed away.

Kaito looked around and illuminated the wall.

The boards there were not part of the retaining wall, but hid a passage or a cavity. That was not unusual, many passages or cavities were secured that way, he thought.

"Mio, take ten steps back.

"Kaito wait, are you sure?" Mio called out,

"Sure, it's not a retaining wall," he said, thinking, "nothing is clear, this is the stupidest thing I've ever done in my short life."

He looked over at Mio, who, judging by the light, must have gone back about 15 meters and was pulling lightly on the first plank.

"Thank God, it comes off easily, without any resistance," he said to himself.

Mio called, "Are you okay Kaito?"

"Yes, come here, the boards are off, no danger, looks stable."

Mio slowly walked forward and shone the light on Kaito, who was looking into the hallway with his usual unreadable, passive expression. She stood next to him, also shining her light into the corridor, startled, backed away slightly and reflexively grabbed onto Kaito, who nearly collapsed under the weight as her legs gave way.

"An almost perfect murder."

"No, not just a murder," Mio said and began to cry.

Kaito understood what Mio meant; the dead woman's torn clothes were still clearly visible in the vicinity.

Kaito shined his light on the almost completely skeletal hand, in which something was glowing. An amulet. He stepped closer and grabbed it.

"What are you doing?" Mio shouted at him, crying and grabbing his jacket.

Kaito stopped, kept looking at the hand and said, "We need proof, otherwise no one will believe us. I'll be careful!"

Mio let go and Kaito took the amulet from the dead woman's hand.

"Kaito, can you please wait here, I have to get something, please, please," Mio said.

"How long will it take?"

"Five minutes, no more."

"Okay, but slowly, that's okay and don't touch the walls, I'll wait."

Mio's lamp disappeared and Kaito shone his light on the amulet.

"15.10.2007 For my beloved daughter on her 18th birthday."

"Perfect," he thought and looked after the two foxes who continued to run into the tunnel as if it was their home.

"Wait, their home?" he thought.

"Hey you two," the foxes looked at him.

"God of man, God of man, what more do you want from us?"

"Were you with the woman when she died?"

"She died, she died in our arms," they said at the same time and began to play again.

"Thank you," Kaito said quietly in their direction.

He looked around, shining his light back and forth along the corridor. Carefully, he walked a few more meters, but he didn't find the ghost of the young woman there either. It was quite possible that the foxes had sent the ghost up, it was part of their nature. But he didn't want to ask, it didn't matter for what was to come. But the echo of her death was still clearly visible. 'The younger and more violently a life ends, the longer the echo remains,' he recited a passage from one of the textbooks. 'This one will burn for a while,' he said to himself.

He saw a light flicker on the walls. "Mio, you were quick," he said quietly.

Mio had two small bouquets and her jacket, which she gave to Kaito.

"Please put the jacket over her and the flowers to the left and right," Mio asked.

Kaito did so without hesitation and thought, "What a kind-hearted girl."

"I can only hope it's Mrs. Maeda too", Kaito thought as they left the shaft together. Once outside, Kaito gave the two foxes the last two bullets, which then vanished in front of Yuma and Mio's eyes, promising to bring them the rest later. With great leaps, they disappeared into the forest of the mountain.

Kaito wanted to tell Yuma that the woman had been alive when she was put there, which would also explain the amulet in her hand, but he saw Mio's face and left it at that.

"She didn't die alone, the two foxes were with her. Maybe she even saw them. But even if she did, no one will ever know," Kaito thought.

The next day, Kaito explained that everyone had to go home, including Dawn. Only he would stay here and negotiate with Mr. Maeda. He had contacted his father, who had used his contacts, and so he learned that Mr. Maeda certainly had nothing to do with his daughter's disappearance. The plan was set. Everyone but him had to get out of the line of fire. Surprisingly, Mio had no objections and immediately agreed. So Kaito could put his plan into action.

Two days later, a package arrived at KatsuCM-Constructions. It was addressed directly to Mr. Maeda and was tested for poisons, explosives and radioactive substances. The result was negative, so the package was delivered to Mr. Maeda's office.

The executive secretary who opened the package immediately thought of a gift that she would throw away as usual. This time it was a jewelry box with an open note that read, "Kaito Tanaka, Spiritual Deriver, Spirit-KT-Science Institute.

"I need something from you, please let me know if you're interested."

A phone number underneath. That was all.

She smiled and thought about the stupid ideas moochers come up with, took the amulet out of the box with her left hand and turned it over in her hand.

A date and an inscription, she thought as she began to understand the engraved words 'For my beloved daughter ...'.

An unexpected, violent pounding of her heart ripped through her body as her right hand slapped her mouth, her left dropped the amulet and she tumbled backwards from the chair with a violent jolt emanating from the center of her heart.

Trembling, she got to her feet as the situation slowly dawned on her.

Today of all days, Mr. Maeda was in an extremely bad mood, and he had important meetings all day long. She had explicit orders not to disturb him.

But, and again, there was that ten-year-old instruction in the room about his beloved daughter. Everything, absolutely everything, that had to do with his daughter's disappearance had to be reported immediately.

Mr. Maeda, who was otherwise so unscrupulous, had taken five years to return to full-time work. During that time, he had fired many employees for minor misconduct because he considered them incompetent.

She was still trembling.

"Will this cost me my job, no matter how she behaves?" she thought.

She also had a daughter and a son, both of whom depended on her. Her job paid well. She had been a secretary for 20 years, took a deep breath and told herself that an order from the boss is an order from the boss, something a secretary cannot ignore or postpone. She stood up and went to the door.

She knocked once, opened the door and entered the room without looking directly at Mr. Maeda. The room was dead silent. Mr. Maeda was probably cursing himself for hiring her. Bending low, she walked towards Mr. Maeda, the note and the amulet in her outstretched hands. Once at the table, she carefully placed both on the table and walked back to the door without looking up.

He'd had a shitty day, especially with the idiots at the shrine he'd wanted to bulldoze for a parking lot, who were now causing legal trouble, and now the chief secretary who was getting old. "I should find some younger vegetables," he thought, looking at the garbage that that useless old cow had just put on his new desk.

What was that? An amulet, it took him a second to recognize the piece on the table. An amulet that looked like..., he froze.

He saw his hand reaching for the object on the table, why did the hand do that, he had not given the hand that command, but it picked it up and held it at a reasonable distance in front of his eyes. The engraving could not be overlooked, he had it ordered one day, he had been there when it was created. He had sent for the master and insisted that it be done immediately.

He looked at the amulet, moving it slowly in his hand, over and over again. It can't be, no, it can't be, he told himself, not noticing how the room, where ten people had just held an important meeting, was emptying.

When he looked up again, there were only two people left in the room.

He picked up the note that had been lying next to the amulet and read it aloud.

"Kaito Tanaka, Spiritual Deriver, Spirit-KT-Science Institute."

"I need something from you, please let me know if you're interested."

He pressed a button and spoke, "Cancel all subsequent appointments, bring this man in, now."

"Call everyone in, now," he said to a man in the room, who left the room quickly.

Kaito was watching television when his cell phone rang.

"That was fast," he thought and answered it.

"Kaito Tanaka, Spirit-KT Science Institute, how can I help you?

"KatsuCM Construction office. Mr. Tanaka, you know what this is about, Mr. Maeda would like to meet with you immediately, when can you be there?" asked a rather ready, slightly hysterical female voice.

"Oh, so fast, that's great, I'll be there in an hour," Kaito said overly friendly with a mocking expression on his face.

"Can it be any faster?"

"Okay, Mr. Maeda really had nothing to do with his daughter's death," Kaito thought and said, "I'll be there in 30 minutes, it won't be faster."

"Thank you, I'll wait."

Since Kaito didn't feel like waiting and wanted to know who was waiting for him, he arrived at the company building 40 minutes later. He saw a security guard standing outside, looking around nervously, and knew immediately whom to approach. "That's the way it should be," he thought, and approached the man. The man looked him up and down, probably indicating that he was expecting someone else and not a high school student.

When the misunderstanding was cleared up, he firmly but kindly asked Kaito to follow him, which Kaito did with a disinterested look on his face. After passing through a metal detector and somewhat reluctantly locking away his smartphone, he took the elevator to the top floor to a reception room where a very nervous-looking woman was waiting for him. She had probably been standing there for a while, as her shoe prints were clearly visible on the rather firm carpet. When she realized the situation, she looked at him for a second as if to say, "What kind of brat is this, is he really the right one?" After this moment of shock, she approached Kaito and said, "Mr. Tanaka, I'm glad you could come so quickly, Mr. Maeda is already waiting for you, I'll show you in."

She knocked three times, opened the door and looked at Kaito's face again.

"The same expression as when he was on guard duty," Kaito thought as he entered the fortunately well-lit room. "I don't think anyone will die today," he said to himself as he entered the room and first looked at the man at the desk. He had expected to see a sleazy rat, as was common in this line of work. Instead, it was a strikingly attractive and charismatic man with jet-black hair, no more than sixty years old, the situation in the room clearly emphasizing his arrogance and position. Four other men were standing around him. The greasy one on the right was clearly a lawyer. The others were probably security guards or confidants.

Mr. Maeda was already in a bad mood when he got up, and it got worse as the day went on. Finding the amulet was the turning point of the day, he didn't even want to know his blood pressure anymore, he had canceled all his meetings. Fuck the IRS, fuck the stupid mayor and all the other losers who wanted something from him. On this day he only wanted to deal with the man who might know something about his daughter's disappearance, the time he had waited to face this man was the longest he had ever had to endure, with one exception, the waiting period during the birth of his beloved daughter. Now he stood there and knew it was a psychopath, an occult idiot. At first he thought the man probably wanted money, which he could give him and then have him beaten up. But he hadn't reckoned with this milky face that was now standing in front of him. He looked down at the amulet in his hand. Yes, it was the amulet he had given her for her 18th birthday, for sure. All right, he thought.

"Boy, where did you find this?" he broke the silence in the room.

"Let's negotiate," Kaito thought, turning away and looking around the room cheekily without paying attention to Mr. Maeda. He always did that, almost automatically, when he wasn't interested in his counterpart or didn't like him.

"A favor for a favor," Kaito said and looked at Mr. Maeda again.

Mr. Maeda snorted at him and made it clear that he wouldn't get out of here without talking. Kaito smiled cynically at him. Mr. Maeda glanced at one of the people Kaito had identified as security which shook his head slightly. Kaito took that as confirmation that Mr. Maeda now knew that Kaito couldn't record the conversation. That was what the metal detector was for. Kaito looked at the lawyer and said, "I demand that the shrine be restored and stay where it is, then I will grant your wish.

"Who do you think you are, you brat?" he shouted at him.

"Just because I'm a high school student and look weak, you think you're above me?" he said, looking at him again.

Mr. Maeda snorted angrily.

"He's probably thinking if I'm a lunatic or someone sent by the Yakuza or if there could be something else behind it," he thought.

Kaito knew that Mr. Maeda wouldn't let him beat him up until this was settled, so he had time to negotiate in his own way.

"So you're a high school student and you say to be a medium who communicates with spirits?"

"That sounds very cheesy, Mr. Maeda, but that's a colloquial way of putting it."

"You or someone else found the amulet by the river and somehow managed to connect it to my family, and now you want something for it? Did those weirdos at the shrine hire you? Have you formed an alliance with them or are you even one of them?"

"For roaring like a lion, that was polite," Kaito thought.

"I don't care about the 'crazies' at the shrine. Money is always good, but in this case, it won't help. I need something bigger and I'll only get it if the shrine stays as it is."

"Why the shrine?" asked Mr. Maeda and Kaito rolled his eyes.

"Because the god of the shrine wants it that way!"

"Did he tell you where to find the amulet?"

"No, Mr. Maeda."

Mr. Maeda looked at him and said in a cold voice, "Then what?"

"He showed me where to find your daughter and the shrine has to be preserved for that," he lied a little.

The room became even quieter. It was clear who had the highest authority in the room. No one dared to breathe.

Mr. Maeda opened a drawer and took out a gun. "9 mm automatic," Kaito thought and recognized the brand immediately, the design was unmistakable.

Kaito remained unimpressed. "Make no mistake, old man," he thought.

"This is the last time! Where in this damn river is my daughter? We've been searching the river for a year," he said slowly, but clearly agitated, turning the discarded gun with the barrel on the table in Kaito's direction.

"In the river? Mr. Maeda, your daughter was never in the river. What about the shrine?" He reached into his pocket. The guards jumped.

Kaito laughed, "Afraid of a high school boy?" he asked into the room, now holding a folded piece of paper in his hand.

"What's that?" asked Mr. Maeda.

"A piece of paper!" Kaito replied coldly and amused.

"What does it say?" Mr. Maeda hissed angrily in Kaito's direction.

"The current whereabouts of your daughter and the circumstances of her death! What about the shrine!"

"What do you mean with all this. My daughter drowned in the river when her car went off the road?"

"Your daughter was murdered. The car was empty when the murderer drove it into the river, and the best thing is, I can prove it," Kaito said calmly while he held the note in one hand out to Mr. Maeda. This was also bold for Kaito, he knew that, but he didn't like Mr. Maeda and he didn't have to consider anyone.

Only the ticking of the clock told outsiders that time was still running in this room. The men, all the men, had stopped breathing and were frozen. Only Kaito turned his head and looked around in amusement, thinking, "You're all dirt, but even dirt could understand if he wanted to, otherwise that's it!"

Mr. Maeda took the gun from the table, pointed it at Kaito's feet and slowly raised it. Now he had the legs in sight, now the stomach, now the heart and finally the head.

He could kill this brat, this madman for his arrogance here and now. If he pulled the trigger, the scary part would be over, there would be enough witnesses to an attack on him and therefore self-defense, but this amulet and the fact that there was not the slightest fear of death in his eyes. The boy simply did not react, not because he was paralyzed with fear. No, he simply had none, especially in this situation. The way he acted, he wasn't some bum off the street who was lucky to find something, he wasn't some simple weirdo or stupid junkie, there had to be more to it than that. He lowered the gun and put it back on the table.

"If you lie to me, I'll kill you," he said to Kaito without a second thought.

Kaito kept a straight face and said, "Agreed, what about the shrine?"

"If you survive, you'll get what you want," he said, gesturing with his hand.

One of the guards went over to Kaito, took the note from his hand and handed it to Mr. Maeda.

Mr. Maeda opened the note, looked from Kaito to the note and concentrated on it. Kaito saw how Mr. Maeda's eyes got wider and wider as he scanned the note. The moment it became clear that Mr. Maeda had reached the place on the paper where he had described the murderer of his daughter, Kaito knew that he had won. Now all he had to do was wait and let the disgusting bunch have their way for a few more hours and he would have what he wanted. Maybe even all of it. Everything to improve Dawn's life forever and make her a part of this society. "Thank you, fox goddess", he thought.

If Mr. Maeda didn't keep his side of the bargain, a demon would slowly consume him in a few months, or he could do it faster, he thought at the exact moment when someone shouted, "Gather everyone, departure in 5 minutes," and he was pushed out of the room.

The ride to the mine was boring - a security guard sat in front of him and next to him. Mr. Maeda was in one of the other five cars.

He thought about provoking them by asking if they wanted to play cards, but that seemed too childish, so he left it at that.

"Five cars full of security guards, quite an effort, either he's with the Yakuza or he's afraid of them. Either way, not my problem," he thought as the vehicles stopped after a long drive before they started climbing up to the mine.

"Come on, show us the way," one of the guards said.

While Mr. Maeda stayed in the vehicle and the security guards formed a protective ring around him, Kaito climbed up to the mine with four other security guards.

"Boy, if there's a bomb in here, you're going down with it," one of them said.

"That's the root of the matter, that's why everyone is so nervous," he thought.

"Don't worry, it's up ahead," he said, and went through the side passage he'd marked to the breach in the wall.

A guard looked in, lifted the jacket with a stick that Kaito had put over the dead woman at Mio's request, said "Damn! Long time no see," and Kaito thought, "You must have been in the police once, must have fallen out of favor!" Kaito said to himself.

The guard informed Mr. Maeda. Since everything was on speakerphone, you could hear how Mr. Maeda wanted to take a look at everything himself against the will of the guards and probably ran up the hill.

"Oh man," Kaito thought, "it'll be a while before that old scumbag gets here."

But Mr. Maeda was there sooner than he thought and now looked at the dirty, dark grave of his daughter.

Mr. Maeda, like Mio back then and probably like everyone here, immediately recognized what must have happened there. The clothes lying next to the body and the position of the skeleton indicated that the person was not already dead when they were placed there.

Unexpectedly, someone sobbed next to him. Kaito turned in that direction and saw Mr. Maeda looking at his daughter's dead body with a distorted face. He tried desperately not to cry in front of his people. Kaito was about to make fun of the old man when he thought about how his father would have reacted if he, Kaito, had been lying there.

"I will go now, everything as agreed," Kaito said and stood up.

But someone grabbed his arm.

"The flowers and the jacket, who put them there?" asked Mr. Maeda with a tearful voice.

"Damn," Kaito thought, "if only Mio hadn't done that, now you're going to get involved. Nobody would believe I was doing this."

"A colleague of mine didn't want to leave without giving her daughter back at least some of her respect and dignity. From me, you can't expect that."

Mr. Maeda let go of Kaito's arm and said, "Bring me Seto, the pig."

The foxes seemed to have described the person well. Death will be a release for Seto if they catch him, he thought, and he had no desire to wait or stay in one place with these people any longer. He left the mine in the direction of the road and wanted to stop by the parking lot again, the night was still young, he had enough time.

He took his smartphone, which he had gotten back from the security guards, texted Mio and Yuma, and made his way to the hotel when he saw that the parking lot was deserted.

It was just before midnight when Kaito reached the hotel. The long way had made him tired. Fortunately, a bus took him the last long remaining part of the way, and he lay down on the bed to rest for a moment, but then he fell asleep and didn't wake up again until the next morning.

Breakfast did him good, he looked at the TV on the wall of the hotel and read the ticker of the news channel.

He smiled when he saw that the police had solved an old murder case and that the brother-in-law of a businessman had turned himself in and confessed to the crime.

Someone must have warned him, probably someone who wanted to prevent a family war within the Maeda clan. His death would have been slow and cruel, but if he was convicted, he would face a quick execution at most, nothing compared to what Mr. Maeda would have done to him if he had found him in front of the police.

After breakfast, he left the hotel for the train station and was back at the office by noon. Mio was probably at school, where he had been absent for some time now, wondering if he should call Mr. Tanaka to sort things out or try it without him.

He would come back on the weekend, check on the shrine, bring the remaining tributes for the foxes and claim his own tribute.

After school, Mio and Dawn, who was spending time with Mio, came by. Contrary to expectations, he only had to tell Mio the story once and briefly, either because there were no ghosts in it or because it had affected her more than she wanted to admit.

Probably the former, because Mio really wanted to go again, even though she knew for sure that she wouldn't see any foxes. She had made that very clear.

Yuma and Mio didn't see each other again for a while. He didn't want to know what had happened and decided to organize train tickets for the trip to the shrine when Mio gave him a letter. He rolled his eyes when he saw the sender. Even a letter from school would have been better than this one with 'Maeda Family' in the return address, even from the old snipe.

Kaito told Mio succinctly.

"The Maedas want you and me to attend the funeral of their daughter."

Mio became thoughtful and Kaito wondered what he could say to get her to cancel. He was about to explain why she had been invited, but Mio replied more quickly, "It's very kind of Mr. and Mrs. Maeda to give us the opportunity to pay our respects to their daughter."

"I thought I was the crazy one here. How can you have such thoughts? You know, these people are criminal scum in my eyes," Kaito thought as he put the letter away and was shocked to realize that he would probably not be able to avoid the visit.

"If your parents don't mind you going to the funeral of a family with a yakuza past or even present, we'll stay an extra day."

"All families are the same at a time like this," she said, leaving Kaito speechless.

The night before the funeral, the three of them returned to the hotel and took a taxi to the shrine.

In fact, the demonstrators and the barrier to the shrine had disappeared, and work had begun on what appeared to be a renovation of the shrine.

There were no workers in sight. Mio approached a man in a suit who was taking notes. He explained that he had been hired by the Maeda family to plan the renovations here.

After he left too, Kaito sent Dawn ahead, who signaled to Kaito that the entrance to the inner area of the shrine was unlocked. The three of them looked around for a good opportunity, took advantage of a deserted moment, rushed in and closed the door behind them.

The room was dustier than the last time, probably because of the surveying work that had begun. Kaito looked around. The Fox was lying on the altar, visibly bored and with a typically divine, arrogant expression on his face. "Nothing has changed," he thought.

"I have come to fulfill our contract," Kaito said to the fox.

He looked up, grinned and jumped at the three of them. Kaito and Dawn backed away automatically. Mio, who couldn't see him, stopped and the fox stood right in front of her. Mio looked at Kaito who went back to the fox and took out the box with the agreed offerings.

But the fox was more interested in Mio than the offerings and sniffed at her.

"Hey, you perverted fox, what are you doing?" thought Kaito and said, "This is where it's happening and leave the girl alone."

Mio looked around and reached into the air, but the fox moved as if it knew where Mio was stretching her arms and said to Kaito, "An interesting human girl you've brought with you. Her aura is beautiful. If you want to become my priestess, human, you'll be safe here," he breathed to her.

Kaito huffed, "You know she can't see you."

"You really mean that," and suddenly a young man stood in front of Mio. His hand touched her chin and he held her head so that their eyes met.

Before she could realize what was happening, she thought "so beautiful" while her body reflexively recoiled.

"This is the perverted fox of the house," Kaito introduced him annoyed.

But neither Mio nor the fox paid any attention to him.

Kaito looked at Dawn and thought, "She told me that Mio's aura is especially beautiful. But for a fox god to reveal himself to her because of it, that's beyond special."

"Hello perverted fox, I'll leave the rest of the offerings here for you and if it takes longer with my colleague, I'll charge you."

With a short movement of his head towards Kaito, he showed him his contempt, flicked his finger once and eight little foxes came out, jumped on the offerings and made a mess of them.

"What's going on, are there more foxes?" asked Mio.

"My children are getting the fruits of the treaty with the monster over there. Which shouldn't exist," and without looking at him, he pointed contemptuously at Kaito.

Mio looked at Kaito, who made a face, and said, "Hey, perverted fox. The deal is done, now it's your turn."

"What do you mean monsters that shouldn't exist?" asked Mio, immediately regretting her question.

"Hey everyone, if you want to blaspheme, do it alone," he said angrily.

Mio tried to deflect and asked directly, "Your children are around me?"

"Yes, close your eyes and maybe you can feel them."

Mio did as she was told and felt a light, warm, very pleasant wind blowing around her, she smiled and when she opened her eyes again, the offerings were gone.

"God of men, god of men, where are our gifts, where are our gifts?"

"I know this from somewhere," he thought and looked at the voices. The two fox children looked at him and grinned.

Now he understood what was going on.

"Hey, perverted fox, it was you who drove all the Ayakashi away from the river or even killed them. That's why there was a veil of dark energy over the area. And then you sent your children to squeeze me even more!"

"You got what you wanted," the fox said reluctantly in his direction.

"Ayakashi could have helped me as well!"

The fox looked briefly in his direction, said, "Light and darkness, the eternal battle," and turned back to Mio, who was overwhelmed by his beauty. Kaito realized that the conversation was useless and looked at the two fox cubs standing in front of him and said, "Rice balls, Rice balls, give us what you promised, human god."

Kaito fetched a second can, opened it and placed it in front of the two fox cubs, secretly glad that the walk to the parking lot by the river was over.

He glanced at Dawn, who in turn watched the offerings with Kaito's spiritual energy disappear into the mouths of the eight fox children.

"Dawn, please stop this," he told her as he saw the embarrassed Mio continuing to worship the fox god and praise her beauty.

Dawn laughed and jumped between Mio and the god.

"We have another appointment when the sun fell again and Mio has to be at the School of Men by the next sunrise and now give my master what you promised," Dawn said forcefully to the fox.

Mio, overwhelmed by the divine beauty of this fox and at the same time touched by his offer, didn't know how to react and was relieved by Dawn's intervention, even if she only understood a hiss and a meow.

"Too bad, you can come over anytime, but then leave that belligerent house cat at home," the fox said, turning briefly to Kaito and then back to Mio.

"Human monsters! The gods can transfer this ability to god candidates. Find a mangy cat god who will accept her and train her. But remember, each god can only train a certain number. Just like my eight would be happy if you became their servant." He gave Mio a smile she would never forget and disappeared before her eyes.

"Hey fox, not so fast."

"What do you want monster, the contract is fulfilled."

Why was he so angry, Kaito thought. The arrogant dirty fox was right, the contract was fulfilled, that was all the fox could do anyway. But it was just too little for the effort.

"How can the gods balance their aura with dark energy, tell me!"

The fox stopped, turned around and said, "Dark energy? What are you talking about, human monster?

"Then how do you erase your aura?" he continued to ask.

He turned away, went to the exit and said, "Thousands of years of training, a house cat never learns that, not in 100 of your lives, monster" and disappeared from his sight.

"Interesting," Kaito thought.

"Mio, you can call a taxi, we'll go to the hotel and then to ... you know who."

Dawn stayed at the hotel, she didn't feel like coming with them, which was fine with Kaito. That would only attract attention and he wanted to avoid that.

The taxi driver knew immediately where and why someone wanted to see the Maeda family today. He wasn't the least bit nervous or tense about it and even began to talk about the family in an unusually relaxed way, but only in a good way.

He was happy about the decision to preserve the shrine and thought that the investigation of the case that every-one was talking about had something to do with it and asked Kaito and Mio if they knew more about it.

Mio just smiled, she would have liked to tell the man the sad tragic story, but the highest commandment of the 'Spirit-KT-Science Institute' was secrecy about all cus-tomer matters and company internals and Kaito took that very seriously, she knew that.

Kaito coolly replied that they were distant relatives who unfortunately only knew what was in the newspaper, to which the driver agreed and apologized for his curiosity.

He spoke for a while about the generosity of the Maeda family, who had done so much for this poor suburb, and about the shock ten years ago that had changed so much. Now everyone hoped that the old times would return.

"Freeloaders," Kaito thought.

"What an honest, kind gentleman," Mio thought.

Mio showed the invitations to the gate of the huge family estate and they were let in. Several people stood at the entrance to the memorial ceremony, but none that Kaito had ever seen before. They handed over the obligatory small gifts and entered the building, each carrying a bouquet of flowers that Mio had bought beforehand, and stood in front of a closed coffin with several pictures of the young deceased in front of it. While Mio placed her bouquet on the left side of the pictures, Kaito realized that he had not seen a single picture of the young woman in all the time he had been thinking about this subject.

She was a very beautiful woman. Each picture showed her in a special way, so that you could literally feel her joy of life.

"As so often, it was the loving relatives who put an end to this joy of life. She probably trusted her murderer blindly," Kaito thought as Mio nudged him.

He understood immediately, placed the flowers on the other side of the pictures, turned around and followed Mio to the rows of chairs for the guests. Actually, he wanted to leave right away. How long was Mio going to sit there, he wondered. This time, he was about to nudge Mio to make it clear that he wanted to leave when a housekeeper, who was obviously employed, approached Mio.

"Mio Yamamoto?" she asked softly.

Mio nodded.

"The lady of the house, Mrs. Maeda, would like to see you. Would you be so kind as to give her some of your precious time?"

"Hey, and what about my time, you hopping jack. I don't get paid for it," Kaito thought and watched as Mio got up and left the room with the housekeeper before she gave Kaito a quick nod as if to say 'don't fuck around'.

The only one fooling around here was Mio, her polite nature and at the same time so carelessly, far too good for this world. And then there was her divinely beautiful aura, if what the fox said was true, then she was on the menu of all demons. In the shrine, she would indeed be safe from the demons. It was even more important that Dawn became a goddess. Until then, he'd better watch out, he told himself, noticing that more people were whispering about him than he would have liked.

Looking around, he realized that he had not seen Mr. Maeda yet. But he left it at that. He was sure that no one would harm Mio here.

Less than 45 minutes later, Mio returned and Kaito saw the image of a hundred thousand yen being flushed down the toilet.

A middle-aged woman, accompanied by several young maids, bowed goodbye to Mio, looked around, caught sight of Kaito and bowed wordlessly in his direction.

Kaito stood up and returned the respect, albeit reluctantly. After a short 'hello back' from Mio, Mio and Kaito said goodbye to the people they didn't know and an older gentleman at the entrance who bore a certain resemblance to

Mr. Maeda. Then they left the mansion and got into a taxi that had probably been organized and was waiting at the exit.

Back at the hotel, Mio explained that the lady was the deceased's mother and had insisted on hearing the whole story from her.

"I'm sorry you had to wait so long. I only told you what you told me about the case here. I didn't mention Mr. Nakamura or anything about Dawn, nor did I mention any other cases. I hope that was all right?" she asked Kaito carefully, who was a little annoyed.

Kaito tried to calm down after all the stress and said, "It's all right, even if they weren't customers. We should get going," he said as he and Dawn lay on the bed of the hotel room and stared at the ceiling.

"Yes please, let's go now, I want to go home," Mio said.

Mio had slept the whole train ride. He couldn't sleep, which was why Dawn was angry with him. Too many thoughts were running through his mind. Especially one where he had to find a cat god, that wouldn't be easy. He would probably have to ask the Order for help again and that was something he did not like at all.

When he arrived at the station, Kaito was about to say goodbye to Mio when he noticed that she looked at him several times and then looked away again.

"What the hell is going on?" he thought and asked, "What's wrong, I can see you want something?"

"I was just thinking about my grandparents. I told you the story once. I'd like to visit them. Sometime. Can you come with me and see if there's an echo of them?"

Kaito looked at Dawn a little strangely, she was about to take it all back when Kaito replied very kindly, "Sure, we can do that, just say when it suits you," but he thought to himself that she probably made a mistake in her thinking, because very few people die in the cemetery itself. But he would explain it to her another time.

Mio was overjoyed, thanked him and said goodbye to Kaito, saying "see you Monday at school" and thinking "what was that strange look on his face again?"

Chapter 9 - WEEKEND IN LONDON

Some time later, on a Friday evening, Kaito stood outside the building complex where his apartment and office were located, walked to the stairwell, and made his way to the tenth floor. As he climbed the stairs to the office, he checked the company account on his smartphone and thought about the rent that was due again on the first of the month.

"Damn, the rent, utilities and Mio's salary are the biggest items, but I don't want to lose Mio," he thought. Since the last big order from Mr. Kato, there had only been smaller orders, and such a big order barely covered a month's fixed costs. "The perverted fox was expensive fun, too," he laughed. The Maeda family had given him a small token of appreciation later, probably on Mrs. Maeda's orders, but a large order would be very welcome.

Should he try to help the police with their work? It certainly wouldn't be well paid, and he didn't want to think about the dirty looks of Mr. Tanaka's colleagues.

He wasn't allowed to advertise, that was the agreement with the Order, and he didn't want to. Too expensive, too inefficient for this business. Mr. Kato's order had confirmed that the Order was sticking to its terms. "It could be that the old bastard is still hiding a lot, but I can't prove it," he thought.

"Well, Dawn, this isn't going to work with the forest project, or do you have any other ideas?" he said to Dawn, who ran up the stairs with him.

"Let's have a race, whoever gets to the top first gets a feast," she laughed and sprinted off. Kaito could only look after her. In her spirit form, Dawn could jump like a cat, even if Kaito saw her as a human cat girl, so he didn't stand a chance, but he ran away anyway, yelling, "Hey, you little beast, you just want to rip me off again, wait later...". He didn't get any further.

"Meow," a normal person would understand, but for Kaito it was a clear "Watch out, we're not alone!"

He stopped running and walked slowly up the last floor. No sane person who knew him would do anything stupid here, he told himself, that would be suicide and looked up.

Dawn was sitting at the end of the banister, her eyes fixed on a target in the hallway.

"Okay, there's someone at the end of the railing, a hu-man or whatever," he thought, turning his head into Dawn's line of sight as he climbed the last few steps.

"A man in a suit, obviously a foreigner, very classy, probably a lawyer, excellent," he thought.

"*Hello sir, may I help you*?" Kaito asked in English.

"I'm looking for Kaito Tanaka, the owner of the Spirit-KT-Science Institute, and I think I've just found him," the man said in perfect Japanese.

"Well, I shall not underestimate him," Kaito thought and said, "Then come in," as he opened the door.

The man watched as the cat, who had not let him out of her sight the whole time and who, it seemed to him, had warned her master about him, strutted into the office and took a seat on the sofa.

"Sit down if you want," Kaito said pointing to the chair in front of the table.

"Thank you," the man replied, stopping demonstratively and looking around in disgust.

"My name is Charles Whitemore, I'm an attorney with KLQS & Partners," he said, paused, walked over to Kaito and laid his business card on the table.

Kaito immediately saw that this was not a cheap thing like his father's, this one easily cost 1000 yen a piece.

Kaito thought, "when is Mio coming,", but he had to see it through now, KLQS & Partner was not just a small law firm, no, it was one of the most expensive business law firms in the world, extremely exclusive.

"Didn't your firm represent Oceanic World Voyages Ltd. a few years ago?" he asked.

Mr. Whitemore turned his head toward him, looked at him and thought, "Well, when I got that completely stupid order two days ago, my heart almost stopped with anger, but I didn't expect this," and then said, "Did you inform yourself?"

"No, I'm just doing my job, what can I do for you?" said Kaito and thought, "Mio please take over the ass, quick!"

They both looked at each other as a rumble sounded and the door flew open, "I'm late, sorry," came from a panting Mio who had apparently run up the ten flights of stairs. When she saw the customer, she quickly straightened up, bowed, greeted him, and said, "May I get you some coffee or tea?"

"Tea," Mr. Whitemore said, smiling for the first time since he entered the room.

He looked after Mio as she went into the kitchen and saw the cat sitting on the sofa, still staring at him. "What a scary beast, nothing like a loyal dog," he thought and turned back to Kaito.

"My client would like to hire you for a job, but a few details need to be clarified first."

Kaito immediately understood what Mr. Whitemore was getting at, pulled a contract out of a drawer and slid it onto the table in front of Mr. Whitemore.

Mr. Whitemore put on a fake smile and took the note, but after a short time, he put it back on the table.

"It's well written, who was that?" he asked Kaito..

"A lawyer, a Japanese lawyer," Kaito said a little annoyed.

Mr. Whitemore smiled again, and again it was clearly artificial.

"It will only be decided on the spot if they can take on the actual job and help my client, until then the costs will be borne by the applicant, then there will be a new negotiation. In addition, your company agrees to maintain confidentiality under penalty of law. Do I understand that correctly?"

"Yes, that is correct. Contract changes only in exceptional cases, after the case is disclosed.

The man was not just good, Kaito knew that now, he was very good. To understand that in such a short time showed his abilities. His hourly rate was probably higher than his.

Mr. Whitemore pulled an envelope out of his jacket and handed it to Kaito. "A letter of recommendation my client gave me for you," Mr. Whitemore said as Mio came in with the tea and handed Mr. Whitemore three cups to choose from. Mr. Whitemore took one of the cups and thanked Mio as he sat down. Mio put one cup on the table for Kaito and then took the third while Kaito opened the letter and read it.

Kaito let the contents of the letter sink in for a while, then looked at Mio, who looked back and forth between Kaito and Whitemore with interest, and said, "Open a new case and put the letter down, please," and handed her the document and the envelope.

Mio looked at the envelope and then said, "Oh, from Mr..." "MIO!" Kaito snapped at her and Mio almost dropped her cup in shock. Mio walked on without a word, startled. What was that, she had never seen him like that before, had she done something wrong?

Mio thought about it. It was a letter of recommendation from Mr. Kato, it even said so on the envelope, the lawyer would know, and even if he didn't, his client would, so why bother? She was unsettled and watched as Mr. Whitemore and Kaito sipped their tea.

"Kaito, that paranoid pedant, as if he suspected a conspiracy here, as if..." now she understood his train of thought. What if the letter wasn't from Mr. Kato at all, but a fake, then she would now have confirmed that Mr. Kato was a customer of this company, or it was simply a test, some kind of privacy test, carried out by a potential customer. "Damn you and stitch you up, Kaito, you know-it-all... Damn, I screwed up, I hope it doesn't go wrong because of me," she thought.

The lawyer sipped his tea again, looked at Mio who flinched, but he just nodded pleasantly and handed Kaito another business card. It was spotless white and only one name was written on it in slightly raised letters, "William Kawn Harrington".

When Kaito read that, he had to swallow as well. He looked at Mr. Whitemore and said calmly, "What could the tenth richest man in the world want from me?"

Mr. Whitemore had had enough of that cranky cat, but now he had to deal with this boy who might even be in school. The only human in the room beside him seemed to be the girl, the boy was more like a machine or a zombie that ate brains and extracted their thoughts, at least that's what he looked like. Or someone had informed the boy of his coming, unlikely, very unlikely. The problem was that Mr. William would never allow someone like that to come near his daughter. But the order had not come from him, but from his wife, Grace Samira. It could only go wrong, he thought with a smile.

Just as the lawyer was about to present the case, Kaito said to Mio: "Come here and take notes."

"Damn," Kaito thought right after that, "I wanted to say that nicely to show Mio that everything was all right.

Mio was now totally insecure and thought Kaito would fire her the next time she made a mistake.

"Let him," she said angrily, pulling up a chair and sitting down at the table.

Mr. Whitemore explained that the Harrington's youngest daughter, Ivy Rose, had been growing weaker and weaker despite intensive medical examinations, and that Mrs. Harrington had learned from Mr. Kato that there could be other causes than health for these symptoms.

Mrs. Harrington wanted him to rule that out.

Mr. Whitemore had to say these sentences carefully, he had never had to say such garbage in his career, let alone organize it. He had won all his last cases, had he somehow upset an important client without knowing it, had he fallen out of favor or why was he sitting here in this shithole with two teenagers and a disturbed cat and had to spout this garbage?

"Is Mr. Harrington okay with this?" asked Kaito.

"No, damn it, never, you little shit," Mr. Whitemore thought and said, "You bring up paragraph three of their contract. In which all legal guardians must sign that they agree to the contract."

"Yes, exactly," and Kaito had another proof of this lawyer's abilities.

"Of course. Mr. Harrington loves his daughter very much."

"A flight to London on short notice won't be easy to organize," Kaito said and looked at Mio, who shifted restlessly in her chair, thinking "why did I act so stupidly, now I would have the opportunity to come to London. Kaito, please forgive me and take me with you!"

"That's not necessary," the lawyer said. A private jet belonging to the Harrington family, who commute between Japan and England, is waiting at the airport and will take off for London at 9 a.m. tomorrow. Arrival would be around 10:30.

"Fast on the way," Kaito said dryly.

The lawyer smiled and thought: "There's the proof that he's not human."

Now Mio broke out, "Please, please take me with you, I've always wanted to go to London," she begged Kaito.

Kaito looked at Mio and said, "This isn't a vacation Mio and of course I wanted to take you with me. The customer is your age, so it's good to have you with me. Otherwise, people won't believe me anyway."

"You've noticed that correctly, you funny human-like thing," Mr. Whitemore thought, "with the girl together you might get a glimpse of Ivy Rose if you're lucky."

Mio was overjoyed. All the trouble she'd just had was blown away, London on a private plane, if she told that her friends. Hmm, but she wasn't allowed to, she just realized, but she was happy anyway.

"Is it a problem if my colleague comes with me?"

"No, there's plenty of room."

"Well, that makes three of us, Mrs. Yamamoto, me and Dawn, my cat."

Mr. Whitemore was about to take a deep breath, but he just managed to control himself when Kaito said, "Dawn will not be more than ten steps away from me, and oh yes, Dawn is very, very important to me too."

The lawyer smiled and said, "Even though we have quarantine rules for pets, this will be fine, just keep her covered until we get outside."

"Mio, do you actually have a passport?"

Mio froze. "Do I need this?"

"Of course you airhead, what do you think?" thought Kaito.

"I'll ask my parents."

"Ask them right away if they agree, no flight without it!"

"Sure thing!"

Why did Kaito have the feeling that this meant 'I do what I want'?

While Mio talked to her parents on the phone, Kaito and Mr. Whitemore went over some minor formalities and signed the contracts.

When Mio came back into the room again, happy that her parents had a passport for her, Mr. Whitemore was about to leave. When he saw Mio, he turned back to her and said, "You know, Mrs. Yamamoto, England has the best tea in the world. I've never been served anything equal, until today, thank you very much." Then he said goodbye to Mio with a slight bow and left the room.

"If only that girl wouldn't hang out with that... oh, whatever he is, then she could really become something, the tea was really excellent," he thought, looking at the old, run-down building he had actually entered about an hour ago to ask a crazy boy for an exorcism. "How low have I sunk?"

"Mio," Kaito said.

"*Yes, sir,*" Mio said with a laugh and Kaito was glad that Mio seemed to be in a better mood again, which probably meant that she would come with him tomorrow and that the problem with the letter would be solved right away.

"Before you pack a suitcase for a maximum of two days, check the validity of your passport and bring your parents' permission." Mio turned grinding her teeth while Kaito said "call Mr. Kato and have his letter of recommendation confirmed."

Mio was getting worried, what now, she wondered, was he still angry or did he think something was wrong?

"How exactly am I supposed to do that?"

"You can ask Mr. Kato directly about the letter, after all, he signed it and since he's not demented, he should be able to remember it, but otherwise keep a low profile. If he doesn't remember, the police will come to the airport tomorrow morning and not us. Because I don't want to get on a plane to London that ends up in Antarctica. But the letter is probably from him, so don't panic, make some small talk and ask him some more questions, anything your 'senpai' might know can help us."

Mio understood the allusion perfectly, but said nothing, instead taking the letter and going to the phone.

"I'll go back to my apartment with Dawn and get everything ready, I don't want to go through this again. Lock up when you leave."

Before Mio could ask what he meant by 'go through this again', he was already out the door and she just thought, "I'll squeeze it out of you tomorrow."

Kaito looked at his watch impatiently for the second time because Mio was already ten minutes later than the appointed time. "Women," he thought, but at the same time he had a lot of respect for her that she was still able to get so much out of Mr. Kato. The job wouldn't be easy, but he'd already figured that out.

He turned to the other entrance and was both relieved and annoyed. Mio came running in carrying a huge suitcase.

"That was so obvious," he thought and narrowed his eyes.

He was about to shout, but Mio stopped him, "I need all this, no arguments."

Kaito took a deep breath and then said, "Okay, gate 102, that's where the private planes take off, let's go."

Mio saw Kaito leave and her eyes fell on Dawn who was walking next to him with a leash.

She couldn't help but laugh and wondered how Kaito would see her when Dawn turned to her and hissed bitterly at her.

Now she couldn't hold back any longer, had to sit down and started to laugh out loud. Dawn was obviously extremely angry and looked demonstratively in another direction while Kaito tried to take Dawn in his arms to calm the situation down. But Dawn continued to refuse, which made the situation even more amusing for Mio.

While various people walked past them, not understanding the situation and wondering what was going on, Mio slowly calmed down and then walked ahead, giggling so as not to have to watch the scene behind her.

However, Mio's interest changed abruptly when they suddenly stepped through the gate directly onto the tar-mac next to the plane.

"We're going non-stop to London now, I'd like to take a picture," she wanted to say and looked at Kaito who was already rolling his eyes again.

"Does he read minds," she thought.

Mio's large suitcase and Kaito's hand luggage were accepted and stowed away. He didn't let go of the second small suitcase he was carrying.

Kaito had told her helping to make sure that no one touched it.

Mio wanted to know why and Kaito's answer was simple: "Because it could be deadly. At first, she had to swallow, but then she thought that Kaito was probably exaggerating. Because she remembered when he had to open his suitcases at the security check and explain to the security staff that he was a painter and that this was all part of his art, it didn't seem to be a problem.

"Or maybe not," she thought, looking at him as he took off Dawn's leash and told her not to scratch the leather, while the flight attendants looked at Kaito and his cat strangely.

Mr. Whitemore arrived shortly after them and then the doors were closed. The plane was pushed backwards out of the parking position and the turbines were started.

Kaito greeted Mr. Whitemore with a nod, which he returned. Meanwhile, Mio bounced up and down in the very elegantly appointed plane and had to be reminded by the staff to sit down and fasten her seatbelt. Kaito could still feel the enormous thrust of the plane as it took off towards London with the sun behind it.

He had hardly slept and would now catch up during the flight, so he kept his eyes closed and only heard Mio talking about her father, how he had taught her everything as chairman of a Japanese tea culture association, and thought, "Yes, yes, if Mrs. Whitemore knew that, Mr. Whitemore," and fell asleep.

After an hour in the air, Mio had inspected everything on board and was on a first-name basis with everyone on board. Now she alternated between looking out the window and at the flight attendants, who increased their cadence every time they passed the sleeping Kaito. It was funny to see Dawn sitting on Kaito's lap, almost petrified, watching over him like some ancient Egyptian cat goddess, scowling at anyone who even approached him.

A few hours before landing, Kaito Dawn sat by the window, pacing twice and getting food and drink. Mio watched as the staff and passengers tried desperately to fulfill his every wish as quickly as possible, just to get some distance back. This obviously left Kaito cold.

After landing, everything went very fast. A car was already waiting. Kaito had hidden Dawn in his jacket and Mio tried not to think about how that would look to someone with spiritual abilities. She didn't want to have another laughing fit, not in front of all these people, so she walked forward, looked at the ground and thought about her suitcase, which was immediately put into the car.

To her relief, Kaito was already in the car with Dawn when she got in and she sat down next to him, smiling.

"Is something wrong?" asked Kaito Mio, who replied with a laugh, "No, everything is fine," while Dawn turned away and hissed softly.

As the car drove away, Mr. Whitemore said, "*Family estate.*" Mio asked where in London they were going now, and Mr. Whitemore explained that they were going to the Harrington estate outside of London, which Mio sadly accepted.

At some point, Mr. Whitemore explained that they had now passed the gate of the estate and would arrive at the main house in five minutes.

It was truly impressive. The scale and elegance were overwhelming.

The difference between European and Japanese architectural styles was clearly visible.

Even Kaito had to admit that. Mio was overwhelmed.

"Now comes the tricky part," Kaito thought as he climbed the stairs to the entrance and waited with Mio and Dawn in the reception hall.

A door, or rather a gate, opened and Mr. and Mrs. Harrington entered, accompanied by a few employees and security guards who wore their weapons openly on their bodies.

Mrs. Harrington introduced herself with a friendly smile in excellent Japanese. She explained that this house was international, not only because of the worldwide network of businesses, but also because of the extensive family connections.

It was clear from Mr. Harrington's face that Kaito was not welcome.

Kaito returned Mrs. Harrington's greeting, as did Mio, who brought another message from Mr. Kato.

"Now comes the showdown," Kaito thought as they all sat in a conference room.

"*What are your qualifications?*" Mr. Harrington asked directly.

"I spent two years in the Japanese Spiritual Order Society, where I specialized in demon hunting and disintegration. Since there were no further training opportunities, I started my own business. You mentioned Mr. Hiroshi Kato himself as a reference. Apart from that, I am a high school student," Kaito said in almost perfect English.

Mio's breath caught, was this the same Kaito whose English lessons during his school days could be counted on two hands? Maybe it was because he knew it perfectly, now it was clear, but where did he get it from? His parents, no, that was a taboo subject. Mr. Tanaka? Nothing against Mr. Tanaka, but that was also very unlikely. His real parents, then? She glanced over at him and saw, as always, the passive, meaningless expression on his face that made people so nervous or angry.

"Twenty of the best doctors in the world couldn't find anything, what are they going to do?" Mr. Harrington continued to ask, this time in Japanese.

"You're right, if there's a medical problem, there's nothing I can do, I'm not a doctor, but that's not part of the contract. But I can tell you in a minute if it's a medical problem."

Mr. Harrington frowned.

"How?"

"Quite simply, if it is not a spiritual problem, it will be a medical one," Kaito said.

"You need a minute for that."

"Yes. Rather less," Kaito said and thought he had déjà vu, this time not with a bitch but with a stubborn goat and thought of the so nice Mr. Watanabe, who put up with everything because he was glad that someone wanted to help him.

"How close do they ... have to get to my daughter?"

Always the same, he thought, "First you order me in and then this," and said, "Visual contact about five meters, that's enough. Demons are easy to spot."

Mrs. Harrington put her hand on Mr. Harrington's and said, "Please check on Mr. Tanaka. Follow me," she stood up and walked to an open door.

The entire staff followed Mrs. and Mr. Harrington down the second floor hallway, and Kaito hoped the house wasn't too big.

Suddenly Dawn meowed for all to hear and Kaito stopped.

Kaito knew now that he didn't need to look into the room they had just passed. Whatever was behind that door had come straight from hell, if there was one.

"Is your house so big that you don't know which room your daughter has?" he asked cheekily, pointing to the door next to him.

Mio was completely shattered, she had been looking forward to a nice day in London and now this. Kaito was once again playing the insulted know-it-all in front of one of the richest people in the world and even worse, in front of his client, she thought.

Of course it was a test, she had understood that and Dawn had passed it. Still, Kaito should do some training in talking to customers.

"I'll put it on the list for his father when we get home," Mio said to herself.

A low grumble and murmur among the people, then Mr. Harrington said, "Oh yes, we changed rooms today."

He went to the door, opened it and Kaito looked into the room for a second or two with Dawn in his arms, then stepped aside.

He knew it was a demon, but an Essentrax, that's something, he told himself. And his servants, created from the life energy of humans, were nothing to sneeze at, either, and they were almost complete, six of them. Like the armored demon, this one had rammed part of its body into the girl's heart, draining her spiritual energy and weakening her. The armored demon was strong but sluggish, this one was fast, it could easily take the girl to her death if it saw no chance for herself. He had enough positive energy, more than enough to destroy this beast three times, the problem was the time it would take to destroy it, only tricks would help, but with this stubborn goat, he wondered? "Shit Happens", or as the saying went. "Never mind, the girl would be dead in two days anyway if nothing happened and he could really use the money. Mio is mad at me again, how mad would she be if he let the girl die. She would tell his father for sure, so then ..." he thought and said, "Let's go back, I'll explain what I saw and what I would suggest."

"We're all ears," Mr. Harrington said when they were all back in the conference room and Kaito was explaining the situation to the Harringtons.

"So you're telling me that a demon has possessed my daughter and she will die if you don't destroy it, and it will cost about 100,000 yen. Why so little, I would have expected 100,000 pounds. What are you going to do? What do you have to do?" Mr. Harrington asked sarcastically.

Always the same game, Kaito thought to himself and said, "I only need 30 minutes, then we are finished and will be on way back again. Can we start?"

"No, you can't. I won't let someone like you within ten feet of my daughter!" Mrs. Harrington put her hand on Mr. Harrington's again and he said, "If you do, let that girl do it," pointing at Mio.

"Ms. Yamamoto is my assistant and can't do that," Kaito said, trying to remain as friendly as possible.

"*I will never let someone like you near my daughter.*"

"*Then your daughter will die a senseless death. I will not come closer than 3 steps*", Kaito said emotionlessly.

"*ENOUGH! We had a deal!*" Mrs. Harrington yelled at her husband.

"If my daughter doesn't get better tomorrow, you will fly home at their own expense and never set foot in England again," Mr. Harrington told Kaito.

"A million extra!" if their daughter is better tomorrow, Kaito countered unmoved.

Mr. Harrington stood up, went back to the room and said: "*You have 30 minutes.*"

Kaito looked at Mio, who looked very disappointed and scared, of course she had imagined everything completely different. Kaito nudged her and said "Come on, we've got 30 minutes" and smiled.

Mio looked at him. That was the second time Kaito had really smiled and she regained her confidence, stood up, clenched her fist and said loudly, "*We must going!*"

Everyone in the room had to stifle their laughter, except for Mr. Harrington and Mio, who didn't understand.

Ten minutes later, Kaito was allowed to enter the room. There were two security guards in the room, one was the man who never left Mr. Harrington's side, the other was younger but looked no less dangerous, both openly carrying a firearm.

Mr. Harrington had even set up distance markers that Kaito was not allowed to cross. "Next time it'll cost a billion yen, asshole," he said to himself.

Two maids, both very young, stood around Ivy Rose Harrington's bed, waiting for orders.

The lawyer, Mr. Whitemore, who had probably been sent as an outside witness, stood a little further away at the door and remained there. Kaito laughed inwardly as he imagined what was going on in Whitemore's head.

Another man, who looked like a doctor and was about sixty years old, also stood near the bed and of course Mr. and Mrs. Harrington. It was noon, the sun was high, the windows were a little darkened by the curtains, but the room was bright. Ivy Rose had probably just fallen asleep. She was weak and tired, the same symptoms as Mrs. Kato's son.

Kaito opened his small suitcase and Mio tried to look inside. All that came out of Mr. Harrington was a contemptuous snort. No one else made a sound.

Kaito took out some small balls that Mio already knew and put them in his pocket. Then he gave Mio four cuboids about the size of her fist. She was to put two of them in the corners of the bed and the other two in the middle against the wall. He looked at Mio seriously and Mio immediately understood that this was very important. Then he took a paper seal and put it in his pocket, closed the suitcase and put it next to the front door.

Kaito began to draw lines and circles on the floor as agreed, grinning as he imagined the face of Mr. Harrington, who actually looked even more annoyed than before, as Mio clearly recognized. Kaito was just about to draw the circles around the edges of the room when the quote "Don't disturb my circles" by the ancient Greek mathematician Archimedes, who was killed for it, came to his mind and he just thought, hopefully there won't be a bloodbath here. Mio drew a circle around the bed as agreed, something they had practiced a few times before, but only because Mio had begged for it then, now he was glad for her persistence. Fortunately, the room was huge and the bed was not directly against the wall in the back third, so there was still enough room for the other protective circles.

He said to the group again. "It would be better if some of you left the room, it could get serious," and he looked at the servants and Mrs. Harrington.

"No one leaves the room," Mr. Harrington said, continuing to look hatefully at Kaito.

"Then I won't be responsible for full underpants or heart attacks," he thought to himself.

His protective circle was about three meters from the bed. Five more were for the housekeepers, the doctor, Mr. and Mrs. Harrington with their bodyguards and Mr. Whitemore. After about 15 minutes, everything was in place. Then he asked everyone to stand in the circles as discussed.

"You have ten minutes," said Mr. Harrington.

"Fuck you, Harrington," Kaito thought as the demon suddenly started to speak.

"What do you want from me, little human boy?" it banged into his head.

"Damn, did he notice my aura, my amulet was supposed to protect me from it and hide the aura," Kaito thought.

He pretended he hadn't heard him; if the demon snapped now, it was all over.

Kaito looked up and said to the group, "Did someone say something?"

"You've got eight minutes, you son of a bitch, that's what I said," Mr. Harrington said, and Mrs. Harrington had to calm her husband down.

Everything was ready, people were standing in the protective circles, and Harrington was looking at his hundred-thousand-dollar watch including stop function. Ignoring the demon, Kaito walked up to Mr. Harrington, toward his circle, smiled at him, and then said cheekily, "No, I didn't mean one of you," and put his hand around the amulet. Everyone standing in front of him, Mr. and Mrs. Harrington, the bodyguards, and Mr. White-more, saw blood ooze from between his fingers when he embraced the amulet around his neck, squeezed it, dropped to his knees, pressed his hand to the circle on the floor, and clearly pronounced "DISINTEGRATION. The two bodyguards had drawn their weapons and pointed them at Kaito. At the same moment the room brightened further, it was already light, but a new source of light came from the bed of the daughter Ivy Rose Harrington and without paying any attention to Kaito, everyone automatically looked towards the source of light and thus towards the bed. The reactions were varied as usual, he heard the maids start to scream and he heard a thud behind him.

The bodyguard who had just aimed at him now pointed his gun at the bed.

Ms. Harrington took a step back, her eyes widening, then tried to move forward. Just as she was about to leave the circle and Kaito shouted, "*Stay in the ring,*" the older bodyguard pulled Mrs. Harrington back into the circle and a loud scream ripped through the heads of everyone present. Still crouched, Kaito turned to see four of the Essentrax's servants break away from their master and run at high speed toward the crowd. Everyone's eyes grew wide with fear as they realized that these things, which looked like deformed octopuses, were leaving Ivy Rose's bed in their direction. Suddenly, the creatures disappeared as they crossed the edge of the bed, and the shock of those present subsided somewhat. Was it all just fantasy or a dream? Besides, the adrenaline rush was probably so great that no one noticed the rapid drop in temperature, but it didn't matter, everything was happening much too fast for that, Kaito thought, as everyone who was still looking towards the bed saw a monstrous, disgusting, greenish-black something hovering over the bed. It had considerably more limbs than an octopus, spreading out in all directions from a disgusting, billowing center. A heavy thud shook the group around Mr. Harrington. A scream and one of the maids slammed into the wall with full force. The creature that had just disappeared now thrashed its limbs at the housekeepers and the doctor, who all fell backwards in shock or collapsed. Some kind of invisible barrier, a few inches from their faces, stopped the violent impact with a thud to their heads, producing golden particles that made the creature glow and become visible. The bodyguards were about to aim at the creature when the muffled sound of a heavy impact, also a few centimeters from them, smashed into their barrier like heavy projectiles hitting a concrete wall.

The younger bodyguard was so startled by the loud impact of the tentacle-like limbs and the reappearance of the monsters right in front of him that he fired his gun in the direction of the monster in front of him, but the bullets went straight through it and into the wall behind the bed. Due to the noise projected into the heads of those present, no one but his superior noticed. Mio stood wide-eyed in the circle behind Kaito, where Kaito also stood, and watched as golden particles fell from the barriers each time the creatures hit them. "Stardust, so beautiful, so aesthetic, as sublime as thousands of fireflies at once," she thought as she watched the spectacle in awe.

Suddenly, Kaito said loudly, "Hey bastard, what about me, you monster?" and, still crouching, raised his other hand in his direction.

"*I can spare your mother if you leave.*" Voices penetrated the heads of those present as if of their own accord.

Kaito laughed out loud and everyone in their right mind looked at him, "*Take her, no one needs a child killer.*" Mio understood the last two words only too well, more than she would have liked, and tears began to wet her eyes, whether from the fear that was slowly rising in her or from what she thought she was hearing, she didn't know. At the same moment, Kaito flicked a small banishing orb in the direction of the demon. "HOLY LANCE," he said loud and clear. Everyone saw something enter the circle and transform into some kind of lance or spear as Kaito rose from his crouch, took a big step forward and said, "Die. The spear flew towards the green-black, ugly demon that, if you looked closely, showed signs of fear. One of the demon's two remaining servants stepped forward and intercepted the spear with part of his body, which shattered into countless particles that lit up the room again.

Kaito followed, a new orb in his hand. He took another step forward, aimed and ... The demon screamed and all the servant demons rushed at Kaito. Mio looked down and saw that Kaito was no longer inside the protective circle. She screamed, but Kaito screamed first, "Dawn, protect me, quickly. Dawn jumped out from behind the circle towards Kaito, but the servant demons knocked Dawn away, who fell, beaten, in front of the bed and took cover under it, while the demons continued to lean on Kaito. Horrible laughter could be heard in the heads of the bystanders as the demons rushed at Kaito. Mio screamed at Kaito, reaching forward to pull him back into the circle, but it was too late, the demons were only inches away from him when he yelled "OBLITERATION". All of a sudden, the entire room was bathed in a blinding light, the minion demons suddenly disintegrating into stardust and the resulting particles illuminating the room so brightly that everyone was blinded. The gruesome laughter that had been heard moments before suddenly stopped, and a rumbling sound could be heard in the room, coming from the direction where the beast was hovering over the bed. There was no face to be seen, only distorted features that could, with a lot of imagination, be reconstructed into something like this. But everyone could see that the situation had changed, and the demon knew it too. The many limbs shot out of the body in a direction that lay behind the monster, where the daughter, Ivy Rose Harrington, should lie, hidden by the demon and obscured to the human eye by the bright stardust of the decaying demon. The limbs pounded into the direction of the girl's body like a machine gun on a tree trunk, 10, 20, 30, no one could count that fast.

"IVY! IVY! IVY!" Mrs. Harrington screamed beyond despair. She tried to lunge forward again, but was again held back by her bodyguard. "Let me go, IVY!" she screamed at him, hitting him with her hand, but he ignored her. Kaito looked at Mrs. Harrington and wondered for a moment if this was the look of a mother who would die for her child. Mio looked at Kaito and then at his other hand. She immediately recognized that Kaito was holding the fifth seal of the pentagram and she felt as if he was pouring all his energy into it. Together with the fifth seal in his hand, the pentagram was aligned to hit the demon with full force. Mio remembered that Kaito had once said that pentagrams were much less effective than banishing circles, especially when they were not properly aligned like this. So how was what she saw possible, she wondered.

"Is this Kaito's true power? Can one person possess so much spiritual energy, can he be so powerful?

Her answer was clear: "Yes, finish him, Kaito! Kill him!" she shouted into the room, looking at the demon who quickly disintegrated.

Ms. Harrington kept screaming "IVY!, IVY!, IVY!" but the bodyguard wouldn't let her go.

How many times the demon struck the daughter's body with its limbs was anyone's guess, but everyone in the room saw the limbs dissolve into golden particles and the demon slowed down. Suddenly, like a soap bubble, it burst into countless more particles of stardust that once again lit up the room around the bed.

Mrs. Harrington had not stopped screaming. "IVY!, IVY!, IVY!" were the only words that could still be heard. The light quickly faded, revealing a view of the bed. Something was vaguely recognizable. A person was sitting up in the bed. A little later, Mrs. Harrington could make out her daughter's face, and her cry turned into a relieved exclamation of "Ivy! But now another person could be made out, sitting behind Ivy, a face with a smile cast into space. Ivy's head was between the outstretched arms of this other person. A young woman with cat ears, Ivy looked at her with wide eyes. Suddenly the room was quiet, very quiet, no one was breathing. The cat girl's hands were directed at the people in the room, or rather at the disintegrated demon that had been hammering away at her just a few seconds ago. Now, everyone in the room could see it clearly. At the ends of the strange girl's palms, there was a kind of empty space where no particles could be seen. Particles that tried to enter this space were magically reflected there as they tried to enter the empty space. The girl with the cat ears had created a kind of barrier by holding her arms and hands protectively over Ivy Rose and pointing them at the demon, stopping the demon's blows with the created barrier.

Dawn smiled at Kaito, who just said coldly and commandingly, "Dawn, over here "

Dawn looked at the girl, smiled at her for half a second and jumped out of her sitting position onto the edge of the bed, then left the particle area with a second jump towards Kaito and turned back into a cat in front of the spectators, landing on Kaito's arm.

Kaito called to Mio, "Now." Mio understood immediately and handed him a drink they had brought. "Cover the girl..." That was as far as Kaito could go as Mio threw him the other bottles in a bag and ran to Ivy. She pulled the blanket over her and pushed her onto the bed. At the same moment, Mrs. Harrington freed herself from the bodyguard, who apparently saw no reason to hold her any longer, and ran to her daughter. Mio yelled to the staff that Ivy needed something hot to eat and to open the windows. But no one moved. One was cowering on the floor, still screaming, and the other seemed unconscious, so Mio ran to the windows herself and opened them.

It was only now that the others noticed the cold in the room and the ice that had formed which was slowly melting.

Kaito called "*Hey*" to the older bodyguard and pointed at the younger one. The older one reacted immediately and shouted "*GUN DOWN*" at the younger one. He took a step toward him, moved the gun, which was still pointed at the bed, to a safe position, took it from him, punched him in the face, and yelled at him, "*Soldier, come to your senses.*" The younger man reacted immediately, realized his mistake, saluted his superior and was sent outside to look around. The bodyguard then took a step towards the doctor who was still cowering on the ground, picked him up with one hand, yelled "*TAKE CARE OF THE PATIENT*" and threw him towards the bed, where he fell again and was picked up again.

Meanwhile, Mio had found a housekeeper to bring Ivy Rose something to eat.

Mr. Harrington still stood motionless, watching his daughter. Mr. Whitemore had huddled against the door and Kaito thought, "At least he's still in the room," and grinned to himself. When Kaito saw that the house was back under control, he went to the door with Dawn, but Mio was faster, jumped up to Kaito and Dawn and said rather loudly, rather too loudly, "Dawn you were just top of my goddess" and picked her up.

Kaito didn't like that at all, because now everyone was looking at them again. But that probably didn't matter anymore. He took Dawn back with a smile on his face and left the room with her in the direction of the exit. He needed some fresh air without the master of the house, whom he hadn't even looked at all this time. He didn't want to give him this triumph.

Kaito noticed that Mr. Harrington was about to follow him, but then he heard someone shout "*DAD*" and saw out of the corner of his eye Mr. Harrington walking towards his daughter's bed. Kaito breathed a sigh of relief and thought "Good little father" and sat down on the stairs by the entrance in the sun that warmed him and Dawn, glad that there had been no bloodbath this time.

A little later, Mr. Harrington came to him, stood next to him and asked him what to do next.

"Your daughter has a very special aura," he said to Mr. Harrington.

He had learned this from Dawn, who had compared Ivy's aura to Mio's, meaning that they were both cherished by gods and threatened by demons.

"The reverberation of what happened here today will keep all the dark spirits away for a long time, but if you like, I can provide you with something that will have an even more intense effect.

"Thank you, please prepare something appropriate, but I meant more the effect of the events on my daughter.

"I'm not a doctor who makes medical diagnoses, but I can tell you that it wasn't a demon that shortens people's lives, so by the day after tomorrow at the latest, her spiritual energy should be fully restored and therefore there should be no aftereffects or late effects for your daughter from the prolonged deprivation of spiritual energy," Kaito said, looking up at Mr. Harrington.

Mr. Harrington swallowed, you could tell what was going through his mind and what questions he had, but he just said, "Sure?"

"That's for sure, spiritual energy recharges quickly, don't worry. For anything else, ask your family doctor," Kaito said and turned away again.

Mr. Harrington called a maid and said that Mr. Tanaka, his cat and Mrs. Yamamoto would be staying for dinner tonight and would be guests of the Harrington house and that any wish could be fulfilled until then. Then he said goodbye to Kaito and went back into the house.

Kaito looked at the maid who looked up startled, it was the same one who had been lying on the floor screaming.

"Didn't Mr. Harrington notice that this maid was at the end of her tether, or did they want to get rid of her?" thought Kaito as he stood up and asked the maid for a place to rest.

After Kaito had told the maid for the tenth time that the guest room they were in was just right for him and he was about to lie down on the bed, he asked again where Mio was and the maid explained that Mrs. Yamamoto had wanted to visit London.

"*Is someone with her*?" Kaito asked.

"*Of course, a housekeeper and a chauffeur,*" came the answer.

"*Wake me 30 minutes before Mrs. Yamamoto returns.*"

"*Yes, sir,*" she replied and was about to close the door,

"Mr. Tanaka, may I ask you something?"

Kaito just thought "Respect, she can speak Japanese too" and said a little surprised "Yes, please".

"Is there a heaven and a hell?" she asked.

How many times had he heard this stupid question, how could he know, how could anyone think to ask him that, or did he look like an angel or a devil?

His standard answer would probably be unfavorable here and now, if it was for someone like Mr. Harrington, but not for this girl, who was perhaps only three or four years older than him and had just been through the shock of her life.

"What's your name?" he asked.

"Olivia Anderson, sir," she replied.

"Miss Anderson, I'm sorry, but I don't know, I haven't met anyone who could answer that question for me, but I do know that something like today is much rarer than other worldly tragedies. Nevertheless, it is important to fight these monsters, whether they come from hell or not. This house will be one hundred percent safe in the future. You don't have to worry about that anymore," Kaito said slowly so that she understood him.

The maid bowed to Kaito, left the room, closed the door, took a deep breath and thought: "What a monster, luckily it's on our side."

At some point, Kaito woke up. He wasn't really rested, but he couldn't sleep either, it was probably the jet lag. Dawn was still watching over him and asked, "Meow, did you sleep well?"

"Sure, let's eat something," Kaito said and started to get ready for dinner.

Later, he met the maid Olivia in the hallway who told him that Mio was expected at the mansion in about an hour.

He told Olivia that he needed someone to show him around the house. Since no one else was available, Olivia had to take on this task. Kaito walked around the estate with Dawn and Olivia, comparing the surroundings of the house with a navigation app. From time to time he asked Olivia about structural features and created a pentagram whose inner pentagon covered the entire house.

"Pretty good app Yuma made for him, but probably a piece of cake for a good programmer," he thought.

He saved the data and everyone walked back to the entrance of the house.

The older bodyguard stood at the entrance. But he didn't want anything from Kaito and told Oliva that the group had returned from London. He nodded at Kaito and left the house.

Kaito asked Olivia where Mio was and she replied that she was probably in the dining room, so he asked to be taken there.

Once there, Mio ran up to him and showed him the photos she had taken.

He didn't know where Mio got her strength from, but the maid who accompanied Mio looked as exhausted as he felt.

Mrs. Harrington came in and was happy to see everyone together, put a large box of chocolates on the table and started eating the first ones herself, putting three on a plate for Dawn to choose from and saying "Thank you" in a friendly tone. Then she took Mio by the hand and led her out of the room. Kaito sat down on the seat with his name tag, looked at the seating arrangement on the table, wondered if Mr. Whitemore, who would be sitting to his left, had found new underwear yet, and grinned slightly mischievously, which seemed to make everyone else nervous.

Eventually Mio returned, having been dressed by Mrs. Harrington in a daring evening gown, and Kaito was anything but relaxed when he saw her. Dawn made a distinct "meow" to Kaito, who just looked at Mio, while Mrs. Harrington and Mio laughed.

Mr. Harrington and the doctor, whose name he didn't know, came in and Mr. Harrington explained that Mr. Whitemore couldn't come because of an important appointment and they all sat down at the table. "So he didn't find new underwear after all," Kaito thought.

The food was excellent and Kaito realized that this cuisine deserved more than just one or two stars. He was really pleasantly surprised and took more than he actually wanted to eat. A little later, Mr. Harrington asked what Kaito would suggest to prevent something like this from happening again, and Kaito explained the procedure with the ley lines and the pentagram to Mr. Harrington, who accepted it all motionlessly.

Meanwhile, Mio and Mrs. Harrington were talking about other things and seemed to be getting along fine when Ivy Rose entered the room. Also dressed in an evening gown, she stepped forward and apologized for being late.

Then she walked over to Dawn, looked at her briefly, bowed deeply and said, "Thank you so much for your help, I am forever in your debt," and bowed to Kaito as well, who just thought, "Yoo, actually the kitten hardly did anything, but that's the way of the world. Just as Ivy was about to sit down next to Mio, her father cleared his throat and she sat down next to her mother on the other side of the table. Then she said, "Dawn was her name, I hope I can keep calling her that, can you tell us how you stopped the demon?"

Everyone else at the table got excited, including the staff, but Mio understood immediately, jumping up and saying to Ivy, "Can you see her divine form?"

Everyone looked at Ivy that she didn't understand what was meant and Mio continued, "Everyone in this room except Kaito can only see Dawn as a cat, including me.

When Kaito saw Mr. Harrington's expression change, he quickly said, "An effect that will be gone tomorrow," and Mio said, "I'm so jealous.

Then Ivy said, "It would be a real shame if I couldn't see Miss Dawn anymore, she really does look like a goddess," and Dawn meowed to the group. Everyone laughed except for Mr. Harrington.

Only ten minutes later, Ivy asked if Mio and Dawn could come to her room and Kaito knew what that meant for him, he would be alone with that scumbag again.

Mio looked at Kaito pleadingly. What else could he do but agree at such a sight. So the three of them left the room and Kaito sat alone at the table with the Harringtons and the doctor. It was the doctor who broke the silence.

"Mr. Tanaka, even though I got the scare of my life today, it was an experience I would not want to miss. If a strange case like that of Ivy Rose Harrington happens again in my career, I will remember today. Do you know how the state of spiritual energies affects a person's health?

It was the honest statement of a man who not only said so, but took the opportunity to really expand his knowledge. Kaito explained to the doctor that, in his opinion and experience, a person's spiritual energy always remained constant, unless it was used as it was today, in which case it would regenerate quickly, and even if it dropped very sharply, nothing more would happen than a strong physical weakness would occur, but it would quickly regenerate again as soon as the person rested. Only if it was completely consumed by demons or Yokai, it would be dangerous and could lead to death. He could give him a copy of a book, but its contents should be read with caution as nothing had been proven.

The doctor, who introduced himself as James Williams, showed genuine interest and thanked him several times. When Kaito then picked out the English partner organization from the Japanese side of the Order, he became more and more talkative and explained that as a child he had believed in aliens and had searched the sky for weeks until his parents had taken the telescope away from him and everyone in the room had to laugh, including Mr. Harrington this time.

Later Mio, Dawn and Ivy returned and Ivy sadly told the group that she would only see Dawn as a cat, hugged her, thanked her again and sat Dawn down on her chair between Mio and Kaito.

Kaito realized that this was a good opportunity to leave and asked to be allowed to make the return trip, which Mr. Harrington immediately accepted, to the grumbling of his daughter.

On the way to the car, Kaito told Mr. Harrington that he would get back to him about protection and got into the car that took Kaito and the others from the estate to the airfield.

Mr. and Mrs. Harrington and Ivy watched the car. Ivy said, "Mio's really great. I've arranged with her to visit her in Japan."

Mr. Harrington just said, "She's welcome to come here, there's always room."

"Maybe I'll study in Japan too, what do you think?"

Mr. Harrington said again, "Ms. Yamamoto is welcome to come here, there's always a place."

Ivy and her mother looked at each other, their eyes met and they knew they were thinking the same thing, "Could it be that this man was afraid of a human for the first time?"

As the car disappeared behind a hill, Mr. Harrington turned and went into the house and thought, "Oh God, what a monster, who knows what else is in there. Spare my family from this incarnation in human form."

The flight back went pretty smoothly, except that Mio was still wearing the evening gown Mrs. Harrington had given her, and she made a fuss of the whole plane, including the pilot. Anyway, she wasn't alone during the flight and had five new contacts after landing. Luckily, the trip home after landing was uneventful, since she had changed at Kaito's insistence.

Kaito wanted to take Mio home, but she refused. He wondered if there would still be trouble with her parents. He wasn't sure if Mio hadn't signed the letter from her parents herself.

It was already dark when Kaito got home and since they had lost the time they had gained on the outward flight, he simply fell onto his bed.

He was still thinking, "If Mio rings tomorrow, he just won't open the door. Fuck English," and fell asleep.

Mio didn't show up, but to his relief, he saw her in the third period of school. She was surrounded by a lot of girls staring at Mio's smartphone, and Kaito thought about the confidentiality clause in his contract.

"Mio's not stupid, she'll think of something," he knew.

In the afternoon, Mio quickly came into the office and immediately wanted to know how Kaito had killed the demon.

He explained that it had been the same principle as the purification, except that he had held the fifth seal in his hand to fool the demon, and that he had not paid attention to his spiritual energy, but had given the demon a full broadside to make up for the disadvantages of the pentagram.

Dawn had deliberately allowed herself to be hit in order to get under the bed so that she could erect the protective barrier on the other side undetected.

"Dawn can set up a protective barrier just like that?" asked Mio.

"All spirits, especially the powerful ones, can use their energy to create a protective barrier against opposing energies; they don't even need to draw a protective circle. Unlike humans, who have to transform their energy with a protective seal or circle first. Gods, but unfortunately also demons, can protect themselves and others in this way, depending on their spiritual strength.

"Can you do what Dawn can do?" Mio asked. "Maybe," Kaito said and smiled.

"Why doesn't the demon protect himself from your attack then?"

"Oh, he does, he tries, but a bullet goes through a sheet of paper, or do you think I'm shooting with cotton wool?" he grinned at Mio and continued, "Divine energy is also more powerful than dark energy."

Mio was angry that she wasn't included in the plan, but she understood the reason, because it looked for her that Kaito was in danger too, the demon must have sensed that.

Mio said that Dawn had told Ivy similar and that it was a demon of the highest order and that she had been unbelievably lucky. And that he, Kaito, only took so long because he didn't want to endanger her life. Otherwise, the demon could have been killed in a second or two, but that time would have been enough for the demon to hurt Ivy or even more.

"Demons always take their victims to the grave when they know they are going to die. Hence the trick. Inside the protective barrier, the demon couldn't unleash its power and therefore couldn't destroy her heart," Dawn had said, leaving a lasting, thoughtful impression on Ivy.

"You could have told me earlier that Ivy and I have the same aura," Mio said to Kaito. "Dawn had told Ivy and also that this was the reason for the demon attack."

"I wanted to tell you later," Kaito said, but didn't apologize, "for what," he thought.

"Ivy and I are soul mates," Mio said, emphasizing that she was coming to visit her here in Japan and had already written to her.

"I don't want to interfere, but you live in different worlds, so be careful," Kaito said.

Mio looked at him and fell silent, but then said, "We live in the 21st century, Ivy needs friends too," and laughed again as usual.

Kaito left it at that.

A few days later, Mio said to Kaito, "Look, there's something wrong with the balance.

Kaito jumped and ran frantically to the notebook where Mio had opened the account application.

"This receipt is comically large, and we have not yet sent the only bill we are still expecting to KLQS & Partner."

Mio was right, the receipt was huge, and it was not from the Harrington family's contractor, KLQS & Partner, but from another company.

"Look up the company on the Internet," Kaito said calmly for the first time, because fortunately it was a deposit and not a debit.

"Could it be an accounting error by the bank? That would be a shame," Mio said.

"Always possible."

"No, it's not an incorrect entry, this company is the asset management company of the Harrington family," Kaito said excitedly, his eyes widening.

Now he understood and said, "Well, we were in England when I said I wanted a million more. There they calculate in British Pounds and not in Yen," and he shouted loudly "*YES!*"

"But you had Yen in mind!"

"Yes, but the bastard didn't know that, and we weren't in Japan at the time, we were in England."

"You mean the father of Ivy Rose, our dear customer," Mio said, smiling slightly. "By the way, Ivy apologized a thousand times for her father."

"Change the invoice to the new amount that was transferred and send it as paid!", he said a little more coldly.

"Somehow I find that a bit strange?"

Kaito gave her a stern look. Mio was about to row back when she noticed Kaito's sinister expression and he said with a smile, "Demon or pay raise, which do you prefer?"

"Pay raise," came out of her mouth and Kaito said smugly, "Good girl," he turned to Dawn and laughed, "Now the forest project can begin.

Chapter 10 - AGE IS RELATIVE

When Mio entered the office a few days later, she met a cheerful Kaito.

"You look motivated today."

"Yes. I have all the installments for my forest project together."

"Right, you mentioned it, what exactly is it?"

"I can now pay for a piece of forest in the mountains here that I bought an option on, and I want to build a place for Ayakashi there."

"A place for Ayakashi? Since when are you interested in anything but demons and Dawn?" Mio asked with interest.

"I wanted to see if Dawn and Ayakashi could live together after all."

"You know Ayakashi are dark spirits, Kaito!" Mio asked suspiciously.

"Sure. And that's exactly why we have to test if her sister and the other Ayakashi wouldn't get along with Dawn after all," Kaito said.

"DAWN HAS A SISTER!" Mio shouts.

"Yes, but she's an Ayakashi."

"Where is she, how does this work, why don't I know?"

"All in good time, now I have to buy the forest first, which is unfortunately more expensive than I thought and the effort is enormous."

There was a knock at the door and Mio called, "Come in."

"Another man in a suit, very good," Kaito thought as Mio came over and greeted him.

He introduces himself as a confidant of the honorable Mrs. Natsuki Endo, who wants a consultation to lift a curse. He does not know exactly what kind of curse it is, but he is authorized to pay the costs for this consultation in advance on condition of confidentiality.

After Kaito had signed the contract with the man, the address had been given and they had agreed on the cost of the consultation, the man went to the door, turned around, thanked him, said "See you tomorrow" and left the office.

"What do you think, Kaito?" asked Mio.

"Well, house calls are nothing unusual. Curses don't really exist. I've never seen one. Usually, it's demons who attack people and then make them believe in a curse. So you should be prepared for a demon. But the name 'Natsuki Endo' doesn't ring a bell, the address seems to be a very large estate, see if you can find out more, so that we don't get into anything stupid."

When they took a taxi from the bus stop to the estate the next day, Mio asked, "So you took your suitcase for the consultation?"

"As we discussed. It's better to be prepared, who knows what's really coming."

Mio spontaneously asked the taxi driver if he knew the address. He said yes and told him that the Endo family owned the big factories in the industrial port here, but that was all he knew.

A maid was already waiting for them and led them into a reception room where all three of them took their seats. A short time later, a woman in her 60s came in, followed by several other people, and introduced herself as Natsuki Endo. Kaito and Mio thanked her for the job and the trust she had placed in them and introduced themselves as well.

Mrs. Endo said that her mother had been in a kind of coma for some time, and despite intensive medical examinations, no one could find anything wrong with her except that she was very old and that her mother had been cursed by a witch a long time ago. She wanted this curse, if it existed, to be removed and asked Mr. Tanaka to check it out.

Dawn meowed and Kaito stroked Dawn and asked suspiciously, "Are you okay, Dawn?"

"Nothing is clear, don't you realize that something is very wrong here!" said Dawn.

But he also realized too. Why this effort, this implausible story, the mother must be over 80, no demon would choose her as a target unless ...

He had a bad feeling. "Of course," he said, "we'll see if a harmful spirit has taken up residence here, but I'll prepare myself for a moment." He opened his small case, took out the amulet and two banishing seals and put them in his pocket while he put the amulet around his neck.

"Follow me," Mrs. Endo said when Kaito signaled that he was ready.

"At least no discussion with the client, that's good," he thought as he followed Mrs. Endo with Dawn in his arms and Mio running behind him, who looked at the beautiful and very expensive decoration of the house and could hardly tear herself away from it.

The house seemed endless. At the end of an unusually narrow and long hallway was a door with a man standing guard and Kaito just thought "If this is a trap, there will be many deaths today" and prepared himself for something unexpected.

Mio, as always lost in thought, looked at the beautiful and very expensive things they passed.

"Sometimes, she really is treudoof," Kaito thought as they reached the door.

Mrs. Endo said, "My mother will be asleep, it would be very nice if you could look in quietly. Kaito nodded and Mrs. Endo opened the door.

Dawn was the first to jump away from the door, meowing softly. Kaito heard Dawn say "AWAY!" and only saw the reason with one eye as he gave Mio a very firm push to the right side of the door with both hands and she bounced hard against the guard standing there, who absorbed her push a bit before Kaito himself used the momentum to jump away to the left side of the door, fell down and was now kneeling on one leg. Mrs. Endo was so shocked that she closed the door to the bedroom again. The guard was startled when Mio landed on him. He was very angry, as you could easily see, and was about to grab Kaito after pushing Mio aside when Kaito pointed his finger at Mrs. Endo and said, "Call the guard back or you'll never see us again."

Ms. Endo was slightly startled and motioned for the guard not to interfere. He hesitated at first in his anger at this possible attack on him and thus on Mrs. Endo, but accepted it.

Mio was about to scream when Dawn jumped on top of Mio, clawing at her and meowing loudly.

Mio yelled "Ouch, Dawn what..." and tried to pull her away.

Kaito said "Mio, stay calm!" in a very commanding tone and she suddenly realized that this was not some stupid prank by a pubescent boy trying to tease her. Was her life in danger? She froze.

Kaito pointed at Mrs. Endo, who was standing in front of the closed door, holding her hands protectively in front of her. Kaito put his hand down again, stood up and said to Mrs. Endo: "We need to talk, especially about the truth."

Without saying a word, Kaito walked back down the corridor they had come from towards the reception room. The guard started to say something, but Mrs. Endo shook her head, thanked him and went after them.

The guard seemed to have raised the alarm anyway, because Mrs. Endo was already expected in the reception room by several security guards and housekeepers. Mio remained silent and looked at Dawn who was standing next to Kaito. "Everything was so harmonious a few minutes ago and now," Mio thought with a bad feeling.

Mrs. Endo looked at Kaito and Mio noticed that she was unusually insecure for the landlady of such a large house; the woman was 60 years old, so she should be much more confident than she was. "What in the world is going on here?" she asked herself.

Kaito asked, "Should we make the round smaller?"

Mio became more and more restless and thought, how could he ask such a thing? But Mrs. Endo understood. She looked around and ordered a maid and a guard to stay and the others to "go back to work".

When the doors had closed behind them, Kaito looked around again and saw fear in the eyes of the housekeeper, but also in those of Mio and Mrs. Endo. He couldn't read the guard's emotions, he was also around sixty years old, probably a longtime familiar, and the housekeeper was probably a familiar as well because of her age. "All right," he thought.

"Mrs. Endo," Kaito began, "please don't lie to me, I know it's unpleasant, but the matter must be clarified. How old is your mother, or rather, who is this woman really and how old are you?"

Mio slapped her hands over her mouth, she had never expected such insolence from Kaito and was about to say something when Dawn hissed at her. She wanted to cry, but she stayed calm.

Mio noticed that the staff did not bat an eyelid, not even Mrs. Endo became angry, as one would expect in such a situation. Instead the old, powerful and rich woman looked very submissive as she looked down at the floor.

She raised her head and said to Kaito, "I am 30 years old and the woman in this room is a seventh generation ancestor, born towards the end of the Edo period.

Mio, who was looking at the floor, heard Mrs. Endo's words but couldn't place them because so many things didn't fit together and thought she had misunderstood them because of the situation and looked at her. She saw the face of a 60 year old woman who started to cry in front of her eyes. She quickly looked at Kaito, who was also staring at the floor, and then at the housekeeper, who ran to Mrs. Endo's side to support her.

Mio looked back and forth between the people, not knowing what to do. Then Dawn jumped towards her and Mio caught her and hugged Dawn. "Thank you Dawn," she whispered to her.

Mrs. Endo sat down at the table in front of them and Kaito did the same.

Kaito saw that it was impossible for Mrs. Endo to speak and began to break the silence.

"Mrs. Endo, if you don't mind, I will complete everything with my words, may I?" he asked.

She nodded and looked down at the table.

"Your 'mother' made a pact with an Exsuctor demon a long time ago, but this one doesn't reduce the life force of the host, but that of its offspring, and then gives some of it back to the host to keep it and itself alive."

He didn't get any further. Mrs. Endo looked up and almost shouted at Kaito, "WHAT ABOUT MY CHILDREN!"

Mio stood motionless in the room as if in a trance, her heart beating like crazy. "Why is it doing that?" she asked herself, it's just a dream. "Wake up Mio, wake up Mio," she hoped to hear, but nothing came, she looked down at Dawn who was looking at her.

"Where are your children?" Kaito asked calmly.

"I sent them to Tokyo," she yelled, far away from here.

"They are safe from the demon there. Its range depends on its age, but no more than 1000 steps."

Mrs. Endo looked at Kaito with glassy eyes and sobbed, "Thank God."

"That was a wise decision, Mrs. Endo," Kaito said.

"What about the other people here?"

"They must be blood relatives so that the demon can access the life energy of these people."

Mio could clearly see the weight of this cruelty falling from the people in the room, even though no one dared to move or even speak.

"Kill that monster," Mrs. Endo said almost in a panic.

"Of course I will."

Mrs. Endo looked at Kaito with wide, reddened eyes.

"What do you want in return? Say it, anything you want!"

Kaito felt very uncomfortable in this situation. Sure, he could always use money, but to negotiate something like that in this situation?

He could bleed someone like Mr. Harrington, but Ms. Endo, here and now?

"Monopolies can be cruel," he thought.

He dismissed his thoughts and said dryly, "We'll come to an agreement!"

"Your 'mother' is about 200 years old, do you know what that means to her?"

"Yes."

Mio wanted to escape, where is the door, she asked herself, where should she go, but she stopped.

Kaito opened his suitcase and thought back to yesterday when they had almost joked about needing it and took out some seals. He closed it, went over to Mio and pressed the case into her hand.

Then he stroked Dawn's head again and held his thumb out to her. She bit into it and drank some of the blood that came out.

Mio understood and didn't understand either. But in this situation, she couldn't say anything anyway and kept quiet.

"The demon is very fast and, unlike the previous ones, it can disconnect from its victim immediately without dying itself. Go to the garden with Dawn and wait for me there, no talking back," he said.

Mio had never been so happy about a rejection as she was today, she just breathed out a 'yes' and left the room with quick steps towards the exit.

Kaito said to everyone present, "The demon is fast, if it realizes it is in danger, it will try to escape or kill someone before it dies itself. You should stay here as well.

"No, I'll come with you. Nao, you stay here. The housewife looked down and nodded.

"I'll come too," the man said. Mrs. Endo gave him a friendly nod.

"If the demon is dead, they probably have a few seconds before their mother dies too, they should know that it's quite possible that their mother didn't know what she was getting into. Demons always lie and cheat, even the people they make a deal with," Kaito said, knowing that it probably wasn't true.

Mrs. Endo had calmed down a bit, now you could see a face that wanted revenge and was determined to be there to find peace.

"Thank you, Mr. Tanaka, I understand, do what you think is right."

Kaito stood in front of the door and told himself that he could have made a pentagram, but this was too much trouble for him. With one hand, he broke a banishing ball into many small pieces, all of which soaked up his blood, with the other, he took off the amulet, cut his palm, laid the amulet sideways on the floor and took a protective seal from his pocket, which soaked up the blood from his palm. With that, he opened the door and, without saying a word, ran toward the demon, who was hovering over a very old woman in his small, dark green, ugly form.

Kaito laughed when he saw the frightened expression on the demon's face.

"This piece of dirt probably sees a 'Demon Emperor' running towards him," it formed in his head.

He watched as the demon rip the connection from the old woman's heart. Then the demon looked around to escape. But it saw only one way out and moved towards the door, from where Kaito ran towards it.

Kaito threw the shards of the banishing orb from his left hand at the incoming demon, who flinched and screamed in surprise.

"Go back to where you came from," Kaito said as he reached the lying demon, who was spitting golden particles from the many hits and began to disintegrate.

The demon struck again with one of its arms and hit Kaito's forearm. The demon laughed, but Kaito just said "Idiot" and the arm that hit him disintegrated into stardust. The demon screamed, and Kaito pressed the protective seal in his right hand onto the main body of the demon, which turned into golden particles with twitching movements and disappeared.

"Have fun with my mom," Kaito thought as he stood up and turned back to the door.

His arm hurt like hell, it could be broken, he thought. He probably wouldn't be able to avoid a doctor's appointment.

Mrs. Endo and the guard stood motionless. Kaito didn't know how much they had noticed, but judging by their expressions, quite a lot.

"Quick, come on," Kaito said to Mrs. Endo, pointing to the woman in the bed.

She understood and went to her mother's bed as fast as she could.

Kaito got up, went to the door, heard "Gomen nasai" and then Mrs. Endo started to cry. He looked back and saw the old woman on the bed slowly turning to ashes and thought, "One of the few unnatural effects that normal people can perceive and that proves the existence of the parallel dimension.

Mio had calmed down again and decided to continue working. After all, she was an employee. So she went back to the reception room. Dawn didn't mind either. Secretly, of course, she knew that she wanted to know how Kaito was doing. "Did he make it?" she wondered.

When she heard his voice from the door of the long corridor, she was relieved.

Kaito entered the room and saw Mio and Dawn standing there.

"What are you doing here?" he asked.

"Dawn gave me permission," she replied quickly.

Mrs. Endo also entered the room and sat down at the table. The housekeeper and the guard were nowhere to be seen.

"Thank you, Mr. Tanaka," she said and looked at Kaito calmly.

Kaito knew instinctively that he had to stay and answer questions.

"Should I call an ambulance or a doctor?" she asked.

Mio noticed that Kaito was holding his left hand.

"It's okay, there's still time, I'll go to the doctor later."

Mio was beside herself and wanted to go to him right away, but Dawn stopped her.

"How long do I have?" Mrs. Endo asked Kaito.

"This kind of Exsuctor demon shortens the lifespan of blood relatives by about half if they're within a few hundred meters. If they've been exposed all this time, they're 60 years old now, Mrs. Endo," Kaito said.

"And my children?"

"How long have they been here?"

"When I realized that the curse of the Endos had struck me as well, about four years ago, I took the children out of the house when they were three and four," she said, her voice choked with tears.

"Well, then they lost a maximum of three or four years, rather less because they were probably not always in the demon's sphere of influence, and with a life expectancy of over 80 years today, that is justifiable if you consider how quickly a life can be extinguished in today's world, even without a demon, and forgive my language."

"I implore you. Don't mince your words!"

"For years we lived with this curse in our house, it was so obvious that something should have been done, everyone before me kept quiet and died. For what? Why? My 'mother' had always placated and prevented action. It was only when she became unresponsive that I had the courage to do something.

Mio regretted being back in the room.

"So I have about 20 years left to live? What should I do in that time, what would you do Mr. Tanaka?"

"I'm a high school student, I don't have the right to tell you that."

"Even if you look like a high school student on the outside, your mind is certainly not, I can see that in your eyes and I want to know from you and only from you what you would do in my place".

Kaito felt uneasy inside, what should he say to Mrs. Endo in such a situation, a woman who had just lost 30 years of her life. Then he said,

"Your children will inherit the Endo legacy one day. Their 'mother' has built it up during her long life, using her great experience, expanding it, and carrying it through all the turmoil of that time until today. In the next 10 to 20 years, make sure that your children understand how to continue this legacy in a far-sighted and prudent, but above all, wise way. That's all I can tell you, Mrs. Endo."

"Thank you, Mr. Tanaka," Mrs. Endo said, which sounded more like a confirmation of what she already knew.

In the meantime, the guard and the maid had returned to the room, the guard holding a box in his hand and waiting for instructions.

Mio went out again, she didn't care what Mrs. Endo thought, she was just a nuisance anyway and it would take her a long time to forget today.

"You look pale, Mr. Tanaka, shall I call a doctor?" Mrs. Endo asked again.

"No, thank you, but if you had a beer, alcohol will help you recover better."

She smiled a little and motioned to the housekeeper.

"Now a quick word about this. This is the necklace my mother always wore," Mrs. Endo said, pointing to the box the guard had opened in front of him.

"She never took it off. It must be part of the curse, right?"

"Well, it may well be that the demon was attached to this publicly very valuable piece of jewelry. Demons know that such items are inherited and passed down in large families. There are no curses, only demons, and this one is gone now, so the piece of jewelry is a normal piece of jewelry again, and you can wear it without hesitation."

"Take it as a gift," Mrs. Endo said and Kaito twisted the corners of his mouth a little.

"We don't accept anything in kind as payment," he said almost automatically.

"It's a gift and ..."

Kaito interrupted, "If I have something that valuable, I'll be arrested, I really can't do that. Sell it at an auction and donate the money or keep it in a safe. Like I said, now that the demon has been destroyed, it's just a valuable, harmless, but very beautiful piece of jewelry," Kaito said.

"Thank you, Mr. Tanaka, my chauffeur will take you to the hospital now, no arguments!"
Kaito walked to the exit, saw Mio sitting there with Dawn and was about to take a sip of the beer that was handed to him, but stopped, put the beer next to Mio and told her, "Take a sip, it will calm you down a bit. Mio looked at Kaito, then at the beer, then back at Kaito and said, "I'm not going to become a drunk because of a damn demon!", got up and walked with Dawn to the gate.

Chapter 11 - BY COMMAND OF THE ORDER

The next day, Mio was back to his old self, or so it seemed to Kaito. He wrote a report, which Mio filed away but didn't read as usual. She didn't ask Kaito for more details about the demon's exorcism and left it at that.

"We still need to renovate the interior this year to reduce the tax burden, can you take care of that?" Kaito asked.

"How much can I spend?" came back Mio happily, who could hardly wait to get started.

"Two million yen for the office and two million for my apartment."

"But your apartment isn't the office," she said questioningly with a mischievous look on her face, "isn't that a bit, well, ILLEGAL!" she shouted loudly and laughed.

Kaito felt caught and said, "This is an office building, no one lives here, I just sleep in the second office from time to time because I have to work so much. The other office is actually for special visits from spirits," he replied with a laugh, thinking with amusement, "damn Mio just knows too much already, but it's nice that she's back to her old self.

"Yoo, with a divine cat. What are you doing in the evening?"

Dawn hisses at Mio and Mio apologizes to Dawn.

The bell above the office door indicated that someone had entered. Mio looked up and said, "Hello Mr. Nakamura, nice to see you, what's new?"

"The troublemaker is here," Kaito said.

"Ms. Yamamoto, when are you going to teach your monster to be friendly with customers, even beat him up if necessary, that always helps," he said with a laugh.

"The Exsuctor demon surprised us all, or how did you get that bandage on your arm again?"

"I don't know what you mean, I fell off my bike, it's just a sprain. I'll be fine in three days," Kaito said.

"You should see a psychologist, Kaito, this is sick," said Mr. Nakamura and walked over to Mio.

"A Muculentus, every pretty girl's dream, that will be your new assignment," he said, addressing Mio directly.

"Stay away from my employee, you horny otaku ..." he continued, "... along with that little asshole?"

"Well, he's big, strong, fast and good now, and still an asshole, so almost right. You're supposed to support him, protect him in an emergency and give his father an honest report. I hope the fox was worth it," Mr. Nakamura said.

"When?"

"This Saturday!"

"Good, the door is over there."

"Ms. Yamamoto, is Ivy Rose coming to visit you?" Mr. Nakamura asked Mio without warning.

Mio was shocked, how does Mr. Nakamura know all this, it can't be, she thought, has the Order bugged the office?

"Then I'll see you all at the Order on Saturday, leaving at 10 o'clock. See you then," he said and went to the door, turned around and said to Dawn, "You look really cute to-day. Did you get new clothes from your master?" and quickly jumped out of the door. Dawn hissed at him, but he was already gone.

"The Order seems..." Mio didn't get any further. "The Order is networked worldwide and has its informants, especially in the higher circles, without whom contracts like Mr. Kato's would not exist," Kaito interrupted her.

"What was that about every girl's dream?" she asked.

"Nonsense, the Muculentus is a kind of slime, and no, it doesn't dissolve clothes, but it's the only demon that stinks like the plague when you hurt it, and since it's quite massive, you have to get close to it to get the full effect."

"Would you like to come with me? The problem is not the muculentus, but ..."

"The little big asshole," Mio finished the sentence.

"I'm used to guys like that from school, so no problem, I'll definitely come with you," Mio said and called up the web-sites of furniture stores on the Internet.

"Mr. Nakamura could have told us that the meeting place had changed and that he wasn't coming with us. We're too early now," Mio said to Kaito as they got out of the taxi at their destination a few days later. It was a house from the order and there were two vehicles in the courtyard being loaded by two men.

Kaito approached the two young men, who seemed to be a bit older than Kaito, around twenty, Mio guessed.

When they saw Kaito, they stopped loading the car and greeted Kaito in a very friendly manner. Kaito called Mio over and introduced the two men as Mr. Shimizu and Mr.

Fujiwara. They greeted each other and continued loading the car.

Kaito explained that he knew the two men from his time in the order.

"You can talk to them normally and they know how far they can go and what to do," Kaito said and Mio thought, "That's probably the highest praise you can get from Kaito," when a loud "Hey you ugly monster, back again" was heard from the side.

Mio turned towards the voice and saw that Kaito wasn't looking at the person but in the other direction and thought ironically "Who could that be?

She saw a man, also around 20 years old, very well built, tall and muscular, with a beautiful face but a very arrogant expression.

"Hey Kaito old chap. Oh no, little boy, can you already use the toilet alone! But all jokes aside, thanks for coming. Dad must be out of his mind to make me work on the weekend, the old bastard."

Mio saw the other two men roll their eyes and get into their cars.

"What's dad thinking, it's stalking day on the weekend and I don't mean spirits, I mean human bunnies or whatever you call your bunny Kaito. Mio was her name, right?"

"Are you as good as you are at shooting your mouth off?" Mio asked the young man.

"Hey, hey, may I introduce myself, Koji Ito, but you can also say Ito-sama, pretty Mio-chan."

"Can I hit Ito-kun?" Mio asked Kaito and a laugh came from the first car.

"I guess the eternal virgin Fujiwara can't keep it together with so much beauty in his car, let's go," Koji said to Mio. Dawn hissed as Koji walked past her to the second car.

"The bedspread is still stuck half-naked to you Kaito. Weren't you going to introduce me to your sister Dawn-chan?" he said with a malicious laugh, sitting down in the car and closing the door.

Kaito and Dawn sat in the back seat, Mio was the passenger and Mr. Fujiwara, who looked rather nervous, was the driver.

"Mr. Fujiwara, thank you for your assistance. Is he always such an ass?"

"Yes, he is not only the son of the leader of the order, but unfortunately he also has very strong spiritual abilities and almost always performs his tasks perfectly, so that no one can harm him."

"Stronger than Kaito?"

"No, no, that's not what I meant. Stronger than anyone else in the order at his age, even experienced hunters pay him respect."

"We'll see," Kaito said as Dawn meowed and everyone except Mio started to laugh.

"Damn, I want to know what Dawn said, too," she said, but then laughed too.

Three hours later, they passed a village and Mr. Fujiwara explained that in this village, animals were repeatedly being mauled. The village elder had contacted the Order when it did not stop. A hunter of the order had then found the Muculentus in a cave about a kilometer away in the mountains, where they were now heading.

When they arrived, Kaito said to Mio: "Always stay behind me, or to be more precise, always be closer to the exit than me. Otherwise, do what you want."

Mio nodded, she knew that Kaito had only said that for her safety, even if he could have said it nicer, but she would probably have to work on that and smiled slightly.

"Here you go, but only for emergencies, otherwise I want it back," he said to Mr. Fujiwara. He took two magic seals from Kaito, thanked him, took a can of water from the cart and went to the other cart.

"Can you take a small can of water with you, Mio?" Kaito asked.

"Sure, one will definitely go, what are they for?"

"For washing later, they'll need it."

Kaito and Mio each took a canister, followed a path after the others who had already left, and soon reached a cave entrance. Koji opened a box he had brought with him, gave them each a lamp and said to Mio, "To make you see the light."

Mio said nothing and they entered the cave. After 50 meters, Koji said, "We'll wait here until the eyes get used to it. Water here on the wall!" He turned the light to a dim red and drew a protective circle around everyone.

Mio was speechless, that donkey had formed a sentence that made sense, or is that standard knowledge, would Kaito have thought of something like that, she wondered.

"That thing will be about 100 meters deeper in the cave, it's about as big, as fast and as limp as a cow, but it can see better than us in the dark. When we first catch it, we can see it through the stardust better than it can see us. Because of its large mass, long range shots won't kill it, but you can both annoy it and distract it from the front with long range shots, creating light in the process. Annoy it as long as you can, keep it at bay or let it chase you and then back off. I'll try to get around it and destroy it from behind with a banishing seal. A hit from this thing really hurts, so if it comes at you, be sure to fall back.

Turn off your lamps now, keep them handy in case we have to flee, only I'll turn mine on and lead the way. Kaito, if you see anything, report it immediately, that goes for both of you too, of course!" Koji said commandingly and wanted to go on, but he stopped, looked at Kaito and said, "What have you arranged with Mio, she can't see him, can she?"

"She stays close to me, behind me," Kaito said.

"Mio, no matter what happens, never get more than ten feet away from Kaito, he's the only one who can protect you if something goes wrong, alright," Koji said and Mio saw a new expression on Koji's face in the dim red light of the lamp that made her slightly worried.

Mio first had to process what she had heard, this asshole, this scumbag, whom she had wished the plague on just 30 minutes ago, was actually worried about his people, about Kaito and also about her. This Koji had actually held some kind of team meeting here and everyone had listened, including Kaito. He also seemed to think a lot more of Kaito than she had thought at first.

"Yes, I understand," Mio said.

"Okay, let's go, slowly, four meters away from me."

The next hundred meters were longer than expected, Mio felt cold and wondered if it was just the cave or the demon. She stayed to the left behind Kaito, Koji was in front of her and the other two in the middle, then suddenly the light went out and Mio was startled. She could see nothing. Suddenly, she heard Koji say that the demon was hiding in a hole in the wall about 30 meters ahead of them.

Kaito set his lamp to the lowest setting, took Mio by the hand and stood on a rock near the cave wall with her and said to Mio: "Cover your eye with one hand and only take your hand away when it's too dark to see and now look ahead, it's about to start.

Mio understood the old pirate trick and covered one of her eyes in time, just as a source of light illuminated the cave from the front.

Reflexively, she blinked her open eye, slowly opened it again and saw the beast. A demon, about twice as big as a cow and ugly, slimy and dirty, she would have been better off staying at home.

As agreed, the two of them shot their banishing bullets at the demon with a slingshot, but nothing much happened, except that the cave, which was much more spacious at this point, but should be completely dark, was very well lit. "What was that, was it my imagination or did it really start to smell like Kaito said," Mio thought.

Mio was about to ask when she noticed that Kaito himself was holding something in his hand, she suspected banishing orb. "Will his do as little damage to that thing as they did?" she thought, realizing that she could no longer see Koji. "Did something happen to him?" she wondered desperately.

Suddenly, she saw a shadow coming from behind the demon's position. Koji had actually snuck up behind the demon and was now attacking it from the other side. However, since the demon was standing against the cave wall, it was impossible to attack it from behind. "Did such a beast even have a back?" she asked herself.

Realizing that its existence was at stake, the demon began to charge the two attackers from the front. They moved backwards with impressive assurance, keeping the beast at a distance and continuing to take turns firing at the demon.

"If they get closer than that point up ahead, we'll retreat as well," Kaito said and Mio nodded.

Mio saw Koji accelerate towards the demon, who was running away from him and aimed at his back. The demon seemed to notice this and suddenly changed direction. Some kind of arm swung towards Koji. Mio was startled, but Koji dodged it almost playfully, jumping over a second approaching arm and hitting the demon with a banishing seal.

The effect was not as strong as she expected and as she knew it from Kaito, but the demon was injured and the cave was lit up as bright as day.

"An injured demon is no less bad than an uninjured one," Kaito said to Mio, who continued to look at Koji.

The stench was getting worse and Mio hoped it wouldn't get any worse.

Mio saw that Koji was fast, very fast, much faster than Kaito, his movements were almost superhuman. The demon's arms slashed in Koji's direction again, but he was already somewhere else, had a new banishing seal ready and slammed it down on the spot where the demon's arm had come from, which then fell in a flurry of particles and turned into stardust as well. The demon's second arm came from behind, and Mio screamed as the arm flew at Koji at high speed. Koji held both his forearms protectively in the direction of the incoming demon arm and was hit with full force. Koji flew back about three to four meters and the demon's last arm disintegrated into stardust.

Koji just laughed, stood up, took out two more banishing seals, jumped over the angry demon and hit him from above with the two seals like an FX action movie.

The demon disintegrated into stardust and the stench became unbearable.

Mio looked at Kaito, who was still looking at Koji, then turned and said, "Let's go back, quick, or we'll have to wash up too.

On the way to the first stop, Mio asked Kaito, "He was good, wasn't he?"

"Good is not an expression, he was more than very good, much better than before," Kaito said appreciatively. Mio only just noticed that Dawn was missing and almost panicked, "Where's Dawn?"

"Stay calm," Kaito said. She's waiting by the water, she doesn't like the smell.

And so it was. The lamps were directed against the wall to provide enough light and Koji said, "Will the old bag be happy?

"Jumping over the demon at the end was stupid of you," Kaito said, "what would you have done if the two seals hadn't been enough to kill the demon?"

"Then I would have endured the pain and slapped two more seals on it. The arms were off, and that's the trick, right, kid?" Koji laughed.

"What about your two forearms?"

He took off his shirt and held his muscular arms out to Kaito. Two bracers with seal inscriptions were clearly visible.

"That hurt the bastard more than it hurt me, and yes, it still hurts."

"Tricky," Kaito said appreciatively.

"Right, now wash up, nobody gets in the car without being clean."

The two men poured water over themselves.

"I don't like wet clothes on me," Koji said and started to undress completely, looking at Mio and grinning. She turned away and walked towards the exit, just before a curve she turned around again and Kaito, who was walking next to her, asked, "Big asshole or hot ass?

Mio was startled, blushed and took a step towards Kaito. But he already knew what was coming and ran out of the cave.

"Stay here, you bastard," she called after him and continued running towards the cave exit.

Koji and the other two came out of the cave later with new clothes.

"Where did you get them?" Mio asked.

"If you were my girlfriend, I would have brought you something to change into too, how about it Mio-chan, are you interested in another adventure?"

"Scumbag," Mio said and walked away, regretting again that she had thought so much of him in the cave.

"Like father, like son," Koji laughed out loud and looked at Dawn, who was standing next to Kaito.

"Dawn-chan, did the Fox God really jumped on you well or was the trip to Sakura-no-Mura not worth it? I would love to raise one of your children, I'm sure they will be wonderful."

Dawn took a step towards him and raked her sharp fingernails over his cheek, which began to bleed.

Laughing, he wiped the blood from his face and said, "As aggressive and boisterous as ever, I like it." When he suddenly made a gesture to flick the blood from his hands at Dawn, Dawn jumped back and Kaito shouted, "Dare to die here," pointing his finger at Koji.

Koji raised both hands in the air and said smugly, "I'm like an angel of light, I would never do something like that," and walked past Dawn and Kaito to the car, laughing.

The other two were so embarrassed that they wordlessly handed Kaito the two protective seals, bowed deeply and also ran to the two cars.

Kaito hugged Dawn and whispered in her ear, "Did you notice?" and Dawn replied, "Yes, I did. Meow."

The ride back was no problem since Koji was in the other car, although everyone in the car was still upset. When they arrived at the Order House, Kaito, Mio and Dawn immediately took the taxi they had ordered.

Koji yelled something like "buzzkill" and had already disappeared into the house.

As they sat on the train, Mio realized that the reason Kaito had left the order must have been Koji or his father. Kaito simply didn't need to be a member, he was just too good for that. All the others had to give in, "the strong eat the weak," Mio thought, and her anger rose even higher.

They should neuter Koji, that rat, Mio said to the group and Dawn meowed in agreement. But Kaito was strangely in a better mood the more he typed on his smartphone.

"What's wrong, aren't you as mad as I am?" asked Mio.

"No, I was having a great day," Kaito replied.

"Huh? Earth to Kaito," Mio said. "You just realized everything, didn't you?"

"Sure," said Kaito, looking from his smartphone to her.

"Mio, did you hear Koji mention the Fox God in Sakura-no-Mura?"

"So what?" said Mio.

"The fox god we were with was in Sakura-Dori, not Sakura-no-Mura."

"Yeah, I know, maybe he misheard or mixed something up. So what?"

"What he said was illogical, it didn't fit together, so I looked it up. There really is a shrine in Sakura-no-Mura, but it's dedicated to a cat god and we're going there tomorrow."

Mio immediately understood that this might have been a Freudian slip by Koji and said loudly, "You idiot, you asshole, you scumbag, I hope you let something slip," and everyone laughed.

Chapter 12 - LUCKY CATS

Kaito waited impatiently at the station, he had bought more expensive tickets for everyone and was very impatient and a little annoyed that Mio was already a few minutes late again. But when everyone had found their seats and the train started, Mio saw that Kaito's mood was getting better and better.

Mio wondered how Kaito had managed to get Dawn to sit next to him instead of in a cat box. On the other hand, how was she supposed to fit into a box and what view would that have on Kaito? She quickly averted her eyes to avoid laughing like on the flight to London.

Exuding a stoic calm while sitting on a cushion Kaito had taken with him, Dawn became the current attraction and object of desire of would-be photographers on several occasions, which Kaito put up with out of goodwill.

Dawn, on the other hand, seemed to enjoy the attention, sunning herself at the window and looking out at the fields passing by.

After changing to the second train, which was almost empty, no one asked about Dawn. They noticed immediately that time passed differently here. The train ride took much longer for a much shorter distance. "Welcome to the Middle Ages," Kaito thought and stretched as he got off and looked for a bus, which took another 30 minutes.

"How likely is it that a god also lives in this temple?" asked Mio.

"There are so many shrines and so few gods, it would be a stroke of luck if this one was inhabited by a god. But I'm in a good mood. Let's take a look around."

The two agreed to meet back here in five minutes and Mio ran off.

Kaito went to the bakery he saw, bought a snack for everyone and returned to the meeting point. "Mio will make it", he thought.

Less than five minutes later, Mio ran up to Kaito and said, "Good news, the shrine is at the end of town towards the mountains, not far from here, and tonight there's a procession in honor of the cat god.

Kaito was once again amazed at Mio's ability to communicate, "How does she do that?" he asked himself over and over again as they made their way to the shrine and ate the pastries.

The shrine was simple but large. A traditional gate marked the entrance, followed by a path with cherry trees on either side. Guardian statues stood in the large square to protect the central shrine and the shrine itself.

Kaito immediately saw the misty, golden beams of light of the purest divine energy that could only emanate from the highest divine beings. Now it was clear, there was a God here. Dawn herself showed it, looking pensive and introspective, almost moved, as she gazed in the direction of the shrine. "How powerful is he?" he asked, smiling cheerfully in Dawn's direction.

But Dawn remained reverently silent, and Kaito said to himself sardonically, "I hope there is still a free seats for an extra servants, otherwise I'll help."

"Bigger than I thought, that's not so good," Kaito said to Mio.

"Why?" came the reply.

"We can't get to the god without attracting attention, not to mention that old priest over there who's already seen us."

"Hey Kaito, a little more respect or I'll have to talk to Mr. Tanaka," it came back mockingly.

"Then we'll talk to him directly," Mio said and wanted to approach him. But Kaito stopped her. We don't know anything about him. We have to find out which side he's on first."

"What do you mean 'which side'?" she asked Kaito.

"How he feels about the Order, because they must have been here before. Come with me," he said and walked towards the empty prayer hall.

"All hell must be breaking loose here tonight for the festival," he thought, smiling at the heretical comparison.

Taking a box of offerings out of his pocket, he said to Mio, "Two teenagers, obviously not from here, with a cat at the cat shrine, which is probably only visited by locals or neighboring villages, we stand out like colorful dogs.

Dawn meowed. "Don't you like the dog comparison," Kaito laughed again and continued, "Let's make the old priest nervous," he sat down, took an offering from the tin, placed it on a bowl he had brought with him as usual and demonstratively carved his finger and pressed it on the offering.

Mio was not very pleased. It was obvious that he wanted to provoke the priest. "Couldn't this have been settled more peacefully?" she asked.

"Shh and come down to me," Kaito said and began to pray a little louder.

"Oh Manitu, oh Manitu ..."

"Hey, that's enough, what the hell?" Mio interrupted angrily.

But the priest was already there, he smiled and said: "It's nice that the youth of today is rediscovering the path of faith and respectfully dedicating themselves to the old traditions. Do you belong to any religious order?

Mio winced slightly at this obviously provocative question, but Kaito just smiled; the priest had said the word 'order' a little too provocatively.

"I resigned, Mr. Ito and I didn't see eye to eye."

"By the way, on my left is Mrs. Yamamoto, a friend of mine, and on my right is Dawn, she wants an audience with the god of this shrine."

The priest was visibly annoyed and told them to please leave and take their offerings with them as he looked down at an empty bowl.

"Someone seems to disagree," and he took another offering and placed it on the bowl. Just as the priest was about to take the bowl away, the offering disappeared before his eyes. He was startled and froze, but after a short time, he regained his composure and thought, "What kind of trick is this brat playing? Kaito said, "I am honored that you are receiving us, would you allow us to enter?"

A violent gust of wind opened the door to the inside of the shrine, and Kaito said to the priest, "Let's talk inside, or do you want to anger your god?

Was it a coincidence, a lousy trick of the ugly, arrogant boy, or was it really a divine revelation? In all his 70 years, he had never experienced anything like this. He had been waiting for a revelation ever since he took over the shrine, but to no avail, and now some brat came along and this is exactly what happened. He could barely contain his anger, but if it was really true …

Kaito placed a third offering on the bowl in the priest's hand and clasped his hands in prayer. The priest pulled the bowl with the offering away from Kaito, held it next to him, looked at it, blinked and when his eyelids opened again, this offering had disappeared just like the previous one. He looked at Kaito who still had his hands clasped in prayer.

"Who are you?" he asked and looked around to see if there were any other people he didn't know on the grounds. No, only these two were new faces.

"How are you, old man..." Mio elbowed him in the stomach and Kaito had to cough.

"Excuse me. Kaito Tanaka here can really see the god of this shrine, unfortunately he is sometimes a bit, well, how shall I put it, rude! But we have nothing to do with the order, he fights alone against demons and for the people, and for this information that there is a cat god here, he saved a fox shrine in Sakura-Dori from demolition," Mio said.

The priest looked at Mio for a long time and Kaito was about to say "Any longer and it will cost you" when the priest said "That was you?".

"I can't see spirits; Mr. Tanaka has mastered that."

"I don't like the order's exorcists."

Mio looked at him a little confused and then asked with a sincere voice, "You would rather let people die?"

The priest realized that this girl was different and asked, "What exactly do you want?"

"I want to go to the shrine and speak directly to the cat god," Kaito said to the priest's face.

The priest thought of the rumor of Sakura-Dori, where a strange boy was seen with a cat just before the Maeda family's long-lost daughter was found and everything changed.

"You wash and change before I let you in," he said after a few seconds.

"Agreed, thank you very much," Mio said quickly and gave Kaito a dirty look before he could say something stupid like 'it costs extra' or something.

"Does this look okay," Kaito wondered as he and Dawn walked back to the shrine from changing. Mio was already there, chatting casually with the priest again. Kaito tried to push away any thoughts of that.

When the priest saw Kaito, he turned to the shrine and went through the still open door first.

Kaito, Mio and Dawn knelt down and the priest closed the door.

"What exactly are you doing here?" he asked.

Kaito took out the box with the offerings, put it on the ground in front of him, opened it and said to the altar, "I wish to bargain with the god of this shrine. My wish is that you give Dawn the power to materialize as she wishes."

The priest became nervous, you could tell he did not want to be made a fool of anymore.

He knelt down and was about to take the offerings from Kaito and put an end to the haunting when it suddenly went dark behind him. The candles on the altar seemed to be extinguished or dimmed.

"You have served me faithfully for so long and now you want to take what is mine?" a voice asked behind him and Kaito thought, hoping that his heart would survive this.

The priest looked up, startled, but realized that the voice came from behind him and turned around.

"That was a strange reaction for a priest, running backwards on all fours with his back to the ground and screaming," Kaito thought as he watched the man's acrobatic contortions. But the priest quickly realized his mistake and a few seconds after sorting out his limbs, he took a dignified stance before his god.

A pleasant feeling flowed through Mio as she looked at the creature behind the priest.

The cat god was stocky and strong, about two meters tall, and looked like a friendly middle-aged man with the grace of a big cat of prey. His face had both human and feline features, with high cheekbones, almond-shaped golden eyes with a greenish glow, two fluffy cat ears, and a huge bushy tail.

His smile radiated a warm friendliness worthy of a god of happiness.

Suddenly, eight small cat servants appeared around the god and rushed towards the gifts, which quickly disappeared into their mouths. Kaito guessed from Mio's reaction that the priest couldn't see them either, otherwise the old man would have gone crazy.

"Tell me, boy, who are you, or should I rather ask what you are?"

"Hi big guy, I'm Kaito Tanaka Spiritual Deriver and head of the Spirit-KT-Science Institute. Oh yeah, and I'm human, so it would be nice if you gods could see it that way too."

"Hey," Mio hissed at him, looking at the cat god the whole time with big eyes like a little child.

The cat god laughed and Kaito said to him, slightly disappointed, "I see you already have eight servants.

"You didn't answer my question, boy."

"I am someone who cares for Dawn more than any other life in this world, and only a servant contract with you can guarantee her safety after my death," Kaito said, emphasizing some words a little more than usual so that Mio wouldn't take them quite so seriously, but he knew that he meant exactly what he said.

The cat god went over to Dawn, held his hand over her and Dawn turned into a cat girl from one moment to the next.

This was too much for the priest. Seeing this, he slammed a head face down on the ground and left it there, and Kaito hoped it didn't suffocate.

"Is this what you want?" the cat god asked Dawn.

"I want to live with Kaito."

"Spirits of light and humans don't belong together."

"I see it differently and it's my free choice."

"In only 80 years the one you love will be gone. What if you can't forget?"

Dawn hesitates.

"I will not, never, just like everyone else who will follow and so it should remain," she said and Kaito thought "hey, hey, slow down, I'm not that old yet".

"You are already very strong for your short existence, much stronger than my eight children."

"And you saved the shrine of Myojin," he told Kaito.

"That was a wise decision, otherwise that perverted fox would have come here later and begged for shelter. Or what did you call him?" he said, laughing so loudly that everyone had to cover their ears.

"Servants must serve their gods, and that includes my children."

"Your servant positions are all taken anyway, perhaps we can arrange something else," Kaito said questioningly.

"What makes you think that the scheming fox said that?"

"Yes," Kaito said, but he was no longer sure what the cunning fox had said.

"Nine servants, one for each of our earthly lives. I'll explain that to the stupid fox when I see him again in a few hundred years, he obviously has a bad memory and forgot that cats are preferred to foxes," he said mockingly.

"Only my children will have the power of manifestation one day."

"Dawn will stay with me, what do you want in return?" Kaito asked the god.

The priest was still alive, Kaito saw, even if it looked like he was dead at first, he straightened up and turned to the god, as did Mio, who noticed and had to smile.

"I'll take the human girl, she'll be my servant," he said, pointing at Mio.

While Mio's reaction was rather confused, and you could tell that if she was going to be a servant, it would be to the fox god rather than the cat god, the priest's reaction was so funny that even the cat god noticed.

"Falling and rising and falling again and worshipping Mio and the god alternately could be an internet hit," Kaito thought, but then he said, "Mio is not up for negotiation."

"Thanks a lot, you ass, why does that sound like you own me?" Mio thought.

"I'll bring you a box of offerings like this once a year, that should make up for your ninth servant, besides what's a lousy 80 years for you.There's also a procession in your honor today, what do you say we make the cat god of Sakura-no-Mura even more famous?"

"I can show myself whenever I want, you should know that, boy."

"But not in the glow of golden stardust," Kaito said slowly, and the god understood and smiled.

Kaito and Mio left the shrine to change their clothes, while the god spoke some serious words to the priest, who then went to Kaito in the changing room, which made Kaito so angry that he threw the priest out of the door.

Mio tried to comfort him, but didn't get far because he started worshipping her again.

Eventually, Mio made him realize that he should talk to everyone normally, and after hard negotiations, he agreed, which was even harder than negotiating with the god himself.

Kaito explained to the still nervous priest what he wanted to do that night and he agreed. Not that he was reluctant, but he was still very excited. He was thrilled with the idea and assured Kaito that they would get all the support they needed.

Looking forward to the evening, he left Kaito and Mio alone at their request.

The sun was slowly setting, casting a golden glow over Sakura-no-Mura. Colorful lanterns lit up the streets and the smell of food and sweets filled the air outside the shrine.

Kaito had prepared everything, the sealing circles were on paper in the shrine, and Dawn was waiting with the god in the shrine.

"Probably doing cat things right now," Kaito grinned as he waited for the procession back to the shrine to end.

It was well after sunset when the palanquin bearers headed for the shrine gate and Kaito went inside and took Dawn in his arms.

"Let's really get going today," he said and kissed her.

"Yes, Meow," Dawn said with wide, happy eyes.

Kaito checked the sealing circles, his amulet, some banishing seals and banishing orbs that he had taken with him for safety and then waited for Mio's signal.

The palanquin was now placed in front of the shrine and the priest stepped forward to perform the last ceremony of the day, blessing the deity and returning it to the shrine in the presence of all participants. At this point, Mio Kaito gave the agreed upon signal.

"ASCENT SPIRITS," Kaito said coolly and watched as spirits of all kinds stepped out of the sealing circle. He grinned at Dawn and she jumped.

Mio was now standing at the gate, watching the priest say the last words to the deity, when suddenly someone pointed a finger in the direction of the shrine and said loudly, "What is that?

Golden particles scattered from the shrine in all directions and burned up before the eyes of those present. More and more people looked, some started to scream, and Mio hoped that panic would not break out. But they were cries of joy, not fear.

The particles reached the roof, where a glow magically attracted people and made them look up.

The glow above the shrine grew brighter, and the screams louder, as the people there saw a figure wrapped in golden particles sitting on the roof of the shrine, looking at them. The figure was now clearly recognizable as a human in cat form, the first smartphones were pulled out and photos were taken, and Mio thought happily, "Awww, forget it."

Then the figure faded again, but everyone could still see in the fading particles that the figure jumped off the roof like a cat with a mighty leap and returned to the shrine.

The particles disappeared and it became quiet, so quiet that Mio thought she could hear the video recording from the smartphones. Suddenly, the first one started cheering and then there was no stopping it, the screaming was so loud that it could be heard everywhere.

The whole night and the next day there was no other topic. Those who weren't there didn't believe it because there was no proof, because the photos and videos didn't show it. But those who were there believed all the more in a divine revelation because there was no evidence, despite the many recordings, because only those who were there could see it, they were the chosen ones, and that strengthened them all the more.

None of this interested Kaito anymore, they were long on the train back home and Dawn told Kaito how the god had given her the blessing of a servant and that she should prepare to take over her own shrine in a thousand years.

Kaito smiled, but something about this statement made him sad and he thought, "A thousand years? Will there still be spirits or people then and how will they live?"

Everyone got off the train and Mio said goodbye with a grateful smile for this wonderful day. Kaito looked at his smartphone that was ringing silently; he had set it to silent ringing in the shrine and hadn't changed it since. It was his father, he answered.

"WHERE THE HELL ARE YOU?"

"At the station? What's going on?"

"STAY THERE, I'LL GET YOU!" he yelled and hung up.

"Damn, what happened? Was it because him, from his past, was it Mrs. Tanaka or her daughter? Damn, sometimes you're really annoying, Mr. Tanaka."

Chapter 13 - SISTERS

He looked at Dawn standing next to him. It was after midnight, he was tired and wanted to go to bed, tomorrow he had school, English the first two hours with the old ..., anyway, he couldn't even laugh about it anymore, what the hell was going on, he thought and waited.

"Get in," Mr. Tanaka said after opening the passenger door of his civilian police car. Dawn jumped in first and then into the back seat. Kaito got in and off they went. Mr. Tanaka put a blue light on the roof and stepped on the gas.

"Hey old man, WHAT'S THE POINT?" Kaito became unusually loud.

"Listen Nao, the mayor's seven year old daughter has been kidnapped, probably by Yakuza, the reason is probably his candidacy for re-election. The nomination has to be made in seven days. If we don't find the daughter by then and he runs, it's a big dilemma."

"You're too stupid to find the kidnapped daughter," Kaito asked, a bit annoyed and tired at the same time.

"Hey, what are you doing, haven't you realized the situation yet?"

"Dawn, clean the little one's ears and you should think about who's going to naturalize Dawn here! We're going to the base. We'll get more information there. Your task should be clear, find her hiding place and with it the girl."

Fifteen minutes later, Kaito entered a meeting room in a building on government property. The fact that she was allowed onto the grounds and into the building so easily spoke volumes. Mr. Tanaka, his adoptive father, was probably more than just a simple policeman or had even better connections than he thought.

"Sit over there and listen, I'll be right with you," he said, pointing to a chair further back in the rows. Many glances were directed at him, but they were more analytical than judgmental and quickly turned back to the meeting table, where Mr. Tanaka also went.

A short time later, someone said loudly, "Everybody sit down, briefing," and the chairs filled up. Mr. Tanaka sat down next to Kaito and pointed to the podium in front of him.

An older, wiry man, a senior officer or official with many stars, probably the commander of a special unit, started first and said, "I'll summarize. The target's security beacon was found on the way to the south forest. The visual, IR and radar drone units scanned both the southwestern and eastern forest areas from the sea to the mountainous regions for a distance of 50 kilometers. Any anomalies found in relation to previous data or other anomalies were analyzed and assessed as negative.

The evaluation of available audio and video surveillance data, as well as smartphone movement analysis and vehicle geotracking data within a radius of 100 kilometers, also provided no clues to the perpetrators' further escape route. The last point of contact remains the tunnel in the south part of the city. There they dived into the sewers and split into several groups. The mantrailers could not find any clear tracks. We now believe that they have moved to an unmonitored area, changed trains, and are now on their way to another city or a safe house. Roadblocks have been activated without success.

Further procedure ..."

Mr. Tanaka stood up, pulled Kaito behind him and said on his way out, "Find the girl as fast as you can, where shall I take you?"

"I can only help you if the girl is hidden in the forest and if it has already been searched, then..."

"Who knows, maybe something has been overlooked, just systematically go through everything that makes sense to you," he interrupted him as they got into the car.

"Take me to the eastern forest, to the leasehold I want to buy."

Mr. Tanaka stepped on the gas, but the drive would take a while, Kaito knew. Should he ask more questions? But in the short time available, it was only possible to search the forest anyway, if the little beasts could be persuaded to do so at all. "Well, if not, threats always help," he thought.

"Wait, father," Kaito said suddenly, lost in thought and wondering about himself. "Buy a bottle or two of sake or schnapps quickly, then it'll be easier to negotiate."

Mr. Tanaka looked at his son for a moment. He had heard a lot of nonsense and garbage during his time in the service and had learned to recognize it. He looked at his son again and understood that he was not joking. He turned off the road and stopped in front of a 24-hour convenience store, stormed in without saying a word, and stormed out with two bottles of sake.

A short time later, he and his car were at the end of a country road. They all got out and walked a few hundred meters together across the adjacent field until they reached the beginning of a wooded area. Mr. Tanaka took one of the bottles he had brought with him, gave it to Kaito and said quickly, "Come on, what now?"

Kaito said to Dawn, "Stay a little behind me," walked to the edge of his lease and yelled, "EVERYONE HERE, NOW!"

Mr. Tanaka suddenly felt a strong gust of wind in his face and heard the trees groan. The wind died down and it was quiet again. It was calmer than before, he thought, and a cold shiver ran down his spine.

Kaito opened a bottle of sake and placed it in a spot at the edge of the forest where it was clearly visible in the bright moonlight.

"I am looking for a girl, seven years old, her name is Nao, she was kidnapped by humans and may be hidden somewhere in the great eastern forest between the sea and the mountain peaks. Find her and take this as your first payment. If you find her, there will be much more," Kaito said and listened.

Mr. Tanaka said nothing. He still wasn't sure if Kaito was just a good actor or if this was all real, but now every second and every bit of help counted. Anything could be decisive. Every possibility had to be considered and Kaito had already solved so many problems in his strange way, why not here? At the moment, he couldn't help much anyway, so he just listened, no matter what happened here.

He looked down at the bottle and thought, "Huh, it's empty. Kaito couldn't have finished it, even if he had distributed it, he would have noticed it. He had seen him open it and put it down. He wanted to ask questions when Kaito said.

"Why not?

"Okay, if you had it, could you do it?"

"Okay, I'll get it, wait here," Kaito said and turned to Mr. Tanaka.

"It's like I thought, Ayakashi can't do much with descriptions of people or names, they need something the girl's aura has transferred to, then they can find that aura. Sorry, I should have said it right away."

"I only understand half of it, where are we supposed to get it from, what would that be?" asked Mr. Tanaka.

"Well, it would have to be an object, not a living being. Something that was very important to this girl over a long period of time."

Mr. Tanaka looked at Kaito and after a few seconds of silence, he asked excitedly, "If a mantrailer already has it on his nose, will it work?"

"Yes, no problem."

"Wait here, I'll be right back," he said and ran to the car.

Kaito wanted to yell "FATHER BEWARE" after him, but he refrained and said to himself, "Mr. Tanaka, drive carefully," and looked at Dusk and Dawn, who were looking at each other from a meter away.

"Dusk, leave Dawn alone, you know she doesn't like dark energy. How's the forest I entrusted to you, has anything happened lately?" said Kaito to another cat-like creature, with much darker hair, dark eyes and clothes just as skimpy as Dawn's, only much darker. He grinned a little, but was too tired for mind games.

"No, except for a few wanderers and schoolchildren who got lost, no one has come by here yet, meow. There are fifteen new Ayakashi, and I've driven away three evil yokai. How about rewarding me, meow?"

"The sake should be enough for now, and isn't it important that you protect your home?"

"Dawn gets divine energy from you and what about me, I want dark energy, meow."

"Jealous cat," Kaito thought and said, "Look around, there's way too much wafting around here anyway. Did you have a fight or did you vanquish the three Yokai?"

"Bah," Dusk said and looked away.

"Has she gotten even stronger, more confident, or is that just my imagination? With the amount of negative energy here, it would be no wonder," he thought and asked a small Ayakashi next to Dusk, "What happened here that there is so much dark energy, will you tell me?" and he thought he knew this little fur ball from somewhere.

"I don't talk to humans and only take orders from Boss Dusk."

Kaito grinned as he recognized the Ayakashi as the one from school, took a step forward, grabbed him, who protested loudly, and threw him full force about 20 meters into the bushes at the edge of the forest, watching with a grin as he picked himself up and cursed. Still laughing, Kaito turned to Dusk and asked again, "What exactly happened here and when did you become the boss?

"Well, find out, great forest master of men, meow," Dusk said, laughing as well and jumping a few meters into the forest.

"If you find the girl by sunset, we can talk about another reward," he said when he heard Mr. Tanaka's car.

A couple of smaller Ayakashi annoyed Dawn and Kaito said to them, "If Dawn strikes and you become stardust, that's your problem, than", which in turn distracted them and Dawn took a leap at them, lunging and stopping just short of them.

The Ayakashi fled screaming and Dawn started to follow them, but Dusk stood in her way, hissing at her.

"Hey you two, stop it, here comes Mr. Tanaka with the aura you're supposed to be looking for and no arguments," Kaito said.

"Who is Dawn hissing at?" asked Mr. Tanaka and handed Kaito a stuffed animal in a bag.

"Dusk, Dawn's sister, but she's an Ayakashi and they don't get along as well as I'd like. I told you that before."

"I don't see Dawn's sister, where is she?"

"Since she's an Ayakashi, you can't see her either, the fact that humans can see Dawn at all is a miracle in itself. It's rare for divine beings to incarnate directly into a body."

"Okay, I don't know what you're talking about, what's next?" asked Mr. Tanaka.

Kaito opened the bag, folded it so that he would not touch the stuffed animal but could throw it, and threw it in a short arc to Dusk.

Here and now, Mr. Tanaka was convinced that the world as he knew it so far was not what he saw. The stuffed animal that Kaito had thrown in an arc towards a bush ... it had, how should he put it ... just disappeared just before it hit the ground, just gone, like enchanting, like a magic trick, or rather like in a comic strip from childhood, where it went 'PUFF' and something disappeared. The moon was shining brightly, the trajectory of the cuddly toy was clearly visible, no excuse that it was too dark or a trick was possible here.

He didn't know what he should or wanted to ask and was thinking about it when Kaito started to speak, "That should do it, make sure you find the girl and no, you can't keep the cuddly toy, give it back.

Another strong gust of wind and the toy fell to the ground in front of Mr. Tanaka as if from nowhere. Kaito picked it up with the inside of the bag, put the bag back over it and closed it. He turned to Mr. Tanaka and said, "I'll stay here with Dawn. I'll let you know if they find anything."

"Are you sure?"

"It's a warm, cloudless summer night and I'm tired, I'll be fine, Dawn will take care of me," Kaito said, going into the forest and looking for a suitable corner to lie down.

He had done this many times as a child. But Mr. Tanaka didn't know that. He only knew the reason, but not the consequences, Kaito thought.

Tired and in no mood to argue, he cut his thumb and gave Dawn some blood, enriched with a large amount of transmuted divine energy. Dawn would watch over him, he knew that, wrote a message to Mio that he would be late on Monday and she wouldn't have to look for him and fell asleep.

"Meow, meow, meow," she made in front of him and he thought he was still dreaming, but he woke up and saw Dawn and Dusk sitting in front of him.

"The two pretty catgirls together, that's cute, what's up?" said Kaito as he stretched and thought about what he was doing here in the forest.

Dusk grinned, "Your master seems to have had perverted dreams, Meow," Dusk said to Dawn and laughed maliciously.

"We found them, and Dusk is just jealous," Dawn said quickly.

"Hey, wait a minute, you ratty would-be messenger of the gods, I found her and where's my reward, Meow?"

Kaito realized the seriousness of the situation. He had completely forgotten about the mayor's daughter and had not expected Dusk to find anything. Now he was wide awake, the adrenaline drove him on.

"Where?" Kaito asked. Dusk stopped her discussion with Dawn and began to explain the way while Kaito moved the satellite view of the map program with his fingers according to Dusk's instructions.

"That should be it, Meow. A house with red wooden walls and a field of flowers around it," Dusk said.

"Kaito looked at the smartphone and thought, "Crap, two and a half years old and winter view," zoomed in on the house he found, turned the smartphone to Dusk and asked, "Is this it?"

"Huh? Meow?" Dusk asked back, looking at the thing in front of her.

Dawn laughed, "Stupid dark forest kitty, don't know what a smartphone is."

"Shut up," he said loudly and they both fell silent. He looked at the picture in front of him, looking for a clear anchor point for Dusk as he asked, "How do you know she's right there?"

"The house seems cold, but her aura is deeper in the center of the house and can be clearly felt, meow," Dusk said.

Kaito shuddered and asked, "Is she still alive in the human world?"

"Yes, meow, I say," Dusk confirmed and Kaito realized once again that Ayakashi who have little contact with humans logically have a hard time understanding human life.

For them, a cold house means that it is uninhabited, that you can't see inside, that the windows are probably barred. Everything should look uninhabited. Probably a trick of the kidnappers.

An aura that is 'deeper' does not necessarily mean that it is buried, but that it is held in the basement of the house.

Now he found a possible anchor and said, "Describe to me the nearest rocks around the house.

"30 human steps north is a pointy white rock and 40 steps southwest is a gray round rock, meow."

Kaito's heart pounded, it was correct, had she really found her? What if the information was wrong and Dusk had just tricked him?

"Are there other people in the house?"

"Yes, four, meow."

"Why didn't you say so?"

"I was supposed to look for one aura, Meow."

"It's all right, thank you," he said, patting her head.

Kaito copied the GPS data and took a screenshot, "and go," he said, hitting the send button on his messenger.

Less than ten seconds later, the phone rang.

"YOU HAVE THEM?" came the question from the phone.

"Look what I wrote. Check that house, I'm 70% sure she's there."

There was silence, then a "wait," then silence again.

"If Dusk says her aura is there, then it's there. We cats can sense auras very well," Dawn said.

"You're not lying to me, are you?" asked Kaito Dusk.

"Do I get a reward if I lie, too, Meow?"

"No, you silly cat, definitely not!"

"100% sure," Kaito said loudly into his smartphone.

"We'll pick you up in 20 minutes," someone said and hung up.

"Reward?" asked Dusk.

"Later, when we have the child alive, you'll get a large amount."

"Meow, but I want it now."

"Like little children," Kaito thought and wrote to Mr. Tanaka to bring some food.

He drew a protective circle in the ground and said to Dawn, "Get two meters behind me," and you, dark kitty, get into the circle, cutting his finger lightly and said, "*DARK ENERGY*".

"Enough, if we get the girl alive there'll be plenty more and I don't want to hear any more until then."

"Meow," Dusk said sardonically and looked at Dawn.

Kaito went to the street and saw that Dawn was depressed. "You'll get something later," he said as she looked down sadly.

"Meow. The lazy would-be goddess didn't do anything," Dusk meowed.

Kaito was glad when he saw an SUV coming towards him and said to the two, "Come along and be quiet."

Mr. Tanaka and another man got out and waved Kaito over.

"This is Mr. Kimura, the head of operations," Mr. Tanaka said and Kaito recognized the man from the briefing.

"What makes you think the girl is there?" he asked, scrutinizing him.

Kaito was angry with Mr. Tanaka, his father, "what was that about, was he supposed to give Mr. Kimura a crash course in Ayakashi science or what did his great police-man father have in mind," he thought.

"Sorry, I have to decline, business secret. I know the hut there, it should be empty," he lied, "you haven't found any trace yet, so another check with a drone would be a sensible and negligible little effort, or am I looking at it wrong?"

Mr. Kimura rolled his eyes, looked at Mr. Tanaka who smiled at him, picked up a radio and gave the order for a VIS/IR drone to double check the transmitted GPS data and said to Kaito, "So you know there's someone in the building who shouldn't be there?

"That's right."

"You won't say how you know that."

"Right."

"Status?" Mr. Kimura asked into the radio.

"Anubis-4 drone in direct overflight, high resolution VIS and IR data available. Analysis commencing, over," a voice came back.

"Final result?" asked Mr. Kimura.

"Final result?" Mr. Kimura asked again and louder.

"One moment, please."

Silence and a short time later, "One person in the entrance area visually confirmed, weak infrared differences signatures indicate possible additional persons in the building, person identification has begun, please give further instructions, over."

"Compare with first pass yesterday, over?"

"That was negative, but not high resolution, over."

"Subject identified, three convictions for assault, no outstanding warrants, over."

Mr. Kimura's eyes widened, "Reconnaissance of the area, transmit data to HQ immediately, over."

"This is Alpha-1, new target identified, coordinates transmitted, prepare ground drones to drop in target area, position special units according to reconnaissance data, over."

"Mr. Tanaka, drive, I'll tell you which way to go," Mr. Kimura said.

Kaito was about to go back into the forest when Mr. Kimura said, "Everybody in the car, even the cat if you have to.

Kaito kept his thoughts to himself and said, "Everybody in, let's go," pointing to the open car door. Dawn jumped into the backseat and Dusk followed her.

Kaito looked at Dusk, who was probably sitting in a car for the first time and looked out of the window with interest.

Mr. Kimura tapped his fingers nervously on the armrest. You could tell that he had some questions for Kaito and wanted to turn to him and grill him, but he didn't and Kaito was quite happy about that.

Mr. Tanaka then simply turned the SUV into a meadow on Mr. Kimura's instructions and drove towards a wooded area behind a meadow hill.

As the car drove over the crest of the hill into the hollow, Kaito was amazed to see that two vehicles with heavily armed special forces personnel had already gathered there, and Kaito had to respectfully acknowledge, "Yes, they were very fast."

A man approached Mr. Kimura, greeted him, and reported that a ground drone unit had approached the house and the tripwires had been identified, but they had not yet been able to get a look inside the house. The man handed Mr. Kimura a tablet with a live visual feed of the area around the house, with the identified person's line of sight permanently marked. A red dot on the image was presumably the position of the ground drone approaching the house from behind.

Impressive, Kaito thought and stroked Dawn.

"Kaito, can you give us a look inside the house?" asked Mr. Tanaka, clearly audible to Mr. Kimura.

"Dusk could," he replied sullenly, not really wanting to give the Special Forces man too much information. He was a federal officer, after all.

"Do you need an inside look?", Mr. Tanaka asked Mr. Kimura directly.

"Sure, as soon as possible. We have no proof that the target is in there. So we can't just storm the house," he said, looking back and forth between Kaito and Mr. Tanaka in disbelief.

"Dusk, look around the house, go to the girl in the basement, look around and pass everything on to Dawn. Don't touch anything and don't draw attention to yourself."

"What do I get for it, Meow?"

"Always the same with these Ayakashi," he thought, took Dusk by the right ear, shook her head slightly and said, "If the girl is rescued safe and sound, you'll get your reward."

Kimura watched, frowned, and said nothing. Hundreds of special forces had combed the woods but found nothing. This boy had found something that had been overlooked, it was the only useful clue so far. So he would pretend that he hadn't seen a boy talking to an imaginary person, reaching into the air and talking to a cat.

Kaito opened the door of the car and a small gust of wind surprised Mr. Kimura who was still thinking.

Dusk was fast, Kaito saw, faster than Dawn. She jumped up the hill, past the special forces who had posted themselves there, and was already gone.

She was probably heading straight for the house now, which was hard to see even from the hill through the trees.

A little later, Dawn meowed for all to hear, and Kaito thought about how he could tell Mr. Kimura what Dusk had told Dawn telepathically.

Dusk and Dawn were sisters, born at the same time from a coherent fusion of positive and negative energy. Ten times hitting the jackpot in the lottery had a higher probability, he knew from Shy.

Even he was only vaguely aware of the abilities the two of them possessed and how they were connected. For example, there was direct telepathy over medium distances. They could not communicate over long distances, but they always knew in which direction the other was.

"It's a shame that they don't get along, because together with Dusk they would be an unbeatable team. The three of us should open a detective agency," Kaito thought and had to grin.

"What are you laughing at, Mr. Tanaka?", Mr. Kimura asked Kaito.

"The girl is in the basement, sitting in a corner, hands and feet tied, but she's fine. Three other people are sitting at a table about three meters away from the girl, between her and the stairs that lead directly to the entrance of the house. The three people are armed. There's a dim light coming in directly above the girl, there seems to be an entrance there, wait," Kaito said to Mr. Kimura, who listened motionlessly.

"Tell Dusk to look carefully from the outside to see what the entrance looks like where the light comes in," Kaito said to Dawn, looking at Mr. Kimura who was watching passively and didn't make a face.

"It's a vertical basement window, protected by a horizontal grate, like you often find in basements. It's mostly covered with branches and leaves," Kaito said to Mr. Kimura.

"Ground unit! Basement window on the north side covered with branches and leaves. Have the ground drone check it out and make visual contact with the target if possible, over," Mr. Kimura said into the radio.

"Rodger, switch to ground drone, over," it came back.

Mr. Kimura placed the tray in front of him so that Kaito and Mr. Tanaka could also see it, and this now showed the view of the ground drone moving slowly forward, while on a second PiP, a picture-in-picture, the person outside could be seen continuing to stand guard in the entrance of the house, looking bored. The drone reached the location that Kaito transmitted to Mr. Kimura.

Dawn meowed and Kaito said frantically, "Tell Dusk to leave the drone alone."

Mr. Kimura frowned again and said into the radio, "Use the sensors only, any manual changes could increase the light incidence and give us away."

"Analysis complete," it came back, "access confirmed, please request authorization to use the Endoscope lance, over."

"Authorized, over."

Then the video switched back. First there was little to see, then a room, and now three people at a table, Mr. Kimura swallowed.

"Tell her to go to the girl and take care of her," Kaito said to Dawn and Mr. Kimura nodded at him.

"Do you see the ground in front of the window? The target should be there, over," Mr. Kimura said over the radio.

"Negative, and breaking the glass is too risky," came the reply.

"Can you see the girl if she gets up?" Kaito asked Mr. Kimura.

"Can you see the target when he is 50 centimeters away from the wall, the target is 120 centimeters tall?" Mr. Kimura repeated into the radio.

"Analysis in progress, hold on," came the reply.

"Positive, the face would be in the drone's field of view."

"Can you get her to stand up?" asked Mr. Kimura.

"Dawn, ask Dusk if she can, the girl is young, maybe she can?" Kaito said and Dawn meowed, she had understood what Kaito meant and told Dusk to try to project her thoughts onto the girl, she should stand up and ask for food and then sit down again if there was no answer. Suddenly, a radio transmission came through.

"Fourth person identified," the radio said, and everyone looked at the tablet. The back of a young girl's head was clearly visible, but only her long dark hair was visible.

Kaito yelled at Dawn, "SHE SHOULD LOOK AT THE CEILING OR THE WALL BEHIND HER."

Suddenly the girl looked up and everyone in the car looked into the face of a frightened, crying girl who sat back down as she winced.

"Prepare access. The safety of the target is paramount. Eliminate three hostage takers in the basement, take no risks, take the fourth alive if possible," Mr. Kimura said into the radio after seeing the girl's face. Kaito considered using Shy, but immediately rejected the idea; what followed was the people's job, and he had already given away too much information anyway.

"Taking hostages is a capital crime, and if innocent people are endangered in the process, this state will not compromise, and that's a good thing," Kaito thought, when suddenly Mr. Kimura grabbed his arm and said, "Do you know what that box is?" He pointed to a box in the room near the girl and Kaito realized that Mr. Kimura feared a bomb that could lead to the hostage-takers' final triumph in case of an attack.

"Dusk, what's in the box next to the girl?" he said to Dawn.

"Air, wood and some dark energy," she replied.

Kaito said it was empty and then explained to Mr. Kimura the best way from the front door to the basement area and mentioned two small barriers the hostage-takers had set up. He relayed all this to the special forces soldier.

"In position, audio link to target established," came the radio.

Dawn meowed and Kaito yelled, "No, don't do that, watch the girl. Damn it!" and he looked at the tray, where you could see that the box was suddenly moving.

"Wait," Mr. Kimura said into the radio.

Mr. Kimura saw one of the men get up and run to the box while his gun was still on the table. He kicked with his foot and kicked the box towards the girl, laughing, "Dirty rat, go to the brat and tease her."

"ACCESS," Mr. Kimura said over the radio as the man on the screen laughed and chased after a rat that jumped out from under the box, the trajectory showing that it was empty.

"Dusk, watch out for the girl," Kaito repeated as he watched the man collapse outside on the PIP screen. A short time later, the image of the basement brightened, the cellar door opened and the men jumped up, two of them immediately fell back to the ground, but the third was only hit in the leg or hip and still moved towards the girl, lowering a gun in her direction and ... Mr. Kimura's breath caught, why didn't the pig fall down, at least they could have hit the upper body, or did the other two intercept the first volley of bullets meant for him ... Suddenly, there was a kind of hissing sound and the man screamed, raised his gun again instead of lowering it, and was riddled with bullets.

Kaito, himself startled by the scene, quickly looked at Dawn. Relieved, he saw that Dawn was sitting next to him. Was it Dusk who had intervened? How had she done that? Had she been able to materialize? No, he thought that was unlikely. He would probably question her later and thought to himself "now he's playing the annoying policeman" and grinned.

Everything else was almost routine, he watched as the units picked up the girl and brought the crying child safely and very quickly out of the house to a vehicle. He thought of Koji, who had acted just as quickly in the cave as these people here in the house, and said to himself, "He would be better off in a unit like this than in the Order. He was about to get out of the car when Mr. Kimura and Mr. Tanaka stopped him and both said the same thing: "Not so fast.

Kaito rolled his eyes and sat back down.

On the way back to the city, he had to endure a few questions, but to Mr. Tanaka's annoyance, he blocked most of them with the words "business secret" and "please fill out an order form". When pressed, he explained that an Ayakashi had given him this information. He pretended to know nothing about the rat, which was more like a bigger mouse, which was a lie, of course, and he was supposed to give Dusk an earful for putting the mouse under the box. But in the end it had helped, she probably wanted a reward for that too.

"That will be expensive," Kaito thought and explained clearly to Mr. Kimura that he should please understand that his own people were responsible for the success of the operation, which he accepted wordlessly after a few more seconds. What was he supposed to write in the official report? His job was done. Who exactly was behind it, how the hostage-takers had gotten so close to the mayor's daughter, and most importantly, how they had managed to disappear and hide here after the kidnapping, was a matter for another department to investigate, and he looked to his old military friend, Mr. Tanaka. Tanaka, who had always surrounded himself with strange people, like himself for example, and now with the high school student in front of him, he thought and let the strange little unassuming boy and his equally strange cat off near the city center at Mr. Tanaka's request.

Kaito strolled through the city center for a while, sat down in a café and thought about what would happen next. His biggest worry was how he would explain everything to Mio and what would happen to him if he didn't tell her when she found out. Then he went to the office. It was afternoon as he walked up the stairs to his apartment and office, "I wonder if Mio was there yet," he thought.

Yes, she was there, watching the news where the kidnapping case was now being broadcast as a special program all over the country. She looked at him and said smugly, "You have some explaining to do."

It was a long afternoon. All the parts of the story involving Dusk, Dawn's sister, had to be repeated three times, and since he had no better answer to the question of why he hadn't introduced her to Dusk than "Because you can't see her," there was trouble.

After about four hours, the scare was over and Mio went home with a happy and satisfied face.

"Dawn, how do you think Dusk managed to stop that man?" he asked Dawn, although he could tell that Dawn was unhappy and jealous because she was playing second fiddle at the moment.

"You should know, shouldn't you?" she replied somewhat sarcastically, "in a stressful situation, and then in uncomfortably confined spaces like this basement, dark, powerful spirits can manifest themselves in people's minds, distracting them and causing reactions. The fact that even we could hear her hissing shows us that she has really grown in the last few years," she continued sulking.

Kaito understood, of course, he should have known that, took a book from the shelf, flipped through it and got stuck on 'Chapter 11. Dark Beings and their Influence on Humans'. "I'll probably read that again," he thought, put the book down on the table, went over to Dawn, hugged her and said, "Starting tomorrow, we're going to raise your status."

Dawn mewed, embarrassed and happy.

Since Mio didn't let up about Dusk the next day either, Kaito made her a suggestion.

She was supposed to bring the rewards to Dusk and tease out just how strong she was. The plan was to give her the reward only if Mio could be sure that it was really Dusk.

Mio was on fire and set off without hesitation. "It will take a while until she comes back," Kaito thought and drew a sealing circle with blood on a large sheet of paper. He knew that the only dangerous thing about Mio's mission was that he had hidden the fact that he was going to supply Dawn with a huge amount of positive divine energy in the meantime and that he didn't want Mio there. "The Aya-kashi in the forest are harmless pipsqueaks compared to Mio when she finds out," he said aloud to the room and Dawn gave a questioning "Meow?

Throughout the day, Kaito had been giving Dawn a huge burst of divine energy, and Dawn had been trying to trans-form as the cat god had told her to. Kaito hadn't expected her to succeed after only one day, something that took the gods hundreds or even thousands of years. But he secretly hoped that they would be able to achieve an effect by the end of the year.

Towards evening, Mio stormed back into the office, over-joyed.

She told him that she had ordered Dusk to sit in front of her five times when she wanted the reward from Kaito, and Kaito laughed at how Dusk had reacted. But after the second time, she felt a presence clinging to her and her body grew heavier and when she took a step back, she heard a soft but insolent voice in her head, "Meow, give me, give me you human female, meow" or something like that. She ordered her again to sit down and show herself to her, but nothing happened.

"You didn't run away?" Kaito asked amused.

"No way, I shook her off and told her once again that I would leave with the reward if she didn't sit down. Then everything was quiet. I opened the box, wanted to put it in front of me, but it was all gone in a flash," she said proudly.

After that, she had called for another 30 minutes to show herself, but the presences had been swept away and she had gone back.

Kaito was glad that Mio was happy and that he would be spared another trip to Dusk. Kaito told Mio that he would take care of Dawn's status starting tomorrow.

Before Mio could combine, he left the office, saying he had to go shopping and saying goodbye for the day.

About two weeks later, Mr. Tanaka suddenly appeared in the office and Kaito had a bad feeling.

"What's wrong?" asked Kaito.

"You, or rather all of you, have an invitation from the mayor," said Mr. Tanaka and Kaito grimaced.

"I wasn't part of it," Mio corrected.

"Mio, you're responsible for making sure that this one," and Mr. Tanaka pointed at Kaito, "is well-behaved, well-mannered, disciplined and oh, you know."

Mio grinned, Kaito growled, Dawn meowed.

"The girl keeps talking about a cat-girl who whispered to her when she was in the hands of the kidnappers. That wasn't Dawn, was it?"

"No, that was Dusk, but there's no way she's coming with us."

"Why?"

"Damn, because she's a dark Ayakashi, she doesn't like people and if anything, she only listens to me, no idea if and what will happen if she comes along," Kaito said, getting louder.

"Okay, but Dawn is coming with you, right?"

"Of course Dawn is coming with me, I won't leave her alone."

"Here's the invitation, see you soon," Mr. Tanaka said and left the office.

Kaito was in a bad mood and left the office without a word. Mio started to say something, but Dawn stopped her with a loud meow.

A few days later, Mio was wearing the evening dress that Mrs. Harrington had given her. When Kaito saw it, he was about to roll his eyes when Mio explained that Mr. Tanaka had given her permission and had even said that a beautiful fairy was desired.

Kaito had dressed rather casually and was already stressed and annoyed, how was he supposed to get through the evening?

A limousine picked them up on time and brought them to the Takahashi's large estate.

Mr. and Mrs. Takahashi were waiting for them personally at the entrance and accompanied them into the reception room where, to Kaito's surprise, Mr. Kimura and two other men were already waiting. "I knew he wouldn't tell me, why should he?" thought Kaito and would have preferred to leave again.

Ms. Takahashi introduced those present. The chief of police, who coordinated the logistics of the special forces, and a professor of child psychology, who treated her daughter, were the two men he didn't know. Kaito was only briefly mentioned as the person who had tipped off the special forces about the hostage-takers' hideout, which Kaito was very happy about. Mrs. Takahashi led everyone into the large dining room, beaming with joy, and personally assigned everyone a seat. Dawn sat between Mio and Kaito, which to Kaito's surprise seemed to surprise only him, since no one in the room was surprised that a cat was given a place at the table. Kaito accepted it and was glad that Dawn was sitting next to him, even though he kept his thoughts to himself.

A little later, Nao, the daughter of the Takahashi family, arrived and, to everyone's surprise, ran up to Dawn, petted her, thanked her and then joined her mother in thanking everyone. "Brave girl," Mio thought when she saw Kaito and noticed that he was taking it all very calmly.

After everyone had toasted to Nao and her successful rescue, they moved on to a leisurely meal. Kaito sat next to Mr. Kimura, who made no effort to say anything, which suited Kaito just fine. The professor's wife was the first to talk to Mio about her evening gown, indirectly telling Mio that it must have cost several hundred thousand yen. Mio glamorously tried not to let the news get to her, which she only half succeeded in, and Kaito excused himself to go out for a moment before he was the one who started laughing this time. Kaito went to the restroom, watching Nao and Dawn playing in a corner of the dining room. Nao was talking to Dawn and Dawn meowed back. A little later, Kaito washed his hands and walked back, just before he reached the dining hall, he heard a voice next to him. "Hey, boy." Kaito looked over. Mr. Kimura stood on a balcony and looked into the starry night over the city.

"Do you want to go back to the table, even though you hate this ideal world of family gatherings as much as I do?" he asked Kaito and motioned for him to join him.

"Did you know that I know Mr. Tanaka from the military?" he asked and Kaito immediately realized that Mr. Kimura knew that Mr. Tanaka was not his biological father.

"No, but I thought you must know each other, otherwise the day would have been different."

"Damn right. You really are a smart boy. That Tanaka is a real phenomenon. He has a feel for situations and people like no other. I'll never forgive him for switching to this ridiculous police service instead of joining the special forces with me," he said, looking at Kaito and laughing.

"I'm sure you want to go home, me too! It's nice that little Nao can laugh again, but I'm done with this family world. Shall I tell you why?" asked Mr. Kimura.

Kaito was about to say "No" when Mr. Kimura started.

"My wife died when I was on a mission for our country, that was back then... never mind, I forgot. She died in the arms of my daughter, who begged me to come back, which I couldn't do at the time, it just wasn't possible. We haven't spoken since. She married a foreigner and left the country I defended, and I have never seen her since. What a shitty world," he said, drained the glass in one go, looked at it and said, "1000 yen in one go, not bad, right?"

Kaito was silent, many thoughts and questions were running through his head, but he could neither organize them nor form a sentence.

"You're probably wondering why I, the old sad man, am telling you this!"

"Yes, exactly, he's right, that was going through his head too," he thought.

"Are you with that cute little girl you brought?"

"No," he said quickly.

"Then make it happen, or find yourself another sweetheart. You'll go far with your abilities, and then you'll need someone at your side!"

"And if you find one, take better care of her than I did, protect her with all your strength," he said and put a hand on Kaito's shoulder.

"I already have a girlfriend," Kaito said.

"Then I won't have said anything and if there is ever any stress in your relationship, think back to this day. The image of how harmonious the Takahashis are now and how divided they'll be when we're gone and make it better. Just go to Nao, talk to her for two sentences and you'll have talked to her more than Mrs. Takahashi did that day," he said, winking at him and walking towards the dining room.

"Sad old man, I will, for sure," Kaito thought and followed him.

Mio was just blossoming and was the number one conversation starter. "Go talk to the others," Kaito thought and looked at Dawn who was still playing with Nao. He went over to Dawn and Nao and said in children's language, "Hello Nao, are you playing well too?"

"Yes," she beamed back, "but she annoys me."

"What does she do?" he asked with a smile.

"When she wants to know something from me, she's a pretty girl and begs very sweetly, when I want to know how she can change, she's a cat again and always meows as an answer."

Kaito fell silent, what had the girl just said? Children, like Mio's brother, could see Dawn in her divine form, but he could only see her in her divine form, not this way and that.

He looked at Dawn who was sitting grinning next to Nao who was hugging her and Kaito started to understand and whispered to Nao, "It's a secret of the cat world, if you're all sweet and keep it to yourself until you grow up and then ask her, she'll tell you how she do it."

He turned around, walked back to the table, grabbed a glass of alcohol, took a sip, and thought to himself triumphantly, "What a perfect day."

A few weeks later, Dawn was actually able to manifest. At first she could only hold this state for a few seconds, then a few minutes, but it was enough for Mio to freak out completely, be in permanent photo mode, and make party plans including school enrollment for Dawn, which of course overwhelmed Dawn. Kaito took away her smartphone, which she got only back when she calmed down.

Dawn could manifest herself in different ways, as a human or a cat person, as she wished. Or she could show herself as a cat person only to small children, because they were even more receptive to spirits than adults, just like she had done with Nao.

"Very practical," Kaito thought and was excited himself.

Each time she was strengthened by the positive energy, the duration of her manifestation would increase. It would not be long before it would last for one or even several days. All this thanks to his enormous powers, which not only the spirit world feared so much.

Chapter 14 - RABEN

Some time later, Dawn went shopping with Mio and occasionally met up with Mio and her friends, whom she introduced as distant relatives of Kaito or Mr. Tanaka, who would now be living and working here in Japan.

One day, the mayor, Mr. Takahashi, presented a very beautiful, flawless woman with a certificate of naturalization for special services to the fatherland and wished her, Dawn Tanaka, all the best for the future.

Kaito was a little annoyed by Mio's enthusiasm, but put up with it for a while and was about to reprimand Mio when the office doorbell rang.

A neat, middle-aged woman entered the room and introduced herself as Yoko Nishimura, manager of Star-AA-Sun, a management agency. She needed an expert opinion on a problem with an artist. But she demanded discretion, she explained as she looked around the office.

Kaito was glad that Mio and Dawn had bought some new things in the office together, but Mrs. Nishimura still didn't seem to like it.

"Snipe," Kaito thought and handed her a contract.

Then she said that her artist Reiko-Lucie Yoshida was being harassed by a Yokai and that Kaito should please explain to the young lady that it was just her imagination or he should get rid of the problem.

She went on to explain that this Yokai would come into her bedroom in the evening when Reiko-Lucie was asleep and disappear again when she woke up.

"Put a stop to it," she said. "After all, Reiko-Y-Lu, as she called her, is at the peak of her career and she have to worry about making money," she continued, simply asking when the woman, and she pointed at Mio, could come over to solve the problem.

"Snipe goulash," Kaito thought to himself, "would that taste good?" he wondered.

Mio grinned to herself, cleared her throat and explained to Ms. Nishimura how a case with a Yokai would generally proceed. Kaito leaned back in his new chair and thought of his English teacher, "What was her name?" Anyway, the similarities between the two were unmistakable. "Maybe the undead has a great-great-granddaughter," he thought and went to the kitchen, "Mio will take care of it," he was sure of that. And so it finally happened. Mrs. Nishimura signed the contract, got a copy as usual and made an appointment to catch Reiko-Lucie or the Yokai.

"God, I was nervous, now we get to meet the super idol Reiko-Lucie Yoshida aka Reiko-Y-Lu herself," she said to Dawn and Kaito, who both looked at each other a little strangely.

"You're not telling me that you don't know Reiko-Y-Lu," she said louder.

"No," Kaito said. "Is that something to eat?" he asked sarcastically.

"You're only allowed to come with us because I made it clear to her that only you can solve the problem and don't you dare make a fool of us."

"Well, look who's talking," Kaito wanted to say, but stopped himself and said instead, "Well, see you tomorrow night, that could be really fun, come on Dawn, let's go buy an idol, ... uh, something to eat," Kaito said and walked to the door and out of the office, while Mio called after him, "what the hell is that supposed to mean, 'that could be fun'".

The next evening, they stood in front of Reiko-Lucie's apartment and were let in by Ms. Nishimura shortly after. Reiko-Lucie was very, very pretty and obviously very charismatic, a typical idol. Even without make-up, she had a self-confident, charismatic elegance.

Her long, straight, black hair reminded Kaito of Dusk, her rather light green eyes of Dawn.

She greeted Kaito and the others rather coolly and asked Mio if she was or wanted to be an idol, which she quickly denied, but obviously flattered her. Then she looked at Kaito, then at Dawn, then back at Mio and Kaito thought "Snipe number two".

Reiko-Lucie then explained to Mio that she had been woken up in the evening by noises in her room and that she had always noticed a strange flickering in the air that slowly disappeared through the open door that was supposed to be locked. She had grown up in the country, and this had happened once before, just before she moved to the city. She could hardly sleep and wanted the thing to go away now.

"So you're sure, snipe, that it has to go," Kaito thought and grinned.

"What's there to grin about," she said promptly without looking at him.

"Well, I think it's an Ayakashi, he probably means no harm. Could it be that you got a gift from him?" asked

Kaito, caught off guard and trying to avoid the real question while catching Mio's evil eye.

"Hm, a few days ago there was a black rose on my bedside table, I wasn't sure if I had overlooked it and then forgot to ask who it was from."

"Do you still have it?" Kaito asked, this time suppressing a grin.

"I'll get it, wait."

"Here."

"Dawn, what do you think?" Kaito asked.

Dawn meowed and Mio wondered why Dawn didn't come to the missions in her new form. It would be much easier for everyone.

"Ms. Yoshida, how about put the Ayakashi in his place?" Kaito asked.

"How am I supposed to understand that? Make him disappear!"

"I won't vanquish him if there is another way. If you tell him clearly, he won't bother you anymore. And if he does, I'll take care of him, free of charge," Kaito said.

"I can hardly see him, what am I supposed to say to a billowing mass of air?"

"You will see him, wonderfully, and then you will explain to those Ayakashi that it won't work that way, forever!"

"Why should I do that?"

Kaito thought for a moment and then said quite impressively to the group, "Because it's a chance for a positive experience you'll never get again."

Reiko-Lucie looked at Kaito and then at Mio and said to her, "He's not messing with me, is he?"

Slightly shocked, Mio replied, "He's a little strange, but he wouldn't do that. His customers are very important to him," and Mio thought, "Don't you dare, you little monster."

"How is that going to work?"

"As discussed, I'll wait here in the antechamber, they're all in your room, I'll call you when the Ayakashi is caught," Kaito said.

It was already after 1 a.m. and the voices from the bedroom faded. Kaito sat alone on the sofa and wondered if the Ayakashi would come today. Dawn was with Mio and the others. Kaito had drawn some circles on the floor. He was sure that he wouldn't need them but "better safe than sorry", he thought. Then he heard the front door open and said a little louder, "How do Ayakashi always manage to open a locked door?" and turned on the light.

It really was a raven, just as he suspected, now they looked into each other's eyes and he could see that he wanted to escape.

"If you run, I'll send you to heaven, and now let's talk. Close the door and come here," Kaito said.

"Explain to me why her?"

The door to the bedroom was flung open and Mio came running in, "Do you have him?" she asked.

"He is right in front of me ..." he didn't get any further because Reiko-Lucie shouted, "There it is, can you see it Yoko?" But Mrs. Nishimura and Mio saw nothing and Kaito shouted to the group that they should stay calm and that the Ayakashi could only be seen by him and Mrs. Yoshida.

"Why are you bothering this woman?" he repeated loudly into the room and everyone in the room fell silent.

Kaito listened while Mrs. Nishimura looked at him angrily, but at the same time she noticed that Reiko-Lucie probably didn't see this as a trick and so she let this stupid action pass. A little later, Kaito explained to those present that it was an Ayakashi who had mistaken Mrs. Yoshida for his long dead partner, since they had the same aura. The raven disagreed and told Kaito that Reiko-Lucie was really his wife, but Kaito silenced him. Dawn and Kaito already suspected this because of the rose, which had a similar aura to Reiko-Lucie's, but this was the final confirmation.

Reiko-Lucie became extremely angry and shouted, "I SHOULD HAVE THE SAME AURA AS THAT THING!"

Mio tried to mediate by explaining that auras were completely arbitrary, like hair colors, and had no meaning, though she knew Kaito saw it differently and hoped he wouldn't talk about Mio's aura.

Kaito cleared his throat and spoke, Mio winced, "He won't?"

"What I'm about to tell you, I mean it. Give the Ayakashi a drop of your blood, then you can see him. If you do that, then you alone will decide what happens to him," Kaito told Reiko-Lucie directly to her face.

Mio was shocked, but that was Kaito. Always good for a surprise.

Reiko-Lucie looked at this boy, whom she found thoroughly repulsive, but it was she who wanted something from him and he wasn't fooling her, she could see that for herself. He saw the thing in front of him, just like she did. He wasn't pretending, he saw it in the same place she did. A cheater would try to hide the position or find out about it and then look that way, but he had been looking in the right direction from the beginning. "A drop of blood," she thought, she had endured much worse to be where she was now and no one would take that away from her, not even an Ayakashi. Still, she wasn't going to make it easy for that arrogant brat.

"I can already see him," she said angrily.

"No, you only see the flickering of his spiritual energy, not his real body, and you only see this flickering because you happen to have the same aura!"

She looked at him and said, "When you lie, you walk the streets naked."

"Reiko-Lucie," Mrs. Nishimura shouted and Mio laughed out loud and said, "I'm sure no one wants to see that," which Kaito acknowledged with a scowl.

"Agreed," Kaito said and Mio couldn't believe her ears.

"Get a needle from the first aid kit, Yoko," she said, looking at Kaito as if he were a disgusting insect.

"How is that supposed to work?"

"Stick yourself with the needle and give it to my colleague. Mio will then hold it one meter in the direction of the front door."

"I won't be cursed by it or anything?"

Kaito laughed, "No." "Not in the traditional sense," he thought.

Reiko-Lucie took the syringe needle out of its original wrapping, pricked the side of her left index finger, and then handed it to Mio, who took two steps forward and then held it a meter toward the front door.

Everyone looked intently at the hypodermic needle Mio was holding in the air. If she hadn't already done so many jobs with Kaito, she would have sunk to the ground in embarrassment, but she waited to see what would happen and suddenly realized that the syringe she was holding between her thumb and index finger had been pulled out and disappeared. A little startled, she pulled her hand back, but regained her composure and stood still.

Reiko-Lucie and Ms. Nishimura continued to stare at the spot where the needle had disappeared until Reiko-Lucie screamed and fell back. Mio and Ms. Nishimura looked at Reiko-Lucie in shock. But there was nothing unusual to see except that Reiko-Lucie had just fallen backwards. Mio reached out to stop Reiko-Lucie from falling, but something was faster and they both saw Reiko-Lucie stabilize herself, float in the air for a moment like a magic trick, and then straighten up. She was clearly staring at something, very close, something that seemed to be right in front of her. "Something that has saved her falling," Mio thought immediately.

"May I introduce Kurohane, the Ayakashi who has been bothering you, now you can tell him what you think," Kaito said to Reiko-Lucie and grinned slightly cheekily.

But Reiko-Lucie stopped listening and just looked at the face of her dreams.

This beauty and elegance, paired with the gentleness and calmness in his deep blue eyes, was something she had never found in any man she had met before.

"Let me be there for you forever," the man before her said, catching her in his strong arms as she fell back, startled.

"Yes," she said, oblivious to the world around her.

Mrs. Nishimura shouted at Kaito, "What have you done, put an end to this, now".

"Should I chase the Ayakashi away, Ms. Yoshida?" Kaito asked smugly.

"Hello Ms. Yoshida, Earth to Ms. Yoshida," Kaito said a little too jokingly and Mio snorted angrily. Reiko-Lucie regained consciousness, straightened up, cleared her throat and said to Ms. Nishimura: "Starting tomorrow, I'll do whatever you want, but now shut up and sit down!" Ms. Nishimura angrily went to an armchair and sat down without saying a word.

"Mr. Tanaka, what exactly does the situation mean for me now?" asked Reiko-Lucie while she continued to look at this man.

"This Ayakashi sees you as the reincarnation of his past love, he will protect you and always watch at your side, but no one but you will ever see him. He will never grow old, but he will always be in danger, as ravens and crows like to be hunted by exorcists for training. Protect him from the humans as he will protect you from the Yokai, or let your paths part here. It's your choice," Kaito said, grinning a little and heading for the door.

"You are welcome to come by in a few days and tell me your decision," he said, opening the door as Dawn left the room.

"Oh yeah, you can't get pregnant by an Ayakashi," he said quickly and closed the door even though Mio was still inside.

"YOU FUCKING LITTLE PERVERT. Stop right there so I can smack you," came from Mio who had now torn open the door and was running after him.

A few days later, Reiko-Lucie actually came to Kaito's office with Ms. Nishimura. He hadn't expected that and was happy about the simple and positive case without any trouble, possible death or danger. He should open a dating agency for humans and Ayakashi and offer couples therapy if needed, he said to himself with a grin. "Hmm, maybe

Mio should do that better," he thought when Reiko-Lucie told Mio that she and Kurohane were together now. Ms. Nishimura accepted everything as long as the performances went well and to do that, they would have a few more questions. Mio made it clear to Reiko-Lucie that she would have to talk to Kaito about this and she accepted, even though she was visibly scowling.

Kaito was surprised by the insight of the young woman. He explained to Reiko-Lucie how she should best behave, what she had to watch out for to keep the danger as far away from her and Kurohane as possible and that living with an Ayakashi would not be easy. Especially in company that was not privy to this parallel world, one had to be very careful. The envy and fear of others would also have to be taken into account.

When Reiko-Lucie asked how he knew all this, a beautiful cat girl suddenly stood behind Kaito's chair, hugged him and said, "Because he's been living with a super cute divine kitty like me for so long.

This time it was Ms. Nishimura who fell backwards off the chair and Kaito thought, "How can this happen to an office chair that costs 50,000 yen?

Mio helped Ms. Nishimura up from the floor, who was staring at the catgirl as if she had seen a ghost, but Mio realized, "Yes, she just saw her first ghost."

Mrs. Nishimura walked around the table to Dawn, looking her up and down and touching her ears gently, but then she jumped and said, "They're real. Dawn was a little confused and Kaito guessed what came next. "Do you want to become an idol?" asked Mrs. Nishimura. "No, she don't," Kaito said energetically and led Mrs. Nishimura back to the other side of the table.

Mio wanted to say something but saw Kaito's annoyed face and left it at that. Mrs. Nishimura and Reiko-Lucie left the office a little later, almost reluctantly, but not without leaving behind three tickets for the next concert, which Mio gladly accepted.

"As long as they pay the bill," Kaito said afterwards. "Touching Dawn costs an extra hundred thousand, put it on the bill."

Mio rolled her eyes but said nothing.

"Why did you do that to Dawn?" Kaito asked angrily and Dawn meowed sadly.

"She wanted to show Ms. Nishimura and Reiko-Lucie that you can be trusted," Mio said, "so stop it."

"Okay, but never change in front of strangers again. The risk is too great. We're already attracting too much attention. Okay?"

"Meow, okay," Dawn said, her ears drooping.

Chapter 15 - SHY

Kaito looked out of the window of his office, he was bored, he hadn't had a customer in two weeks. He felt like a shark tooth dentist and laughed as he thought about sending Yokais to people's homes to get more business. He could also use Dusk and her subordinates. He quickly dismissed the thought, "It's not proper," he told himself.

Then he thought about the dinner with the mayor and Mr. Kimura. It was clear to him that Mr. Kimura had only talked to him at his father's request. What did his father want? Maybe to get him together with Mio? That was out of the question, he had to know that, they were too far apart, they only had this one thing in common. Was it his fixation on Dawn that didn't suit him? But he realized that he wouldn't find out, so he left it at that.

Dawn and Mio had just gone shopping and should be back soon anyway. He had even been persuaded to take her to the concert of, what was her name again, oh yes, Reiko-Y-Lu, together with one of Mio's friends.

She was living with the raven Ayakashi now and it had been going well for a while, he would never have thought. Love must be great, he thought when the smartphone answered. He looked at the display and saw that it was Mio trying to reach him.

"It was probably about the color of the furniture again," he thought and replied.

"DAWN HAS BEEN KIDNAPPED!" she yelled into the phone without waiting.

Kaito had to process her words, then froze and said, "Explain what happened.

"DAWN HAS BEEN KIDNAPPED! We were on our way home, she was still in her cat form, when a man behind us grabbed her from me and threw her into a car parked next to us. Then he ran away and the car drove off," she almost screamed into her smartphone.

"I'll call your father," she yelled again and hung up.

"No, wait," Kaito said, but it was already too late.

"Damn," he thought and dialed his father's number himself, but it was already busy.

"Okay, the time seems to have come," he thought and looked out of the window again, this time not at the sky but at the taller buildings about 500 meters away.

"Someone will die today, tomorrow at the latest," he thought and said, "Shy, take a look around the rooms in that building over there with the window facing us and report back to me.

It was unlikely that anyone would kill Dawn right away. Those who would kidnap her out of hatred for him weren't that stupid, he knew. The others were the ones who wanted to possess Dawn because they knew how extraordinary, desirable and unique she was. A man like Mr. Harrington or Mr. Kato might be able to afford it, but he didn't believe any of them could do it. One loathed anything spiritual, the other, according to his theory, wouldn't mess with the gods at the end of his life. That left only one. The sleazy, arrogant scumbag from back then. Someone who put his personal and professional success above the law of the land and was in a position to enforce it. Probably, really, a department head of a government agency, just as he had introduced himself here in his office at the beginning of the year, powerfully trumpeting, insisting on cooperation, only on his terms, of course.

Kaito was looking for the key to the bicycle lock, found it and put it in his pocket when the office door flew open and Mr. Tanaka burst in.

"He was quick, did he have a guilty conscience or is it fear in his eyes," Kaito thought and sat down on the sofa.

"Kaito, Mio told me everything, I'm looking for Dawn, you don't have to do anything," he said.

"I guess you're here with me now, or who's looking for Dawn?" Kaito asked sarcastically.

"I'll call some people and we'll find her for sure."

"I'll find her without you," he thought and said, "I want her back by tomorrow morning," because he knew that with every hour that Dawn was in the grip of this madman, it was getting worse for her, and Kaito had just gotten confirmation from Father that the kidnapping was state-sponsored, why else would he be pulling strings.

"Don't do anything stupid," Mr. Tanaka said to Kaito.

"I would never do that," Kaito said, smiling at his father.

Mr. Tanaka walked over to him and said again, "Promise me you won't do anything stupid, please."

"I promise not to do anything stupid," he answered Mr. Tanaka directly.

"Why don't I believe you this time? If you do something yourself, I can't help you and Dawn," he said and went to the door.

"I want her back in the morning," Kaito said as Mr. Tanaka opened the door.

"DON'T DO ANYTHING!" he ordered again and closed the door.

"I've never done anything stupid, Father," he said to himself, grinning a little as he thought about the mine in Sakura-Dori and watched out the window as Mr. Tanaka got into a car and drove away a little later.

"I hate biking," he whispered to himself a little later as he unlocked the bike and set off in the direction of East Forest.

Mio kept calling him, but he only picked up once and explained her to go home because it was too dangerous for her, then he put her on ignore in his smartphone.

It took him a long time to get to the forest and what he saw there made him really angry. Mio was standing there.

He was about to yell at her when he saw her coming towards him in tears. She was shaking and could barely get a word out except for 'I'm sorry' and 'I'm sorry'.

Instead he said, "It's not your fault, it could have happened at any time. I need to find out where she is now, and if you keep blaming yourself it will distract me too much, so stop," and took her in his arms. After a minute, he stood up and walked to the edge of the forest. "HERE DUSK, NOW," he called.

"Meow, what is it?"

"You know what it is, go find Dawn."

"Meow, what do I get for finding my stupid sister?" she said, jumping in front of him.

Mio calmed down a bit when she realized that he could find Dawn quickly with Dusk's help.

Kaito was really angry at Dusk. He imagined pushing Dusk against a tree and squeezing her throat, screaming at her that he would wipe out her existence if he didn't get Dawn back unharmed, and he wondered if he really would have done that if Mio hadn't been standing next to him.

Instead, he walked a little closer to Dusk and said slightly angrily, "You live in my forest, here I am your god and I order you to find Dawn so that you can continue to live well here and, if you are a good catgirl, get a reward from your god from time to time, especially if you and Dawn stick together and understand each other. What do you think?" he said slightly threateningly, scratching his finger, reaching for Dusk, who jumped away in fright and said, "She's far away."

"That's fine, dear kitty. Shy, come here!"

Dusk was about to say something like "Not the monster ..." but Kaito said commandingly, "Shy, as discussed, take her with you, find Dawn's whereabouts together with her and then come back to me," and Dusk disappeared before his eyes.

Mio had calmed down and Kaito told her that Shy and Dusk were now looking for Dawn. All this would take longer and she should go home.

At first, Mio wanted to know what Shy was all about, but Kaito didn't give in. He put her on her feet and told her to take her bike and ride into town with him, which Mio did.

Mio kept trying to find out what exactly was going on and if a customer had done this.

Kaito answered in the negative. But he understood that she wouldn't stop asking without an answer and would put herself in danger. So he explained to her that it was probably a government agency that wanted to research and exploit Dawn's abilities. Mio listened. She was angry, but now she understood the situation.

"How long have they been after us?" she asked.

"Minimum a year," he answered and heard Mio swallow.

He wondered if she was angry with him for never telling her. But even if she was, it wouldn't have stopped Mio from working with him on the cases.

It was already dark and quite cold. "Autumn," Kaito thought as Mio said goodbye and he made his way home.

It had been dark for a long time when he tiredly arrived at his apartment. He should have ordered Dusk here instead of going there, but no matter, in a few hours, he would know where she was and then it was up to Mr. Tanaka, he thought, staring at the ceiling, but despite his tiredness, he couldn't sleep.

All he could think about was that disgusting man's face and what kind of fool had put such an idiot in such a powerful position. After all, they weren't living in the Middle Ages or a dictatorship. The longer he thought about it, the angrier he became until he noticed that the rising sun was slowly illuminating his room.

Where are they, Kaito wondered, when he suddenly heard a meow next to him.

He turned his head. "Was that Dawn?" he asked himself, hope flooding through him.

It was Dusk and Shy, of course it wasn't Dawn, how could it have been her.

"Where is Dawn?" he asked.

"Far north, very far, deep underground," she replied.

"Coordinates!" he ordered angrily. Dusk didn't understand the word, but began to describe the route. It took him about two hours to find the location on the satellite map. Now you know I found you," he said to himself.

"Do you want to walk back or should Shy take you?" he asked Dusk, but she had already jumped out of the window without saying goodbye and Kaito thought, hopefully she still knew we were on the tenth floor.

"Come here Shy! Have you seen the building?" he said questioningly and looked to the foot of the bed.

A black sphere or round disk, you couldn't really see it because of the lack of contours, hovered over the end of the bed. It looked like a black hole, like an ideal black body with no structure on the surface. Even to him, it was just a circular black disk.

"Yes," it sounded in his head.

"Then listen to me carefully," he said, knowing that he would have to explain everything in detail to this monster. It was very intelligent and its knowledge surpassed everything he had ever seen, but it probably wanted to annoy him and didn't understand simple commands easily. You had to

give it clear commands, otherwise it could become dangerous, like one hot summer day when he had ordered Shy to
get him a drink as a joke, and suddenly there was a strange
refrigerator in his room. He never found out why he did it,
and he didn't care.

But there was one thing he had to do first. He had to call
his father and tell him what he had done, he had promised
him. He called him, "Hello father," Kaito answered.

"You call early," Mr. Tanaka said.

"I told you I wanted Dawn back with me in the morning.
Do you have her?"

"Still working on it Kaito."

"What do you know so far?"

"Like I said, I'm still working on it."

"You haven't achieved anything yet, admit it father."

"It's not that simple," Mr. Tanaka told him.

"Father, the people in this country you are so proud of
have committed a crime and violated the constitution they
are supposed to protect. Go to the mayor, tell him to use his
contacts. He owes Dawn a lot. Make him realize that," he
provoked him.

"It's not that easy Kaito, what do you think a simple
mayor can do? Look, give me some more time, I can handle
this," he said with a slight huff.

"Dawn doesn't have that much time."

"Kaito, what are you doing?"

"I'm sorry, Father," Kaito said and hung up.

"It won't take long", he thought, looking at the round
black disk that still floated motionless above the foot of his
bed in front of him and had answered "yes" in his head a
few minutes ago.

"The building Dusk showed you, where Dawn is being
held, is a building where people go about their business.
There is a fence around the building, between the building
and the fence there are just a hundred human paces, the

order I am about to give you applies only to the area inside that fence, as well as 100 paces below the fence and above it towards heaven and earth. Do you understand?"

"Yes," it rang in his head.

"Good," he thought, the distances mentioned didn't matter, but the creature now knew the area in which it could rage and carry out its orders. That was important, because the damage had to be limited.

"Dawn's safety is the highest priority. Bring her back to me unharmed. To do this, you will enter the building and eat anyone who gets in your way or could be dangerous to Dawn on the way to her. You must never compromise Dawn's safety. Therefore, you will eat your way to her as quickly as possible and when you have found her, you will bring her to me immediately and wait for further orders and now fulfill your mission," Kaito said to the black disk that disappeared before his eyes.

Father would probably be with him in an hour or half an hour if he wanted, but Shy would have solved the problem by then. Shy, the only real monster. Hundreds of demons were nothing compared to this creature. In modern times, the few who knew this being at all called it 'Creator God', almost a thousand years ago it was called 'Worldshifter'. This old name, Kaito thought, suited this being much better because it explained its unimaginable power with a single word.

Realizing that there was nothing more he could do, he closed his eyes and fell asleep.

Kaito had a dream that he really wanted to forget, why today of all days, he thought, when he saw his old self at the age of six running to his father and screaming: "Father, father help me, the monsters".

Father reached out his hand and punched Kaito in the face with full force, causing him to fall backwards and stay down.

Then another scene. He saw his mother walk up to him and say, "Your father is never coming back and it's because of you, you alone. She took a swing and hit him so hard that he fell to the floor, dazed. She went into the bathroom and ran some water, he could still hear it, but he couldn't get up, everything was spinning. Then the mother came back and picked up the dazed boy and carried him into the bathroom.

"What are you doing, Mom?" he asked. "We're having a bath," she said and dropped him. "Look at my beautiful dress your father gave me, you've ruined it for me," she said, pushing him under the water.

He woke up in a soft white bed, nurses he knew from TV coming and going, whispering over him.

Kaito stood and watched these scenes with utter coldness. He knew them, he had seen them so many times that they were already boring him. He knew what was coming next and thought, "Why don't you let me wake up?"

"Run for your life, you bastard," a voice behind him said, and his 13-year-old self started running, followed by three teenagers from his school. It was cold and it was hard for him to move forward on the snowy meadow. Suddenly he fell, but there was no ground and he kept falling. Eventually he hit the ground. He didn't know how far hc had fallen. He couldn't move, and everything hurt.

He had forgotten how long he had been lying there, at some point his eyes got used to the darkness. He could move a little, but every movement hurt. He focused his eyes and saw a black disk that stood out against the dark background, about two steps away from his head and he breathed, "You filthy Yokai, why can't you let me die in peace."

"You can see me, human?" the disk said.

"Of course I can see you vile creatures, leave me alone."

"Never in all these eons has a living being been able to see me when I didn't want to. Give me your blood and I will serve you."

"I'm dying right now, you useless bastard, in case you hadn't noticed," and he was suddenly glad that he could at least yell at a Yokai before he died.

"Why are you dying?" it came back.

"Oh, screw you, why don't you get it and then get out?"

"I will give you knowledge and power. I will carry out your orders in the human world for a thousand of your lives."

"You're a fool, why don't you just take my blood?" just came out of him.

"Come to me, that's the only order I'll ever give you."

Kaito laughed, the cold had probably frozen the pain, but his body was almost stiff. He said, "That sounds good, you stupid animal," tensing his muscles once more, tried to turn around and rolled a bit towards the black hole. Even the pain his father had inflicted on him over the years wasn't as great as this. He screamed louder than he had ever screamed before, he didn't know for how long, all he knew was that he passed out and woke up in a hospital room.

"Alabaster colors," he thought as he saw the wall. Strange, how did he know that word? A nurse said to a doctor, "Multiple fractures, pulmonary laceration plus a heparperforation, it's all taken care of." The doctor looked puzzled, said, "Okay," and left the room with the nurse.

"Hey, why can I understand everything they say?" said Kaito, lying very weakly in a bed and looking up at the black round thing hovering above him.

"Knowledge and strength as well as 1000 of your lives I will serve you in the human world, that was the pact between us."

"You know that a human has only one life?"

"No, but I will carry out your orders for a thousand lifetimes."

"You don't want to understand, but can you find the one boy who drove me into the hole?"

"Yes."

"I want him gone, do it!"

"Yes," the monster said and disappeared.

Kaito didn't know how many times he had seen this scene before, "wake up, wake up," he said to himself and thought, "is this the punishment for my rash revenge back then? "I'm sorry, boy whose name I have long forgotten, I shouldn't have done that back then." Then he remembered how he had once ordered Shy to eat a demon, and Shy had reminded him that he would only serve him in the human world, not the world of spirits.

"It would be so easy if it weren't for this restriction. Why did Shy say it like that, was there a deeper meaning behind it, and why not the other way around? No humans, but demons? Why had he agreed to it back then ... well, he probably had no other choice at that time. But it was annoying. At least he had been able to negotiate a few small exceptions for more blood later, he told himself and yelled again, "WAKE UP! WAKE UP!"

Meanwhile, Mr. Nakajima was standing on the bottom floor of a newly built high-security laboratory of a military intelligence research unit in the northernmost, most uninhabited and inaccessible part of the country, yelling at two of his scientists in a lab.

"For the last time. This cat is an Ayakashi that can transform into a human, and you will prove it. Make it transform or you are no longer welcome in this country," he said, turning and walking through the airlock gate, the huge, barrel-heavy steel doors closing behind him. This made it clear to the two scientists that they would not leave this room until they had done their work and that Mr. Nakajima didn't really care if it was an ordinary cat or a real Ayakashi. Kazuo and Satoshi looked at each other and thought, "You old bastard, kiss my ass."

They went over to the cat, looked at each other again, and Satoshi asked, "What else can we do?" Kazuo was at a loss and shrugged. All investigations had failed, even the electric shocks demanded by the boss had done as little as good persuasion. The four guards at the back of the gate, who were constantly making stupid remarks and laughing at them, could also wring the cat's neck by their own. One of them said, "Shoot it in the leg or chop it off."

Kazuo was furious, this was not what he had imagined. He thought of how he had seen all the monsters as a child, Ayakashi, ghosts and so many others, and how they had frightened and annoyed him back then and how he had been glad that one day, they just disappeared. And then, in the first year of high school, he remembered again, and his interest grew in what it was all about? Were they a child's dreams or nightmares or was it really real, was the world bigger or different than he thought? That's what he wanted to know. After graduating, he was struck by a job ad for a parascientific experiment. He was immediately hooked and volunteered for an experiment with a government organization in a country he deeply admired, a country that had given him so much and to which he and his family owed so much. He stayed there, and his first assignment was on a farm deep in the beautiful, warm south. Several ghost hunters had gathered there. Those who could see them and those who pretended to. It was an amusing time, watching these parties fight among themselves and learning in the process. For a short while, he felt like he was seeing the spirits again, but then the old chief left the department and Mr. Nakajima came, and the good ghost hunters left as well. They seemed to be smarter than him. Was he just too ambitious or too simple-minded? He should have cancelled the job at least six months ago, when he was supposed to move to that high-security lab that was quickly set up and kept top secret. Why? Why hadn't he done that? Now he had this asshole as his boss, was at the end of the world and had to let him yell at him. His old boss would never have done that, he would never have allowed anyone to take a young girl's cat and then boast about it. He was ashamed and said, "Well, kitten, I guess we both have a problem now. Kazuo and Satoshi placed all sorts of technology in front of a massive-looking box made of tempered glass, made up of various parts that seemed to be very sturdily nested together and secured with a lock. Inside this box, a cat lay huddled in a corner, not moving. Kazuo started various measurements from long wave to IR to X-rays, looked at the results and said, "Kitty, the devices clearly say that you are a cat and nothing other than a cat. So if you're not a cat, let's work together and help each other," and laughed at himself.

The cat looked at him stoically from the corner. "It's no use," he said. He looked at the guards, who laughed at him, and at his colleague, who shrugged.

He pulled up a chair and said, "I don't know what else to do, I don't want to hurt you, kitten. Can't you just vanish into thin air and disappear, you can normally do that, then we'd all be helped?" He sat up, hoping that the cat would just disappear in front of his eyes.

At the same time, two armed guards stood outside the gate of a large, secluded building somewhere in the middle of nowhere. They were laughing and joking. One of them said, "I'm bored, I'm sick of this wasteland. Three years ago I could shoot at enemies 'Tack, Tack - Tack, Tack' and four less. It was really fun to watch them fall."

"Yoo," said the other, "but I'm getting old and I can feel it in my back and killing isn't much fun anymore. That's why I'm glad that the old man used his connections and was able to place our mercenary troop here. Now we're here, guarding ghosts and making a lot of money, and we have more than enough free time, too."

"Do you believe in this Ayakashi nonsense?" the younger man asked.

"With this salary, I also believe that the boss is an alien, if that's what he wants."

"Yes," the younger one thought, "the salary is unbeatable and together with the amount of free time one can have a lot of fun, so why not" and looked over to his buddy who had brought a chair. He had made himself comfortable in it, even though it was already cold, freezing cold, and looked up at the sky where snowflakes were falling, illuminated golden yellow by the security lights on the gate and sinking to the ground.

"If something doesn't happen soon, he'll fall asleep and I'll have to stand guard alone," he thought, and said, "Hey, I've got..." as a thud was heard.

It took about five seconds for the older one to open his eyes, look at the younger one and say, "Did you slip, you idiot, what were you doing..." but he didn't get that far, he looked at two single legs standing in front of him in the snow where his buddy had been. Startled, he fell backwards from his chair, hit the radio on his chest with his right hand and yelled "ATTACK! ATTACK! ATTACK! Unidentified object at the main entrance! We are under attack!"

"What was that?" he thought and saw the massive gate at the entrance to the fence, capable of stopping even vehicles, deform before his eyes, no, it was pulled together, dissolved and disappeared. The space around the gate moved into place, how could that be, everything was solid, it looked like rubber that had been compressed. Then everything suddenly jumped back to its original position, but in the middle, where the gate was, there was a hole, a hole about six meters across. Was it an enemy with a cloaking device or some other new kind of weapon? He picked up his assault rifle and fired the magazine in the direction of the hole. At the same time the man in the control center heard the word 'attack', he looked at the monitors for the main gate and saw a huge hole in the entrance of the fence and one of the security men shooting at the hole. He was still thinking, "What the hell is he doing?" when the guard disappeared before his eyes and there was some kind of distortion on the screen that disappeared after a second.

Intuitively, he hit the alarm button. It only took a second for the alarm to be heard throughout the building, all the way down to the tenth floor of the high-security lab.

"ATTACK! ATTACK! ATTACK! THIS IS NOT A DRILL!"

"ATTACK! ATTACK! ATTACK! THIS IS NOT A DRILL!"

Voices echoed through the rooms and the alarm sirens wailed unmistakably.

"ESTABLISH COMBAT READINESS!"

"ESTABLISH COMBAT READINESS!

the announcement changed, only to start again.

The security guard at Headquarters looked at the monitors in the entrance area of the building and at the same moment saw the structure of the building at the massive main gate that shielded them all from the outside world contract. The gate bent, no, it was compressed, it disappeared and the concrete around it took the place of the gate and suddenly everything jumped back to its original position as if the space had been eaten away and then filled again with … NOTHING.

The phone rang as he looked at the monitors in disbelief. It was Mr. Nakajima, "WHAT THE FUCK IS GOING ON HERE?" he yelled.

"We're under attack," the guard said without thinking, continuing to stare at the surreal image on the monitors.

Kazuo on the tenth floor was talking to the cat when he heard the alarm and jumped. He thought about it and thought, "This can't be, we're in Japan, in a remote research lab in the middle of nowhere, very far away, a lab that nobody knows about and even if they did, who would be stupid enough to attack us here, that would be suicide. The lab is guarded by a special unit and is nuclear bomb proof. If foreign powers or enemies want to spy on us, it will be via satellites or overflights with spy planes or an agent trying to get information in the next town. Nothing more."

He looked at the cat, then at the door, then back at the cat and said, "Did you have anything to do with this, did your owner have anything to do with this?"

The cat stared at him. The guards in the room were in a frenzy, barricading the gate and taking up positions where they would be harder to hit.

It came over the loudspeakers again.

"THIS IS NOT A DRILL, AN UNKNOWN OBJECT IS AT-TACKING THE BASE."

"ATTACK EVERYTHING THAT DOESN'T BELONG HERE," came another command from the loudspeakers.

The guards became nervous and stared at the cat.

Kazuo stood demonstratively in front of the cat and said, "Leave her alone, she belongs here. This was Mr. Nakajima's express order, he brought her here personally.

The guards turned back to the gate as the loudspeaker announcements resumed.

"THE OBJECT HAS PENETRATED THE BASE. IT IS ON THE FOURTH LEVEL AND IS MOVING ITS WAY DOWN IN A STRAIGHT LINE."

A guard yelled, "What the hell does 'moving straight' mean? There's only one elevator between levels and it's blocked when the alarm goes on," and they looked back at the cat.

"THE OBJECT IS ON THE SEVENTH LEVEL AND IS EATING ITS WAY DOWN IN A STRAIGHT LINE."

"Damn it, what the hell is going on up there, kill it," one of the guards yelled into his radio.

"What do you think we do, we fire everything we have at an invisible target. The shots just go right through. We can't even see it. The only thing we know is that it probably can't go through solid walls, it has to break through, it..." was the last thing the guards heard before the transmission faded into static. Now it was clear to everyone in the room, there were no soldiers from a foreign country coming towards them, and that meant they wouldn't be fighting humans, Key thought.

He, Key, squad leader of his four-man unit, was down here today with this bunch of stupid scientists. Scientists were funny idiots, they always squealed so nicely, and unlike the animals, it was enough if he threatened them. Sometimes he wondered what would happen if he shot them. Actually, he had been looking forward to this day's work; these guys were just too funny. Time passed faster with them and it was warm down here.

"And now something like this," he snorted. They were like rats in a trap down here. Key thought the situation was something out of a horror movie. An opponent without a body, without mass, but still capable of destroying its enemies. What was the weak point of this thing to look for, as always in horror movies, if there was one. They had maybe ten seconds or less to find it. Or was it just an exercise and in a moment the door would open and his comrades would laugh at him? No, certainly not, for what he heard made him shudder.

They were on the tenth floor and could hear the shots of heavy machine guns hitting concrete, even though they were trapped behind a meter of reinforced concrete. This was Coo's unit, only they used such heavy weapons. They were strong, they were fast. In the mercenary war ten years ago, they had wiped out entire units and what now, they were on the ninth level and absolutely defenseless, Key thought, staring at the huge, massive airlock in front of him.

It became quiet.

Key looked at his men, who had all taken up the best position in the room for close combat. For hand-to-hand combat against humans.

"Something stood in front of the massive gate. But it wasn't a human," he said to himself.

The gate was massive, nuclear bomb proof, would it hold?

He looked back at the two scientists who were still standing in front of the cat in the glass dungeon, talking to it. He would have preferred to shoot them, but they would probably die with him anyway. The best thing to do would be to get the cat out and hold it up to the monster, but he didn't have a key, Mr. Nakajima did. The windows of the box were bulletproof, he could try, but what if the thing attacked just then? Better stay in position, he thought, wondering how it would get in, said "Load the weapons!" and everyone could hear the machine guns being loaded.

Would the thing blow the gate inwards like in horror movies, melt everything down like a dragon, or corrode everything with acid like an alien?

"Come here, you bastard," he shouted in the direction of the gate as it began to flicker and get smaller and smaller and the space around the gate with the concrete walls bent and deformed and in the end only concrete took the place of the gate. Until suddenly the concrete walls snapped back into place like a stretched rubber band, leaving a six-meter hole where the 40-ton gate had once stood. A huge thud rumbled through the room.

For whatever reason, swirling dust seemed to indicate an object in that spot, and Key understood that the enemy was there.

It didn't matter if shooting didn't help, what else could they do? "FIRE," he yelled.

The shots bounced ineffectually off the wall on the other side of the missing gate.

"Damn," Key thought, looking around to see if he could still see the thing, "where did it go?" he said to himself, firing in different directions, kicking up dust.

He looked to his right and started to laugh. Tai was gone and all that was left of Tac were his legs. He looked at Gos. All that was left of him was one hand.

He aimed at the cat, but he didn't care anymore, the two Jumping Jacks wouldn't survive anyway. Kazuo shouted "NO" and Key pulled the trigger, but there was nothing, his hand, his forearm, all gone, along with the gun. With his other hand, he drew his backup weapon and tried to aim, and Kazuo saw the man he hadn't spoken to for more than three sentences vanish before his eyes. He looked at the cat and said, "I'd like to let you out, but I don't have the key," then walked over to the wall and sat down.

He heard Satoshi shout, "NOW WE KNOW! WE'RE NOT ALONE!" and saw him run into the room with his fists raised. "That's stupid of you," Kazuo thought, but he didn't have the strength to stop him and saw Satoshi disappear with a thud as well. He was more than just a colleague, they had started together, he loved science fiction and still loved the mystical like he did and now he was just gone. He couldn't take it anymore, closed his eyes and put his arms around his knees.

He thought of his mother, his father who had done so much for him, his girlfriend he had met at the university, he didn't want to die, what could he do and started to cry.

He heard another soft bang, like the other times when people had disappeared, he knew what it was. That creature was eating the space. With each bite, the space that wasn't eaten bent around the space that was being eaten, and when the thing bit off and swallowed the room, everything else jumped back and a kind of vacuum was created in the place left behind, which suddenly filled with air and caused a bang, almost like thunder in a storm.

He heard the cat meowing and hissing, apparently escaped from the glass cage. Had the monster destroyed it? He knew what the hissing meant to him. He began to pray and wait, but nothing happened except that the cat continued to hiss. Was he already dead? He opened his eyes. No, he wasn't dead, the cat was still hissing, hissing like crazy, but not at him, but in the other direction. It was standing two meters away from him, hissing towards the gate.

Was the cat trying to save him, to protect him? What would she gain? He thought, "Why don't you run away, cat," but she didn't seem to be in any danger. She hissed at the monster, which was probably less than ten feet from him. The cat seemed to keep it at a distance, running left and right in circles around him, as if trying to keep the monster away from him from every direction as it tried to get past the cat.

"Leave him alone," Dawn yelled at him, but Shy wouldn't listen, he kept trying to get to the human behind Dawn without seeming to hurt Dawn.

"Leave him alone, damn it, what did your master tell you to do?" she kept yelling, protecting the young man from having his soul erased.

"You're not talking to me. Well, I'll tell you one thing. If you disobey your master's command, there will be consequences."

But Shy still didn't listen to her. Dawn knew for sure that Kaito had given her protection as a prime directive, that was clear, but what then? What was his next order. He wouldn't let Shy eat people randomly while she was in danger here, he would get her back immediately, she was sure of that.

"All right," Dawn thought and yelled at him, "do as your master says and take me back to him right now. Kaito's order must have been something like that, she was sure of it.

Shy stopped and Dawn calmed down.

Kazuo saw the cat sit down, but she was still staring at a point in front of him.

"Was that a good or bad sign, would he survive after all?" he thought and remained transfixed.

Kazuo continued to stare at the cat and when he blinked, the cat was gone. He started screaming and pushed himself backwards, but there was the wall, so he slid along it behind the glass box. He kept screaming, he had just had so much hope, but now he was in the corner, that was as far as he could go, he started to laugh, closed his eyes again, said "Thanks kitty, for the few extra seconds" and thought of the one he loved.

Kaito awoke to a soft meow and looked up to see Dawn snuggled up next to him, pulling the covers over herself. He felt her warmth, put his hand on her head and stroked it as he thought, "Always this stupid dream. He looked to his left, there was Shy floating next to his bed, and he thought, "You really are the only scary thing in this world," and looked at the dark, inky black circular surface.

"Shy, at the beginning of the year, just before the last snow had melted, two men came to my office. One told me that I had to obey him unconditionally, threatened me, and the other destroyed some of the inventory. Do you remember this?"

"Yes," came the answer in his mind.

"Both men were supposed to be in the building, in the area I had designated for Dawn's rescue. Did you eat one or both of them?"

"No."

"Go back to the room, look for the two, if you find them, destroy them and come back, if you don't find them, come back as well, and in both cases get into a waiting position. Move," he said and watched as Shy disappeared.

Kaito noticed Dawn hugging him tighter, stroked her again and said, "I'm glad you're okay. He closed his eyes and fell back asleep.

A short time later, he was awakened by a rumbling sound, probably coming from the stairwell. He didn't know exactly how long he had been asleep. "That was fast, let's see who it is," he thought. The door to his apartment was being forced open. Fortunately, he hadn't locked it and Kaito thought, "Who do you think it is? An idiot, his father or his idiot father?

To his relief, Mr. Tanaka rushed in.

"What have you done?" he shouted directly at him.

"What have I done?" came the reply.

"Dawn's back, I see. So you know exactly what you've done.

"What do you think I've done, explain it to me."

"You know exactly."

Kaito laughed and said, "Since when do accused have to confess before the charges are read to them, or are we living in a Kafkaesque world already?"

Kaito realized that Father had not understood the allusion, but he waited.

"Twenty-seven dead. That's the charge," Mr. Tanaka said.

"Wow, he's really gone on a rampage," Kaito thought.

"As of today, you have 27 people on your conscience."

"They're not the only ones in the world, unfortunately," Kaito thought, "Well, tell me who told you that and I'll tell you what you want to know, Father."

"Mr. Kimura called me.

"Oh, I hope he's still alive, that would be a shame, he was actually quite nice," Kaito said casually.

"He has nothing to do with this. He got a call because someone knew he was in contact with you, and that man is a high-ranking military intelligence officer who learned that one of his divisions had been attacked."

"Wow, you know bigwigs, and you're telling me all this right here, right now, in this room. To a high school student. Father."

"Don't call me father, you monster. They'll arrest you and charge you."

Kaito had to laugh so loudly that his father had to wonder if he had lost his mind.

"Arrested for what?" he asked his father.

"For killing 27 people!" he said loudly.

"Actually, I would have expected a policeman to understand what it takes to hunt down kidnappers. You should go back to police school."

Mr. Tanaka was furious and charged at Kaito.

"Shy block him," Kaito said and a black wall appeared in front of Mr. Tanaka. He was startled and fell backwards to the ground.

"Shy back."

Mr. Tanaka yelled, "What the hell is that?

"Meet 'Shy'."

"What's that?"

"You asked me back then, just before Mrs. Kato's assignment, if there was anything more powerful than gods or demons. That's exactly what it is, a World Shifter."

"You said then that the probability was so low that there had never been any contact with humans."

"I notice there are gaps in your memory. I said 1 in 100 billion for 'relevant points of contact', and so far there have been about 100 billion people living on our beautiful Earth."

Mr. Tanaka's eyes widened, "You made a pact with such a monster?"

"Be a little nicer to Shy. He's the guarantor that I can go about my work as normal and help the people who have hope in me, without having to worry about what's important to me being taken away by parasites who think they're above the law. I didn't expect it to be the state itself breaking its own laws, I thought it would be a client or acquaintance. But that's the way it is now, and I was just going by the words Mr. Kimura said to me on your behalf, 'Protect what's most important to you'. Do you really think that I'm so stupid, so foolish, that I would walk through the history of the world with my eyes open, presenting something as desirable as Dawn everywhere, negotiating with mobsters, with the richest people in the world, who could wipe out a person with the snap of their fingers, without being prosecuted, and without having anything up my sleeve to protect what is so important to me? Do you really think, Father, that you have a son who is that stupid?"

It took Mr. Tanaka a long time to understand these words, but he did.

"If you are so powerful, why did you kill them?"

"Oh father, you should know."

"Don't call me father, you monster."

"What happens when you take back property from a tyrant that he just took?"

"Stop playing games."

"Well, what happens when you break into the tyrant's heavily guarded palace, kill 27 of his guards without a trace and without any casualties of your own, and then take back your property?"

Mr. Tanaka's eyes widened again and he shouted, "You killed those people just to make an example?"

"No one will accuse me, or do you think they will admit that there is a parallel world from which I took a monster to do this? How ridiculous does that sound? Can you imagine what would happen in this country, in this world?"

"They will kill you!"

Kaito laughed again. "Maybe the arrogant, stupid lacquer monkey who was put in this office by the previous government would have done that. But he no longer exists. Do you know who his replacement is?"

"No, you tell me," said Mr. Tanaka, sitting on the floor in frustration.

"I don't know either, I searched all publicly available government documents for his appointment. The only thing I could find was a single letter 'Q' and a date indicating his appointment as Deputy of the Military Research Division 30 years ago. This letter is probably the only subtle clue he has given us about his character. Together with his 30 years as a deputy, it is clear that this man is both feared and respected. He is the real secret man behind this department, and thanks to his intelligence, he has remained so to this day. Someone like him would never jeopardize his life's work," Kaito explains to Mr. Tanaka, who now seems rather passive and weak.

"Shall I tell you what will happen? Nothing will happen. It will be covered up and in a few years one of these gentlemen will contact me, he will make a request and I will accept it, apologize and that will be it. That's how the world of power works. Power is everything," Kaito said.

Mr. Tanaka got up, went to the door and said, "I don't think we should see each other any more in the near future, you're old enough to live on your own and you're already standing on your own two feet. Goodbye," and left the apartment.

"I will continue to protect you and your family, I owe it to you," Kaito said, knowing that Mr. Tanaka couldn't hear it anymore.

At the same time, far away in a bug-proof room in a government building, President Matsumoto sat watching a video on a laptop of people being devoured by an invisible enemy in a laboratory, unable to do anything about it, thinking, "And I'm supposed to believe this kind of FX shit, screw you all, I've got better things to do," and was about to get up when a man entered the room. Mr. Matsumoto looked at him and thought, "What a disgusting little guy with a smarmy look on his face and ridiculously small glasses on his way too big head that magnify his way too small eyes to twice their size when you look through them. The way he approaches me is repulsive enough."

"Isn't it a beautiful day, the sun is shining, the birds are chirping, the children are playing lightly and happily in the park, and then this successful project I want to tell you about. Have you seen it?" the man said, pointing to the notebook.

Mr. Matsumoto was annoyed by this ridiculous dwarf and said, "It's raining cats and dogs, it's two degrees Celsius, and this shit can't be real," also pointing at the notebook.

"You must let your feelings speak for themselves, Mr. President, may I introduce myself?"

"No, the gray eminence 'Q', I suppose, and now explain this shit to me," pointing at the notebook again.

The man nodded and smiled at him, sending a shiver down Mr. Matsumoto's spine.

"No wonder no one has wanted him as a department head for 32 years," he thought.

"What you see there is exactly what happened, nothing is embellished, isn't that wonderful?"

"Damn it, you want to tell me that there are such monsters here in our world, in our beautiful country of Japan. How am I supposed to explain this to people who are already protesting about a road detour? There's an election in a year, and now we have 27 dead in a lab that my predecessor spent a lot of money to build."

The man tilted his head to the left and said, "By your predecessor, right!" He tilted his head to the right and said, "As well as that idiot Mr. Nakajima, my former department head.

Mr. Matsumoto found this gesture extremely disgusting, but only said, "What are you trying to tell me?

"There was an accident in the research lab that killed 27 people, unfortunately including the incompetent department head who was pushed through by the incompetent former president. He screwed everything up. Now you come along as a savior and publicize this moronic waste of money, publicly declaring that Mr. Nakajima disregarded everything and wasted taxpayers' money on dangerous experiments and that now, after three years, they can finally put an end to it when this fool went too far. The evidence is all there, we just have to get it out," she said, slipping Mr. Matsumoto a piece of paper.

"Do you know how much this will cost us?" asked Mr. Matsumoto.

"The project will be completed successfully five years early, there's enough money left over to compensate anyone who knows too much or ..." the man pauses and laughs.

"What does 'successful mean'?" exclaims Mr. Matsumoto.

"The goal of the project was to detect supernatural beings, it could hardly be better than this," and the man again pointed to the notebook in front of him.

"Mr. Nakajima would have been pleased with this ending. Unfortunately, he passed away during this crowning finale and was unable to attend the victory celebration. I'm sure he would have given his life for this, he was always like that. May God have mercy on his soul," he said in a sad tone and smiled.

Mr. Matsumoto tried not to get upset and then said, "What's next?

"After integrating the remaining project funds into the budget and settling the hush money, uh, I mean after the money for the victims and survivors has been paid, there will still be some left over to keep parts of the electorate quiet. Give out medals, I have some names for you, of scientists who can prove everything about how horrible the department head acted."

"You're a disgusting scumbag yourself," Matsumoto thought, but he knew it wasn't a bad idea and he should reconsider that plan.

"If what I see on the video is true, what should we do with the boy who sent the monster, or is that a lie?" said Mr. Matsumoto, pointing at the notebook again.

"No, no, you're well informed. We're not doing anything, that's for sure."

Mr. Matsumoto swallowed a little and asked, "How am I to understand that, he seems to be a danger, shouldn't we take him out?"

"The boy is a clever fellow. "Oh, if only I were in his place," the man sighed.

"Sure, you disgusting thing, so that you have even more power than you already have," Mr. Matsumoto thought.

"The boy did exactly what you would expect a young man to do. He protected what was important to him. To make sure it doesn't happen again in the future like it did a few days ago, we will leave him alone and protect him ourselves and, of course, keep an eye on him," he said with a smile.

"I will help him to realize his dream, to find an Ayakashi forest and a shrine for his beloved sweet catgirl, and if we really need him, I will tell him all we have done for him, apologize to him, and he will accept the mission I will ask him to do for the good of this land that promises freedom to his beloved catgirl."

"Why don't we just get rid of him?", asked Mr. Matsumoto, who was not comfortable with the whole thing.

"Do you have a little more time, Mr. President?"

"Start already!"

When the boy was six years old, his mother had tried to drown him in the bathtub, the neighbors heard the screams and called the police, who found the mother drowned in the bathtub with her head down. The ceiling lamp, which is normally attached with three screws, fell down and hit the slightly drunk woman on the back of the head, leaving her unconscious with her head in the tub. Well, this lamp was probably only attached with one screw. Still a strange coincidence, especially that the boy could be revived and the mother could not. Wasn't it?

In middle school, he was bullied by classmates who chased him into the woods, where one winter day he fell into a deep hole. If it hadn't been for a man named Mr. Tanaka, who was driving there that day for a short detour and got into an accident with a deer, which caused him to get out of the car and then hear the screams of a child, well, the boy wouldn't have been found until summer, if he had stunk.

With Mr. Tanaka, the boy blossomed, using his powers on a wide variety of people, including those of dubious reputation, without showing the slightest fear. Somewhere along the way, this very kind boy had made a pact with this monster, a monster who might have told him 'I'll serve you for 1000 years' in return, we don't know. Now do you see why I think we should appreciate him?"

Mr. Matsumoto didn't quite understand yet, but he had a very uncomfortable feeling in his stomach.

"Explain further," he said.

"This boy, who is so friendly to everyone and puts up with so much, much more than he should, commands the monster with a tone as if it were a machine. Why?"

"Tell me."

"Because the monster doesn't care, it serves him now for 1000 years, no matter what."

"He will be dead in 90 years at the latest."

"Yes, but not the monster," and Mr. Matsumoto's stomachache came up stronger than before.

"Are you saying that he ordered the monster ..." asked Mr. Matsumoto.

"... that after his death, he should destroy everyone responsible for his death. Yes, it could be like that. A theory, but a possible one. The boy is not stupid, Mr. Matsumoto."

Mr. Matsumoto felt sick thinking about the consequences.

"Then do something," he almost shouted at the man.

"That's exactly what I told you, we'll get him on our side, on the side of light. That's what they say in science fiction, Mr. President," he said, laughing at him.

"If you lied to me today," Mr. Matsumoto threatened.

The man stood up, knowing the conversation was over, folded the notebook on the table, took it and said, "No way, Mr. President, and I'm taking this with me. As he walked to the door, he thought of the 26 mercenaries he had sacrificed for his grand plan. The mercenaries who had only ever caused trouble were perfect for something like this. He would get rid of the rest of them or integrate them into the new unit that was already waiting in the wings. It was all for his plan that could change the world and Kaito Tanaka would be a part of it, whether he liked it or not. It was just a shame about the one truly dedicated scientist who loved science fiction so fanatically, a real shame, but there was nothing he could do about it.

"Just a moment," Mr. Matsumoto said, and the man replied without turning around, door handle in hand, "what else can I do for you?"

"Rumor has it that someone put that fluff of ghosts in Mr. Nakajima's head. Who could that have been?"

"No idea, Mr. President, no idea."

"Congratulations on your promotion. We better not meet again!"

"Thank you," the man said and closed the door behind him.

A few days later, Kaito was lying on the bed with Dawn, watching the evening news, which summarized an initial report on the accident at a research lab that had killed 27 people.

The then head of the department, Mr. Nakajima, was the main culprit in the accident, according to all those interviewed, and the president complained loudly on television that Mr. Nakajima had been appointed over the heads of the Diet in the last legislative period, and now emphasized that with the approval of the Diet, the deputy had taken over the office on a temporary basis and was working with the commission to investigate the accident.

Kaito wrote Mio a message, "It's all right, do you want to join us again?"

"Yes, and let's celebrate our birthdays," came a quick reply. Kaito smiled and stroked the meowing Dawn.